A SPY WITH SCRUPLES

GARY DICKSON

RIVER GROVE BOOKS

This book is a work of fiction. Names, characters, businesses, organizations, places, events, and incidents are either a product of the author's imagination or are used fictitiously. Any resemblance to actual persons, living or dead, events, or locales is entirely coincidental.

Published by River Grove Books
Austin, TX
www.rivergrovebooks.com

Distributed by River Grove Books

Design and composition by Greenleaf Book Group and Kim Lance
Cover design by Greenleaf Book Group and Kim Lance

Cover images used under license from:
©istockphoto.com/portfolio/viktor_gladkov;
©istockphoto.com/portfolio/NiseriN

Publisher's Cataloging-in-Publication data is available.

Print ISBN: 978-1-63299-263-5

eBook ISBN: 978-1-63299-264-2

First Edition

To my wife, Susie
Ours is a conspiracy of two.

"In life, you don't get to do what you want, but you are responsible for who you are."

—JOHN-PAUL SARTRE

One

A LETTER THAT ARRIVES UNEXPECTEDLY CAN'T BE good news even when presented on a silver tray. Scott thanked the young hotel clerk, one of the many scrubbed village demoiselles who staffed the reception desk at the hotel. He examined the mysterious envelope, which somehow had seemed important enough to be forwarded from their home in Geneva to their honeymoon hideaway in the south of France.

As he considered this unwanted surprise, he looked across the table at his wife, the former Countess de Rovere, but now just Desirée Stoddard—having lost the title gained from her first marriage as a result of marrying Scott. In her elegant way, she took the silver tongs to place one lump of sugar into her cup and two into Scott's. Eight weeks pregnant, clothed in the soft linens of Provence, her blond hair tousled, those crystalline blue eyes glistening, she epitomized the qualities that defined her: secure, aristocratic, and French, even after marrying a mere mortal, an American, such as Scott. She would always be a countess to him.

"What's that, my darling?" she asked.

"It's from my draft board."

Until this letter's arrival in paradise, the newlyweds had been enjoying a peaceful morning in a bucolic setting, lazily brunching on breakfast pastries with real butter and home-preserved fruit jams under the canopy of the large-leafed plane trees that sheltered the hotel's courtyard and dining area. The Mas des Alpilles was a restored farmhouse, an estate *de seigneur*, rising three floors and surrounded by extensive grounds, including its own orchards and vegetable and flower gardens. It was a corner of heaven in Provence, unpretentious and so French for a honeymoon.

"Aren't you going to open it?" she asked.

He tore at the flap and removed the contents, a one-page letter: "You are hereby asked to report to the United States Army base in Augsburg, West Germany—the nearest American post outside neutral Switzerland—on September 28 to undergo a physical and psychological examination." It was postmarked July 26, 1964. On the positive side, Scott noted that his presence was requested rather than ordered, leading him to presume that he wasn't in the army yet.

"What does it mean?" Desirée asked.

"I'm not sure." He wasn't going to explain to her the intricacies of the Selective Service System, otherwise known as the draft. That would only worry her. It was the law that all American males had to register with their local draft boards on or before their eighteenth birthday. Most received a classification of 1-A until a physical exam proved them unfit for service or, in the case of students in good standing, a deferment—2-S—was granted, or 1-F for those with a physical disability. Scott had been 2-S during his undergraduate years in the United States, and this status had continued when he became a graduate student in Switzerland. All changes to a student's status—such as moving to a new address, choosing a new field of study, a decline in health, getting married, or having a child—had to be reported. Scott's recent marriage to Desirée triggered a review of his 2-S classification, which could possibly result in a change of his status. At times these reclassifications could be quite capricious as each draft board followed its own set of rules.

"Now that you're married, they can't draft you, can they?"

Obviously, she didn't know that unless it occurred before 1964, marriage didn't exempt men from the draft. But then why would she? Otherwise marriage would have been an alternative that most might have taken.

"Let's not jump to conclusions. It's probably routine," he said, trying to reassure her. But at the same time, he knew that the reason to be concerned was the very fact that his file was being reviewed and that they now wanted him to take a physical. It wasn't exactly a sign that it was a routine review, but discussing it with Desirée wouldn't change anything.

"I'm not jumping to conclusions," she said. "I like to plan ahead."

The little war in Southeast Asia begun during the Eisenhower administration had increased in the early days of Kennedy's tenure and now resembled a powder keg under the Johnson administration and his hawkish cabinet. The escalating problems, although a world away—two worlds away—increased his risk of being reclassified and drafted, but he didn't want to alarm his new wife. Being French, she was already acquainted with the futility of any war in Southeast Asia because the French military had suffered one of its worst defeats some ten years earlier in Indochina. And as she reminded him on a regular basis, "It's foolish to get mixed up in it. Any Frenchman would tell you that. Any European would tell you that."

A first-year graduate student in the University of Geneva's international school, Scott wasn't ignorant of either the history or the politics of Southeast Asia. As a matter of fact, he and Desirée had met by chance the previous September on his initial trip to Europe on the transatlantic liner, SS *United States*.

While the attraction had been immediate and mutual, Scott had resisted calling on her, given the improbability of beginning a relationship considering the number of differences between them: she was twenty-nine, and he was twenty-one; she was an aristocrat, and he was upper middle class; she was rich, and he received a generous allowance from his parents; she was Catholic, and he was Protestant.

Their whirlwind romance from the following January to July and his conquest of one of the most sought-after and beautiful women on the continent became very public as a result of the paparazzi chasing them as they jetted to Saint Moritz, Cannes, and Paris. After a few months, their photographs began showing up in the newspapers and fashion magazines. Overnight Scott became a celebrity through his association with her. Her friends, but most of all her mother, opposed the marriage and were joined by Scott's parents when they learned that their academic and professional aspirations for their son were being interrupted by a romance with an older, more experienced woman. They cared not a whit that she was a countess or that she was rich. Everyone wondered what the countess saw in the young American. Scott had too.

Then Desirée became pregnant. This new reality quashed the opposition of all detractors. A special dispensation came from the Vatican that accommodated the bride's desire to marry a non-Catholic in the Church, and the ceremony was hurried to accommodate the bride's condition and demands of decorum. They had been married for just over a week, and now this.

It was apparent to Scott that the reporting on the looming war by American papers was more jingoistic than the cautious and more pessimistic editorials published by French papers such as *Le Monde* and *Le Figaro.* He was well aware of the increasingly ominous nature of the conflict in Southeast Asia, accentuated by the Gulf of Tonkin incident that had occurred just a few days before. His classmates had similar anti-war opinions, complicated by the fact that they were mistrustful of America's intentions, particularly as they pertained to foreign intrigues. Vietnam was precisely one of those adventures so difficult for Europeans to understand. They weren't buying the domino theory, not for a minute. But they were very attuned to colonialism in whatever guise it took.

As they were dressing for dinner that evening, Desirée said, "Worrying about it won't change anything."

"I don't know. Once upon a time I worried about something more or less continually until it changed for the better."

"And what was that?"

"Your ex, the Venetian playboy. I worried until, boom! He was gone."

"Worrying had nothing to do with it."

"Prove it."

"I loved you. He didn't have a chance."

"Maybe he's the one who should have worried more."

"I'm sure he did."

"But not enough."

"Could you be serious?"

"I'd rather not."

"Then I will be."

"Ladies first."

"All right. This unpleasant turn of events can't be ignored, but we will get through it. In a few weeks you will go to Augsburg. Meanwhile, we'll prepare the house for the baby's February arrival. And we'll begin to develop some options."

"Options? What options?" Desirée was always two steps ahead, but she didn't have any idea what she was pitted against this time. Scott guessed that she was thinking that he would, if drafted, refuse to leave Switzerland, where no extradition treaty with the United States existed, and avoid being sent to the war. What she couldn't know was that his background and education had stressed honor, duty, and country to the point that refusing to report wouldn't be an option no matter the consequences. But as the reality settled in, he couldn't predict what he would do. This war wasn't like previous wars. It was unpopular, particularly with the young, and it was difficult to understand or even believe that the United States was threatened by a dispute occurring some eight thousand miles away. Nevertheless, it was obvious that any decision he made would likely disappoint someone.

For the evening, they had determined to fight off the uneasiness, to proceed as if they had no problems. A romantic dinner would take place as planned. And dining at the Mas meant eating outside in a space bordered by the house, the trees in the courtyard, and a low wall that trailed along the side opposite the driveway. Simple wrought iron tables and chairs on a raked gravel and pea stone terrace spoke of an uncomplicated lifestyle of ease and relaxation. In the fading light, small hurricane lamps lit the courtyard with a soft candle glow.

As usual, Desirée looked stunning. In the south of France in the summer, white is the preferred color, and the countess—he still called her that—wore it well, carefully combining silk and cotton with lace and muslin. She draped herself in a mysterious and sexy mantle that accented the colored stones of her summer jewelry—turquoise, coral, and lapis lazuli.

It was mid-August, high season, and the small hotel was fully occupied: a few families with small children, two other honeymooners, and three older couples whom the staff treated with a deference that indicated they had been coming to the establishment for years.

Scott knew that they—Desirée at least—had been recognized, first by the staff, and then by one of the wives of the younger couples. After their wedding in Paris, they had escaped the paparazzi waiting for them outside the Ritz by hiding in one of the hotel's laundry trucks until they were a safe distance from the hotel. Desirée's chauffeur, Gustav, had met them and driven them to this hotel in the south of France, a world away from their usual bustling life and games of hide-and-seek with the press.

They took a table in an intimate corner. The service was measured without seeming so, perfect without being obsequious, more like a remembered melody that, when hummed, each note follows a pattern that one already anticipates, always in time, always on pitch.

Before Desirée's pregnancy, they would have enjoyed the shellfish, foie gras, *ecrivisses,* and bottles of champagne, but tonight they ordered a turbot simply grilled with rosemary. Although she insisted that he not be restricted by the limits she imposed on herself, he was careful to try not to exceed her restraints and then only at the margins.

After coffee, they walked hand in hand along one of the paths toward the adjoining garden where the pool was located. Scott wrapped his arm around her still-small waist, pulling her closer to him. She folded easily into contours that were familiar and reassuring. He led her to a discreet alcove where the border walls came together. A stone bench situated in a spot invisible to the main garden offered them the privacy required to indulge their passion to the point where decorum dictated that they retreat to their suite. They had always been good together, even at the beginning of their relationship when forces that considered them ill matched assaulted them on all fronts. Now they had a new challenge.

The next morning Desirée, always up before Scott, puttered around, making just enough noise to hint to him in her playful way that it was time for him to get up. Still reveling in their intimate evening interlude, he resisted.

"You know, neither I nor the baby will break. You don't need to worry so much," she said, alluding to his tenderness and perhaps awkwardness of the night before.

"It's my first baby," he said. "I'll be better on the next one."

"Slow down, my prince. You're sweet, and I love you for it. I'll tell you if it is too much. I don't want us to become vanilla."

"But I love vanilla. A pod stripped of its essence. Savoring each seed, a bit of heaven on the tongue, don't you think? It's sexy."

"You're incorrigible," she said in her most sexy French.

"Incorrigible or impossible?"

"Aren't you hungry?" she asked.

"I'm always hungry. Do you want to ring for room service or venture down?"

"I thought we might go into the village and find a little café."

"Is that what you did with your parents so many years ago?"

"Yes, but just my father. My mother always had room service. On special occasions, we would chase butterflies afterwards."

It was only a short distance to the village, Saint-Rémy-de-Provence, and Desirée knew her way around, although she hadn't returned for a number of years. A time lag existed in this corner of France, and there hadn't been many changes to the lazy, do-nothing pace of life that had played out for generations.

They stationed themselves in a small café on the Place de Saint-Rémy, small round tables and wicker chairs splaying out onto the public space and sidewalk. It was serene and quaint with the

Provençal blues and yellows on the tablecloths and decorating the pottery cups and plates.

They ordered café au lait, croissants, and delicious caramelized *palmiers* and watched the few tourists and townspeople wandering through the square.

"You're unusually quiet this morning, my darling," Desirée said.

"I was thinking that we should save the butterfly expedition until we have the little one to help us. And how would you feel if I said I'd love to be home where we can get back to a normal life?"

"I think you're really anxious to get to Augsburg, take the examinations, and get it over."

"I can have no secrets."

"Why would you want to?"

Two

SCOTT TOOK THE TRAIN FROM GENEVA TO THE ANCIENT Bavarian city, Augsburg. He rented a small car, stayed in a modest hotel, and made it an early evening, although dreading the next day made it difficult to get to sleep. It felt strange to be ordered about, submitting to the demands of others, without any knowledge of what would take place.

His departure from Geneva had been disproportionately difficult for a two- or three-day trip. Desirée's puffy eyes pronounced her verdict; she was upset. Plans for their married life weren't turning out quite as either one of them had imagined. First, she became pregnant before they were married, and then this draft business could not be easily resolved by money or influence, although neither of those options had yet been attempted. She made efforts to understand, but it was difficult for her to grasp that Scott was simply being caught up in the system precipitated by events some eight thousand miles away. Many young American men struggled with the same situation or worse.

The next morning, he drove out to Gablingen and the American army base on the edge of the city. The base was a huge facility populated by rather grim buildings and temporary quarters of corrugated steel streaked with orange oxide. He was surprised to see only a few soldiers, none in formation, walking or sitting around, appearing to be without purpose. It was easy to find the hospital and clinic facilities using the map provided at the entrance gate and the signs in English and German posted at every intersection. At the reception desk, they guessed who he was, and a Sergeant Campbell led him down the hall to an examining room.

"Undress down to your skivvies, and pee in this cup," the sergeant said. "The doctor will be with you in a few minutes."

An hour passed, and the door opened. Scott saw a man in his forties, obviously a doctor and a captain, with two silver bars on his collar, a stethoscope hanging around his neck, and a white coat. He said, "I'm Dr. Claiborne."

Dr. Claiborne had a folder with a sheaf of papers in triplicate that he began to fill out as he asked Scott questions concerning his health history and that of his immediate family, took his blood pressure and weight, listened to his heart and lungs, depressed his tongue, scoped his ears and nose, made him cough twice to check for hernias, and tapped his extremities for reflex response.

During the exam, the doctor commented that Scott was an excellent specimen, and then said, "It says here that you're in the university in Switzerland. I bet that's nice."

It was clear from the doctor's tone that he thought Scott was a spoiled brat, who was probably in Switzerland avoiding the draft. Scott considered mentioning that his Swiss adventure had begun before the war had intensified, before the draft had been enforced, but what would be the point? It might help him feel vindicated, but the doctor wouldn't be interested, because it wasn't something he wanted to believe. He remained silent and passive, but deep down he was sensitive to being thought of as a draft dodger. After all, he was just following the rules. He had always followed the rules.

After the physical, Sergeant Campbell directed Scott to an adjacent building, an annex, where he would take the mental exam. Scott walked down a corridor of closed office doors until he came to one with a sign that read, "Test."

He knocked on the door and was asked to enter. Captain McLean greeted him and indicated that he would be giving Scott the psychological and IQ tests.

He led Scott to an adjoining office that contained a few school desks. There were three tests as part of the overall examination—the usual language and math portions and an IQ and psych portion that used elaborate and semi-elaborate puzzles and recognition sequences to quiz the test taker. Each test was allotted a specific time of somewhere between forty minutes and an hour. Scott had taken many tests of various kinds and felt that he had probably done rather well on these, although the thought did occur to him that perhaps he should deliberately fail. But he guessed his failing wouldn't have been believed and would have identified him as a smart aleck.

At the end of the tests, Captain McLean indicated, just as Sergeant Campbell had, that in three or four weeks he would probably hear from someone back in the States regarding the results.

BACK AT THE HOTEL, SCOTT CALLED DESIRÉE. "HOW DID THE exams go?" she asked. "Were they nice to you? Did they give you any indication on why you are being tested?"

"Not a word. They didn't volunteer anything. It was by the book. But you'll be happy to hear that they said I was in great shape. I would have preferred that they had found a heart murmur or something, but no such luck."

"Perhaps you should have held your breath."

"I'm taking the night train. I'll be back by eight o'clock tomorrow morning. Will you wait in bed for me? We'll have breakfast together."

SCOTT'S TRAIN ARRIVED IN GENEVA ON TIME, EARLY IN THE morning. It had been a rough night, although he had his own sleeping compartment. As the train braked, slowed, or, worse, stopped, he risked either being thrown out of the bed or jammed against the wall of the cabin. Plus, at six feet one, his head touched one wall and his feet the other.

He could have asked Gustav, their chauffeur, to meet him, but Gustav was getting up in years, and asking him to get up so early seemed unnecessary, so he'd decided to take a taxi. Another benefit of taking a taxi was that chauffeurs and large black limousines attract the press, although it was unlikely they would be loitering about early in the morning. Reporters were notorious night owls.

He gave the driver the address, and as it was early there was little traffic, and they were soon on the road beside the lake. "Sir, the address you gave me is the home of the Countess de Rovere," the driver said.

"Quite right," Scott said.

"She recently got married, I think."

"She did."

"She married a young American. That must be you."

"Right again."

"She's very beautiful. I've taken many people up to her house over the years for balls and parties."

"She is beautiful."

At that point they arrived, and Scott gave him a greater tip than necessary. He assumed the driver knew that he had probably broached being indiscreet, but there was no point in penalizing his exuberance. The driver seemed appreciative to be off the hook.

He found her in bed, as beautiful as ever. She was sitting up, surrounded by silk pillows of alabaster white monogrammed in an elaborate design of her initials. Her blond hair framed her face and caressed her shoulders. A pale blue peignoir of lace and silk invited a closer inspection. She was waiting for him. He would not disappoint her.

"I hope you're not too tired," she said.

"I'm tired, but not that tired. Give me a minute for a quick shower," he said. "Let's have breakfast in bed."

Over the following weeks, they didn't discuss the tests or the potential draft. Waiting wasn't easy, and waiting for the unknown was even harder. Scott had no way of knowing why he had been summoned to Augsburg. He was certain he had passed the test, and he knew that since he was a student, married, and expecting a child, those factors made it unlikely that he would be called up, but no one was ever sure. With any change of status came risk. The draft boards had tremendous latitude to make their own decisions, and they didn't need to justify them. Firming up his student status—his only legitimate provision—became a priority.

Three

WHILE SCOTT WAS AWAY, DR. HOCHSTADT, HIS UNIversity counselor, had sent a note requesting that he come to see him when he returned. Scott hoped the note indicated that a discussion about his status as a student in good standing was the reason. Now it was more important than ever since his draft situation was so tenuous. When he had begun his studies at the University of Geneva the previous fall, he had been a dedicated student. But once he'd launched his pursuit of the countess at the start of the winter semester, he had increasingly abandoned his studies. Courting her became full time.

Desirée's estate on the Lake of Geneva was only fifteen kilometers, from the city, and it didn't take Scott but twenty minutes to arrive in the center of town and the University of Geneva. Dr. Hochstadt's office occupied one of the oldest buildings near the Cathedral of Saint-Pierre, a dominant landmark of the city.

Scott had been summoned to his counselor's office once before, in February, when Dr. Hochstadt had come across a newspaper photo that pictured Scott and Desirée embracing at a gala in chic Gstaad. The photo explained without a word why he was missing so many classes.

The professor's office remained the same. Shelves of books dominated the space with piles of periodicals and newspapers stacked randomly, indicating many projects were underway but incomplete. Some volumes appeared to be of a Gutenberg vintage and others had pages still uncut from the publisher. His wooden desk too was running over with unruly papers and thick files stacked to such a height that a visitor sitting in the wrong chair in front of his desk might very well not have an unobstructed view of the professor. Dr. Hochstadt in his characteristic Swiss manner came right to the point.

"Monsieur Stoddard, reports indicate that congratulations are in order on your marriage. But more to the point, now that you've married the countess, there are questions as to whether or not you will have the inclination to pursue your degree."

"I understand that my recent extravagances may have undermined my reputation as a serious student. But I will tell you that, given the opportunity, I would like to renew my courses, and I will not make it a secret that it is in my best interest to do so for many reasons, not the least of which is to maintain my student deferment in respect to the military draft in the United States." There was no use in hiding the truth. It was more than likely that the professor would be sympathetic to his dilemma.

"We've no doubt that you have the ability to succeed, but do you still have the ambition now that you are so well positioned?"

Well positioned was a sly euphemism that Scott had heard often enough from friends and even casual acquaintances in one form or another. Freely translated it suggested that having married Desirée—she from a wealthy Swiss and French banking family and a member of the elite with homes in Geneva, Paris, and Gstaad—he would no longer need to pursue his own interests.

"I realize that I have a lot to prove at this point," Scott said.

Dr. Hochstadt nodded. "It appears that the situation in Vietnam will end in an ugly mess. Most Swiss, myself included, are squarely against this foolhardiness. We can be persuaded to allow you to continue, but the expectations will be high. More *extravagances*, as you term them, would not be viewed favorably. We only have so many spots."

"I understand completely."

"Why don't you think about it and give me an answer in a few weeks? There's no rush. You wouldn't want to start again until after the baby comes. Next fall might be a good time, at the earliest."

News traveled fast, but how? Even the paparazzi that regularly chased Scott and Desirée across Europe hadn't caught on to the notion that she was pregnant. It was only in the last couple of weeks that the pests had realized that they were back from their honeymoon. It had been a welcome respite. Once they learned a baby was on the way, the photographers would likely return to camping out on the main road a short distance from the couple's driveway.

As he walked back to his car after the meeting, Scott was relieved that he could maintain his position as a student in good standing. While Dr. Hochstadt had been more than fair, Scott could count on him to enforce what was expected of every student. But he had been tacitly cleared of neglecting his studies prior to his marriage. Now he would need to redouble his efforts and make sure that Dr. Hochstadt's confidence was deserved.

When he arrived back at the house, Desirée was just finishing up with her decorator, who was designing the nursery. Scott was only allowed the bare minimum of information regarding the details. It was to be as much a surprise to him as it would be to the newborn.

"Was Dr. Hochstadt cooperative?" she asked once they were alone.

"He seemed to be understanding, but he questioned my seriousness due to my being so well positioned."

"My darling, don't be so sensitive. They're jealous. Besides, you forget that you were the only American accepted into your class in the international program. They hardly want to lose you."

"You're right. Perhaps I should have asked permission to skip a few more classes. You never know when we might want to go to Saint Moritz."

"True. You know the Chesea Veglia Ball is January 21."

"Speaking of the end of January, somehow he knew we were expecting a baby."

"That's good. I think it can only help."

"I thought you might be more interested in how he knew."

"But I do know."

He didn't ask because he didn't want to know. Desirée was practiced in moving behind the scenes, manipulating desired outcomes. She, unlike Scott, had grown up in a milieu where the rules were not for everyone.

Four

SCOTT KNEW FROM THE POSTAGE STAMPS DEPICTING Paul Revere that the letter he held had been sent from the United States. The return address printed in the upper left-hand corner read, "Department of the Army." He dreaded opening it and reading the contents, not only because it might contain bad news but, more to the point, if it did contain bad news, then he would need to share it with Desirée. And she would ask for more explanation, more details, going over and over it, and yet there would be no recourse except to follow the instructions. Desirée came from a different world. Her history was that of European aristocracy, privilege, and entitlement. It was difficult for her to imagine that someone could order her or anything she considered hers around, and Scott fit into that category.

Before joining Desirée in the upstairs living room, he read the letter, a one page, two-paragraph communication. In essence, it said that he had to be reexamined on the intelligence and psychological portions, the first being incomplete. Instead of reporting back to Augsburg, he was now to present himself at an army base outside Stuttgart, Germany. His appointment was three weeks away, but there wasn't a number to call, or an agency to contact to reschedule if he needed to. It was a command, not an invitation. And what was meant by "incomplete"? Had part of the test results been lost? There was no one to ask about that either. He was, however, warned that retesting would require a full day, perhaps two. He didn't like the sound of it, even though he didn't fully understand it.

Desirée arrived at home late in the afternoon. She had been to lunch in Geneva with her mother and one of her mother's friends. Scott heard the front door close and the click, click, click of high heels coming up the steps.

"Scott, Scott where are you, my darling?" she called out.

"I'm here in the library," he said. "How's your mother?"

"Worrying and fretting," Desirée said. She wore a chocolate-brown jumper of generous proportions with a goldenrod, long-sleeved turtleneck and brown calfskin boots that extended up under her skirt.

"What's she worried about?"

"Everything. She wasn't happy that photographers had followed me to the restaurant. I think they got her picture too. She'll be mortified if it appears in the paper. And one of the reporters, one of the regulars, shouted and asked if I was pregnant. Naturally, after that, that's all my mother talked about. What are you holding in your hand?"

"The latest from my draft board. It seems that part of the test was incomplete, and they want me to go to Stuttgart and take another test."

"That's ridiculous. Did they lose your test?"

"They didn't say, and there's no one to ask. I have no choice but to take another."

"When?"

"Three weeks from now."

"How can they win a war if they can't keep up with your test?" Desirée looked at him carefully, as if she were trying to detect if he was withholding anything from her, or if there was some telltale sign that he was more worried than he said. He braced for this visual inspection, aware that she was sensitive to his facial expressions. She didn't say anything, so he presumed he had passed and she was satisfied. For good measure, he left the notice on the coffee table in front of the couch to indicate that he wasn't sparing her any bad news. She didn't pick it up, perhaps satisfied that there wasn't anything else.

His departure to Stuttgart gave rise to another difficult parting. It was more onerous for her than him. She had to watch him leave and be anxious of the outcome, and they were both powerless to alter the course. Scott was sure that the uncertainty of the situation was shared by Desirée. They had not contemplated having to deal with this kind of anxiety in the first months of their marriage. Neither of them could have predicted the lives they had anticipated would be so threatened.

Gustav drove him to the Geneva airport. As they turned onto the main road, the reporters began snapping photos. All at once they lowered their cameras, having realized, he assumed, that Desirée, their main interest, was not in the car. After arriving in Stuttgart on a Swissair flight, he rented a car and checked into a small hotel for the night. The following morning, he drove to the base, Wallace Barracks, at Bad Cannstatt, near Stuttgart. The base had been used by the German army in the Second World War but had been taken over by various brigades of the U.S. Army. Overall it was unimpressive. One administrative building after another and nothing to indicate that there was a fighting force nearby—no tanks, no artillery, and not many soldiers.

Nevertheless, security was much tighter than it had been at Augsburg. There was a wall and fences, double gates and barriers, and MP checks to pass through. At the main entrance, Scott presented his letter and his passport as identification. A telephone call was made and his credentials verified, then a sergeant drove him over to building 4301 in a jeep.

Several noncoms stood at an information counter directing anyone with business at buildings 4301–4310. After presenting the letter again, he was duly led down a hall by one of the duty sergeants to an office with a sign that read, "Colonel Bendix." A knock on the door, and they were told to come in. The colonel returned the salute of the sergeant and told Scott to sit down. From his credenza behind a gray, metal utilitarian desk, the colonel grabbed a thick sheaf of booklets.

"These are the tests," the colonel said. "Twelve exams on various subjects. Each booklet is marked on the front with the allotted time. You can finish early, but you can't go on to the next test until the time for each booklet is up. Understood?"

"Yes, sir," Scott answered.

"The tests will last about six hours in total," the colonel said. "Shall we get started?"

"Six hours? The last test was a couple of hours. What happened to those tests?"

"They don't tell us anything. We just follow orders."

Scott didn't say anything, but he couldn't help but wonder how the previous three tests he took weeks before, ruled incomplete, could suddenly morph into a battery of tests requiring six hours to complete. He learned soon enough. While still adhering to a multiple-choice format, the tests explored a wide range of disciplines and subjects: vocabulary, mathematics, physics, chemistry, tools, manufacturing machines, languages, and even aircraft attitudes and controls.

He had never experienced the breadth of subject matter covered in the tests. It went far beyond his experience, and there were many sections where he had to rely on his best guess and his intuition rather than actual firsthand knowledge of a subject. Nevertheless, he did have the advantage that his father owned a large manufacturing business that used many tools and machines, so he presumed that his guesses might be pretty good. And against his mother's wishes, he had taken flying lessons when younger, which made him no stranger to rudders and ailerons.

But while taking the tests, he couldn't help wondering what this was all about. The scope of the tests went way beyond any he had ever taken. But he also knew that it was useless to ask. He was familiar with the protocols of respect and rank as he had attended an elite military prep school. It all boiled down to doing what you're told without protest or comment.

Around four-thirty in the afternoon, he completed the last of the booklets, turning it in quite a few minutes before the allotted time was up. Colonel Bendix, eyeing him in disapproval when he turned the test in early, took the booklet and put it in an envelope with the others Scott had completed, sealed it, and told him that he was finished and could leave. He said that someone would be in touch.

WHEN HE ARRIVED BACK IN GENEVA THE NEXT DAY, SCOTT didn't tell Desirée of the nature of the tests. He let her think that he'd simply retaken what he'd taken earlier. Naturally he continued over the next several weeks to worry about what was really going on, but there was no one to confide in, no one whose counsel he could seek. And he couldn't involve Desirée in the speculation without upsetting her.

Five

THEIR PRE-MARRIED LIFE HAD BEEN FILLED WITH GAIety, going to parties and balls in Gstaad, Paris, and Cannes. Based on Desirée's pediatrician's recommendation, they were reduced to staying at home most of the time, and he had insisted that light exercise, rest, and abstinence from alcohol were best for the mother and the arriving baby. Scott observed these same restrictions because he didn't want to tempt Desirée, nor let her see him enjoy what she couldn't.

On the fifteenth of December, Celine Montaigne, Desirée's best friend, came by train from Paris. Scott went with Gustav to meet her at the station. He was on the platform when she stepped from the train. The paparazzi were there to photograph whomever he was meeting. They probably figured out that it was one of Desirée's friends. He pushed forward through the crowd to take her hand luggage. She was one of the sweetest, most gracious people he had ever known. They'd had a slow beginning, because she'd wanted to make sure of Scott's intentions toward Desirée, but once convinced, she was his advocate. Scott had even been indirectly instrumental in helping Albert, her soon-to-be husband, get up the nerve to propose. And it was already decided that if Scott and Desirée's baby were a girl, her name would be Celine.

Once they were inside the car, Celine said, "Desirée is really worried about this draft business. Can't you do something?" This was the typical European elite's way of looking at a problem. How can you get out of a predicament through money, connections, or some combination thereof?

"I'm not even subject to the draft at this point."

"Yes, but she tells me that you've been to Germany twice taking tests. What does all this mean?" Desirée and Celine had no secrets between them. This was a plain fact that Scott had to accept. Fortunately, Celine was a person of the highest character, and she and Scott had their own little mutual respect relationship.

"It's bureaucracy. It's a mill where the wheels grind, and they grind fine."

"Albert knows a lot of Americans in Paris because of his medical practice, and he tells me more and more stories about some of his patients' sons either being drafted or suddenly having to join another service to avoid the army. Everyone hates this awful thing in Southeast Asia."

"Let's not discuss it with Desirée. She's already worried."

"I won't, but if she brings it up, then I will have no choice."

Over the next few days with Celine at the house, the mood changed. There was laughter again and giggles and talks about the future. Celine and Albert, a Parisian cardiologist and a witness at Desirée and Scott's marriage, were engaged and to be married in May in Paris. The girls passed their time together talking about the baby and its projected impact and the impending marriage. This was a welcome respite for Scott and Desirée from where their thoughts had settled over the past seven weeks.

ONE AFTERNOON, SCOTT WAS IN THE STUDY UPSTAIRS READing. The stairwell afforded a perfect transfer of the conversation Desirée and Celine were having downstairs in the salon. He wasn't paying too much attention to them until he heard Desirée say, "He can't leave me and the baby. I won't let him."

"But how can you stop him?"

"I'm not sure, but I have a few things in mind."

He listened a while longer and then decided to go down the back staircase, through the laundry, and out into the garden. Later he would come through the front door. He couldn't let either of them know that there was a possibility that he had overheard their conversation. Obviously, Desirée was further along in thinking about the problem than he had imagined. She had great intuition, and she'd always had an uncanny sense of his and other peoples' intentions and preoccupations. She was a great ally, but he was trying to spare her the same worry that he was experiencing. Apparently, he was doing so without success. It pays to be wily when you are married to someone who can read your mind. Now he just needed to figure out what she was up to.

THE DAY AFTER CELINE LEFT FOR PARIS, SCOTT AND DESIRÉE drove to Geneva in the evening to have dinner with David Blum, an old friend of Desirée's family, and his wife, Francine. Scott had only met them once a short time before their marriage. It was a little unusual for Desirée to make plans for them without consulting him, but he didn't think much about its significance.

"It was so nice to have Celine here for a few days. I've missed her," Desirée said. "She worries about us and the draft mess."

"I know. She even asked me to do something."

"I think David might be able to do something, if you'll let him," she said.

Uh-oh, Scott thought. David was an attorney, and it was quite possible that Desirée and he had already developed a plan if the worse happened.

They later joined the Blums at Le Mistral, a favorite restaurant of old Geneva. Le Mistral was nothing spectacular in the décor department but made up for this deficit by its authenticity and the quality of its food. David had arranged for a table in one of the alcoves formed by the stone arches that bordered the dining room.

Francine, an Egyptian from Alexandria, was a beautiful woman with dark hair and pale green eyes. She was a curator at one of the fine art auction houses in Geneva. Naturally she gravitated toward Desirée, asking the countess about the baby and the due date and whether she was hoping for a boy or a girl. David listened and from time to time offered a few comments about children based on his experience with their own, a boy and a girl. The family lived outside Geneva on the opposite side of the lake from Scott and Desirée, and from the conversation Scott learned that they were equestrians.

They had decided on a whole snapper, roasted in the oven with a full complement of steamed vegetables, and a Dézaley, a dry white Swiss wine. As they began to dine, David took the lead. "You know, Scott, here in Switzerland, each male citizen must serve in the army."

"I did know that."

"But of course, we never fight wars."

"Very smart," Scott replied. "Send the old fellows first and there won't be any wars."

David laughed. "Desirée tells me that you could become subject to your military draft." Scott nodded, realizing that his suspicion was correct; Desirée had been busy again. He could sense her looking at him, but he didn't reveal any emotion. It was apparent that she was more worried than he.

"You could become Swiss or even French since Desirée has dual nationality and avoid the war altogether," David said. Obviously, he had been given explicit orders. "I could look into it for you. It wouldn't be easy, but with the right connections and a sympathetic audience, it could be accomplished."

"That's a great idea," Desirée said. "Don't you think so, Scott?"

Scott thanked him but assured him that there wasn't any threat at this time. He could see the disappointment in Desirée's face, and it was confirmed that she had organized the dinner just to precipitate the very discussion he didn't want to have. All of it was her idea. That was clear.

"In any case, give me a call if you change your mind," David said.

Six

Every Thursday, Scott played tennis at an indoor club on the outskirts of Geneva where Desirée was a member. He didn't have a regular game, but he found that if he showed up in the morning around ten, there was always a match available, singles or doubles. And sometimes his best friend, Jean, would be there, and they would play a best of three sets. He arrived at the club a little after ten one morning, and as he was getting out of his Porsche, a man in an overcoat came up to him and said, "Mr. Stoddard."

Scott answered, "Yes."

The man handed him an envelope, turned quickly, and darted among the parked cars, got into one, and drove off.

He quickly opened the unmarked envelope and read: "Next Thursday, 11:30, Auberge des Chasseurs, Echenevex. Don't mention this to anyone, not even your wife. Destroy this note."

Scott looked over his shoulder and slowly scanned his surroundings, expecting Jean to pop up laughing hysterically. But no one was around.

Thursday could not come fast enough. Scott left the house at the usual time to play tennis, he said, but of course he was going to the designated village just over the border in France. He was careful not to arrive before eleven twenty-five. He wanted to be punctual, but not anxious.

The Auberge was a white stucco affair in the architectural style of a chalet. Echenevex is a town on the heights above the Lake of Geneva, and the inn had a marvelous view of the lake and the French Alps beyond. The day was clear and crisp.

As he got out of his car, an American in a black overcoat, about six feet tall, close to forty years old, and with an athletic build, approached him and said, "Glad you could come. I'm Stephen Wainwright."

"What's this all about?" Scott said.

"Let's go in and have some lunch. I'm starved. How about you?"

Wainwright spoke perfect French without an accent and asked for a discreet table in one of the booths in the dining room, near windows overlooking the snow-covered meadow.

"We're lucky to have such a glorious day as this in December," Wainwright said. "Don't you think?"

"Yes, very." Scott had decided that there was no use in pressing the issue. He would outwait Wainwright. It was obvious that the man had an agenda that could not be advanced beyond the timetable he had planned.

They ordered the same thing, the veal with morel sauce and noodles, a Swiss specialty. Wainwright ordered a bottle of Bordeaux, and although each was poured a glass, Scott noticed Wainwright didn't drink any, so Scott accepted the challenge and didn't drink any either.

"I'm sure you're wondering what this is all about. Rest assured, it's good news. I've been sent to tell you personally."

Scott wanted to say, "Then, tell me goddamnit," but he didn't. Instead he said, "Good news, from whom, from where, about what?"

"On those first exams you scored very high, so high in fact that a more thorough retest was necessary."

"So, perhaps I passed that too?"

"Passed? Jesus Christ, son! You made the third-highest grade ever recorded on the test. And this is a test that's been given to thousands and thousands of people over the last fifteen years."

"They couldn't just send me a letter?"

"No, a letter wouldn't do at all."

"Are you from the draft board or the army or what?"

"At this point, Scott, let's just say that I'm a representative."

"A representative of . . . ?"

"I've come to tell you news—good news, great news—and to set up additional meetings for us to talk over some very important issues. Issues that need to be kept completely confidential and cannot be discussed with anyone, not your wife, not your parents, not your priest or lawyer. No one."

"What's this all about, Wainwright? Stop playing with me."

"I don't have to tell you what it's about. You already have it figured out. Do you fence?"

"Fence? No."

"Join the Société d'escrime de Genève. It's difficult to get in, very upper crust. Ask your wife to help you become a member. We'll meet here again, at the same time, the first Thursday after the New Year. Got it?"

Wainwright paid the check quickly with cash and left. The wine remained untouched. Scott needed a stiff one, so he drank his wine and then took the bottle and poured himself another full glass.

He was glad it would take a bit to get back to Geneva. He needed the time to consider the morning's events, and what it all meant. But the more he thought about it, the less clear it became. The facts were that he had essentially done too well on the test. The result had attracted some attention from God knows where, and now he obviously was being courted—or enlisted depending on your viewpoint—into some kind of secretive enterprise. But on the other hand, what did he know about these things? Dare he say it? *Spying*. That he knew nothing might make him attractive.

Christmas was a quiet time. If Desirée weren't so pregnant, they would have gone up to her chalet in Gstaad for the ski season, which ran from Christmas until mid-March. They would have hosted a number of dinner parties, been invited to more, and would have attended balls in Gstaad and Saint Moritz. To compensate, Desirée had one of the top florists from Geneva come and decorate a tree and the house throughout. They did have a few people over for casual dinners, her best friends and now his. New Year's Eve was quiet too, just a candlelit dinner, the two of them, no champagne—a first—and early to bed.

January first fell on a Friday. Scott had to wait the week for his meeting with Wainwright. Of course, he had not mentioned any of this to Desirée, and he couldn't help but feel a little guilty as a result. From the beginning of their relationship, they had both been very honest, even direct, and what he didn't tell her she usually guessed anyway, so there wasn't much use in keeping secrets from her. She was a few years older than him, more sophisticated, and in some ways devilishly clever. He had always valued her counsel as she had never guided him astray and had helped him overcome some of his natural inclinations that were based on his own insecurities. Now he had not only to hide something from her, but as a result, would not have the benefit of her advice. He was on his own.

Late Saturday afternoon as they were sitting by the fire in the downstairs salon, Scott overheard Desirée making plans over the phone with her mother to come to lunch the following Thursday. This was helpful—almost too convenient—because it meant that he could take his time with Wainwright. Desirée knew that Thursday was his tennis day, and generally, when the match ended, the men would have lunch together to prolong the camaraderie. With her mother around, he wouldn't be missed.

When she hung up, Scott said, "Desirée, I was wondering how you would feel if I looked into learning a new sport. I read an article in a magazine at the tennis club about how many tennis players have improved their games, their footwork, and their reflexes by taking up fencing."

"*L'escrime?* Are you sure? It's very difficult. It's a good way to get *piqué*, you know, stabbed. It doesn't seem very American."

"I don't plan on getting stuck."

"I'm not sure it's something you plan."

"There seems to be a really good club right here in Geneva, La Société d'escrime de Genève."

"And known throughout Europe. It's very difficult to get in. Most of the members are Swiss, and the ones that aren't are probably former Olympians or national champions."

"Could you say it's impossible?" Scott secretly was not disappointed. He could tell Wainwright that he couldn't become a member and perhaps the lark would be over.

"No, impossible is not a French word, my darling. My father was president of the club, but he resigned when he and my mother divorced, and he went to the United States. But Uncle Pierre is a member of everything. Maybe if I called him . . ."

"He can't refuse you."

"Fencing, really? Are you reading *The Three Musketeers*? I hope there'll be time for the baby and me too."

On Wednesday afternoon, he went to Geneva to his favorite bookstore, Payot, to buy a book on fencing. If he had to take up the sport, he should probably know something about it. Being a novice was always an uncomfortable position.

When he returned, Desirée was upstairs in the bedroom lying on the chaise lounge. "I called Uncle Pierre and asked him about you joining the club. He was as surprised as I was, but he said if it was something you were sure about, then he would ask around."

Seven

On Thursday morning, he left the house at the usual time to play tennis. As soon as Scott pulled the Porsche into the small parking lot of the Auberge in Echenevex, Wainwright was out of his car. He was wearing a nice cashmere black overcoat and a dark gray scarf, but his shoes were classic wingtips. He hoped Wainwright wasn't trying to fool anyone. He looked so American. He needed some help with his spy wardrobe. "You're right on time," he said. "I like that."

They took the same table as before, but this time Wainwright made a show with the maître d' and the waiter of the many maps and brochures of houses for sale in the region near Geneva. Scott presumed that he was pretending to be a realtor.

They both ordered the entrecôte with French fries and another bottle of Bordeaux, but as before, Wainwright waited on him to imbibe first. Scott didn't bite.

"What about the fencing club?" Wainwright asked. "Is your wife working on it?"

"Her uncle is."

"Oh, yes, Pierre de Bellecourt. A good person to know."

"So why am I joining the fencing club?"

"Because it's good cover and good exercise."

"And what if I say that I'm not interested in fencing. And I get plenty of exercise otherwise, and why would I need cover?"

"Well there's always 1-A, and as you know, once 1-A, you could be drafted."

"That sounds like a threat."

"No one is twisting your arm. You might not be drafted. Some people are lucky."

So this is how it was done. They don't twist your arm or threaten to harm you. They only pose uncertain consequences that are more anxiety producing than threatening. He wondered if they had thought about the fact that he could simply refuse them and ask for asylum in Switzerland. They had probably considered that option but thought him incapable of doing it. "I'll need to think about it," he said.

"Don't think too long. And if you're thinking of stiffing us with some kind of asylum nonsense, think twice about your reputation and the impact on your family back in the States. Nobody likes a draft dodger, particularly where you come from. Concentrate on being a patriot, Scott."

"When can we talk again?"

"You might not see me again. But you can still contact us."

"How?"

"Get a copy of the *Tribune de Genève* every Wednesday. In the classified section under items for sale, look for cameras, then for Rolleiflex, and the seller's name, Georges S., and a telephone number, such as 22 40 21 23. If you want to ask a question, or you want to leave a message, you go to Payot, the bookstore, the Shakespeare section. You pick up a book of the sonnets, turn to sonnet number 123, the last three digits of the telephone number in the ad. An answer to any inquiry you've made will be there. Replace the book at the end of the section on the right. Someone will already be in the store watching you. Don't ever speak or make eye contact with this person. If you have a question, leave it in the third Bible from the left on the third shelf from the bottom in the Book of Revelation. When we have an answer, we'll place a new ad in the paper. You must always read the answer, tear it up, and discard it, preferably down the toilet in the store. We will work toward developing a more integrated system of communication as you progress."

"You seem to know a lot about my habits," Scott said. "Can I at least know who I'm supposedly working for?"

"The right side. The less you know the better."

Eight

SCOTT FOLLOWED UP WITH DESIRÉE'S UNCLE ON MONDAY. Uncle Pierre, Monsieur de Bellecourt, the head of a family-held private banking firm that had included Desirée's father prior to his death, had been the peacemaker, assuaging the various factions that initially had opposed the marriage of Scott and Desirée. Given his qualities of character and personality and his important position in the financial sector of Geneva, it was not surprising that his influence spread across many of the city's business, cultural, and social spheres.

When Scott called, Uncle Pierre pleaded that he was in a hurry, but invited him to lunch at the club the following day. His answer had to be yes.

The next day, as Scott was putting on his coat, Desirée said, "My darling, I hope all goes well today. But don't be too disappointed if it is not possible right now. Perhaps Uncle Pierre needs more time to bring some of his friends around to the idea of making an American a member of the club, particularly one with no experience. Remember, they don't know how cute you are."

"Well that's not entirely true. I've been fencing with you for a year now."

"Touché," she said.

"I promise I will be gracious no matter the outcome."

"I'm not worried about your graciousness. I'm worried about your disappointment."

"Well, I'm counting on Uncle Pierre's desire not to disappoint you. That's a better bet."

He left the house in his Porsche by the front entrance, but he outmaneuvered his pursuers when he reached Geneva. He arrived a little too early, so he circled the block a few times before entering the courtyard of the club on rue Dancet, in the old part of Geneva, near the university. It was a building of some five floors, and he entered by climbing a few steps. Just inside he found a foyer and a reception desk. He indicated he was to meet Monsieur de Bellecourt, and a valet led him through the mahogany paneled doors into a lobby of sorts where Uncle Pierre was sitting in a large leather armchair reading the *Tribune de Genève.*

"Scott, my boy, so good of you to come. I hope you're hungry. Tuesday is venison day here at the club."

"Yes, thank you for inviting me. It's good to see you again."

They took the well-appointed elevator to the second floor, where there was an intimate dining room, a male bastion of exotic woods, leather, and dark colors of suede. They were seated at an intimate table for two a little out of the way, although Pierre gave a nod of recognition to the few members who were already having their lunch.

The waiter came and took their order. It didn't take Pierre long to launch into the matter that brought them together. "My dear Scott, I have made some inquiries regarding proposing you for membership to the club. To be clear, some people I've spoken with find it a little odd that you have an interest in fencing. I must say that I find it rather peculiar myself. When I was young, my brother and I were more or less forced to enjoy—if that's the mot juste—the art of fencing. But in general, it's not something one takes up at your advanced age," he said with a smile.

"I agree that it may be preposterous for me to even contemplate it, and most of all I wouldn't want to embarrass you or Desirée, but I do have an interest in trying my luck."

"Well, here's where you—we—stand. I have found the necessary sponsors for your membership, the main one being a Monsieur Sean MacAllister. Sounds Scottish, but couldn't be more Swiss, three generations. His father was a close associate of mine, now deceased. Sean is about twenty years your senior, but he is still a very good swordsman. I think you'll like him."

"You've really been too kind on my behalf. I can't thank you enough."

"Oh, you really need to thank Desirée. It's her they don't want to disappoint. They are asking about her. They want her to have her baby, and then they want the parties and the dinners to begin again. They miss her terribly."

"I understand completely. I miss that Desirée too."

"Sean will contact you. Now let's enjoy our venison. You know it's not the venison I'm after, it's the spaetzle with the jaeger mushroom sauce. And by the way, the members are concerned about the club being monitored by the paparazzi. Do they still follow you and Desirée?"

"They followed me today, but I went into the parking near the Hotel des Bergues and lost them when I came out the other side. I'll be careful not to lead them here."

"Well done, my boy."

Back at the house, Desirée asked him about lunch and what had happened. He gave her the short version. "I expected it to be a lot more difficult," he said.

"Uncle Pierre has a way of getting what he wants," Desirée said.

"I think it runs in the family."

"Louise Goosens called today and brought me up on everything going on in the world I used to be so much a part of."

"Uh-oh," he said.

"Why uh-oh?"

"Because I'm sure Louise could not resist giving you the Stefano report." Stefano was Desirée's ex-husband, the playboy Italian count, who despite his philandering could not believe that he could be so summarily dismissed, and the marriage annulled by the then countess in spite of his begging her to return to Venice. Up until the last moment before Scott and Desirée were married, he had continued to pursue Desirée with promises and entreaties that were for naught, even to the point of enlisting the Archbishop of Venice to intercede on his behalf. He had even tried physical intimidation of Scott, but they had managed to keep that confrontation out of the papers. Louise Goosens, who belonged to the same international set as Desirée, was always in a position to reveal firsthand details of loves lost and regained, infidelities and trysts, as well as the mundane vicissitudes of current divorces.

"She did tease me with an irresistible tidbit."

"Is it something you're dying to share, or should I pretend disinterest as to what his latest exercise in self-debasement might be?"

"Louise says that when he learned that I was pregnant he wept, because he knew that whatever hope he held was futile."

"I'm glad he's beginning to adopt a policy of reality rather than the dream world he so often inhabits."

"I told Louise in a gentle way that I didn't want to hear any more about Stefano. She may have been a little offended."

"Probably embarrassed. I wish you hadn't told her that. I so enjoy hearing about my rival wallowing in his defeat."

"You're so mean," she said with an ironic pout as she poked him in the ribs.

Nine

THE FOLLOWING MORNING, SCOTT GOT A TELEPHONE call from Sean MacAllister asking him to come to his office the next afternoon at two o'clock. It was a modern building by Geneva standards, located on l'avenue Général-Guisan, one of the major streets on the Left Bank.

He had expected an elaborate office, but when he entered there wasn't even a receptionist. Monsieur MacAllister must have heard the door open and came out from his own office, greeted him, and ushered him in. He was impeccably dressed in a gray pinstriped suit, a man of some assurance and size, his posture erect, almost of military bearing and, with the hint of the Scot, reddish-brown, wiry hair.

"I'm so glad you could come on short notice."

"It's very nice of you to meet with me."

"I understand that you're interested in learning *l'escrime* and joining the club."

"I am. I need to tell you, though, that I'm a complete novice, so it's quite possible that I don't know what I'm getting myself into."

"I'm quite sure you don't know what you're getting yourself into, but of course that is exactly what makes you a good candidate for membership."

"I honestly hadn't thought of it that way."

"There's a lot to learn, but over the next few months, if you apply yourself, you will become a swordsman of some talent. You're intelligent and athletic. You will do well, I predict. It will take me a couple of weeks, but your membership will be official by the end of January. I'll call you when it's done, and we'll have lunch at the club. I'll show you around and develop a plan for your instruction."

"I really don't know how to thank you. You've been very generous."

"Not at all. Besides, your real estate agent, Wainwright, speaks highly of you."

Fortunately, Scott didn't flinch, and he guessed that MacAllister had saved this tidbit to the end just to see if he would react to an abrupt revelation. Scott said goodbye, thanked him again, and said he would wait for his call.

THE NEXT TWO WEEKS WERE HELL. HE COULD TURN THESE things over in his mind a thousand times, but there was no more clarity at the end than there was in the beginning. He read the *Tribune* every Wednesday, looking in the classifieds for Rolleiflex cameras, but there was nothing. There wasn't any information for him to pick up, and therefore no questions that he could ask. He felt someone was testing him to see if he would be curious or anxious enough to call and break the silence. He kept his patience.

DESIRÉE NOW WAS AT HER MOST UNCOMFORTABLE PERIOD. The first of February was upon them, and she could go into labor any day. Still the two of them, even with all that was going on—and in Scott's case, so much he couldn't reveal—were relishing their time together and enjoying the fact that they were partners and lovers.

MacAllister called and left a message asking if Scott would join him for lunch on the first Wednesday of February. Scott called the number to say he was available, and a woman answered, took his message, and asked if instead he could come to Monsieur MacAllister's office an hour earlier. They would go to the club together afterward.

When Scott arrived at MacAllister's office, there was no receptionist in sight, but out came MacAllister. "Congratulations. You have been invited to join our little Société d'escrime, a little scream, a little crime," he said. It was a lousy pun.

"Thank you, and perhaps you might tell me exactly what the dues are and what my involvement might entail."

Taking Scott by the arm, guiding him to a chair, MacAllister said, "A couple of months after the baby is born, you will receive a 1-A classification from your draft board in the United States."

"Who do I have to thank for that?" Scott asked.

"Please hear me out. Otherwise we will be late for lunch. A few weeks after that, you will receive a draft notice."

"It would be a lot easier for me to understand if you would just tell me what you want me to do. I thought that if I cooperated with you then I wouldn't be drafted. But I'm confused now as to how this can possibly work out."

"Okay, just listen to me. When you receive the draft notice, you will tell your wife that you can't leave her, you can't leave the baby, and you are against the war in Vietnam, so you have decided not to obey the draft notice and will remain in Switzerland."

"Well, you're right on everything except about not obeying the draft notice. I couldn't do that even if I disagreed with the war."

"And why not?"

"Because . . . you wouldn't understand."

"But the fact is we do understand, and that's why you've been chosen. We don't make a habit of misjudging people's loyalties."

"Am I that predictable?"

MacAllister didn't answer this question, leaving Scott with the impression that they believed that they had him figured out.

"Your wife will propose that you become Swiss or French or both."

"She already has."

"Once it becomes common knowledge that the countess's husband, the young American, has renounced his citizenship, has refused to be drafted, and has taken Swiss and French citizenship, no one will suspect that you are an agent working for the American government."

"How could you ask me to do such a thing? What about my friends?

God, what about my parents? What will they think? I'm not even sure Desirée will respect me."

"Knowing you're doing the right thing by helping your country. Naturally, in the short term there will be some disappointment. But you'll know the truth, and sometimes that has to be enough."

"But why me?"

"Good question. First, you have the intelligence and raw IQ necessary to learn what you need to know quickly, and you have no connection to the military. Your past is pristine. Second, your social position as a result of marrying the countess is unique, and her contacts and influence allow you to move rather effortlessly and without suspicion among aristocrats, diplomats, financiers, and the international set. You can listen, you can learn, you can . . . well, we'll think of things."

"But what about my studies at the university?"

"I'm afraid that will have to wait. Anyway, you won't be needing the student deferment. You can work on your degree later. I'm sure Hochstadt will understand. We're looking right now for something more suitable for you, something with a good cover. But now we need to go to the club. I want to introduce you to some of the members."

Hochstadt will understand what? More suitable, and what might that be? None of this made any sense to Scott.

MacAllister had been a celebrated dueler in his youth and was still an aficionado of the sport and a trustee of the club. Scott could not have had a more knowledgeable or better-connected person to introduce him to the members and the staff. Before the afternoon was over, he was set up with an instructor and had purchased his fencing attire—the gloves, a mask, and most importantly, an épée. He was glad to discover that the clothing was armored with hard inserts that protected the wearer from being stabbed or cut. As a result, it was heavier than he'd imagined.

His instructor, Wilhelm Kruger, was a Swiss German from Zug, the smallest canton in Switzerland. Kruger was a master in the sport, having won many national and international titles. MacAllister assured him that he was in good hands, and he asked Kruger to make sure that Scott made steady progress on both the technique and conditioning required. Scott should come weekly, Kruger proposed, and MacAllister quickly agreed. German Swiss are known for their work ethic, their myopic devotion to their duty as they see it, and their absolute dearth of a sense of humor. Scott could expect no mercy from this five-foot, eight-inch, 160-pound taskmaster.

MacAllister and Kruger suddenly switched from French to Swiss German, exchanging a few words that ended in a chuckle. They were playing with him.

He wondered if Kruger was part of the team. Now he was suspicious of every introduction. As a matter of fact, how did MacAllister insinuate himself into Scott's admission process? Was Uncle Pierre involved as well? So many questions, yet no one to ask.

Ten

On Valentine's Eve, around ten in the morning, Desirée's water broke. Gustav drove them to the Clinique des Anges, where Dr. Pelz, Desirée's obstetrician, was waiting for them.

Desirée's contractions began and intensified once she was in her suite. Dr. Pelz had coached him, and Scott had read about the process, but nothing had prepared him to see her in such excruciating pain. It was obviously worse for Desirée, but no one could know how much Scott suffered seeing her wracked in misery.

At five-fifteen in the afternoon, little Celine, a precious bundle of some six pounds and one ounce, was born. Mother and baby were pronounced in perfect condition, although Desirée might have disagreed. It was a miracle of nature, maybe with God's imprint, that a mother could, within an hour after enduring the pain of childbirth, hold her baby and smile and coo with such love and doting.

Scott sat on the edge of the bed while Desirée held little Celine close. Madame de Bellecourt, Desirée's mother, had donned her surgical mask to enter the suite, but her eyes told the story. She leaned in close and embraced her daughter and told her how proud she was and how beautiful her baby was. Scott hoped that Celine would have those glorious aquamarine eyes that blessed the Bellecourt women.

There was a knock at the door. Scott opened it slightly, and there was Uncle Pierre. Dr. Pelz had already advised that Desirée should have only two visitors at a time, but Scott could hardly enforce the limitation on Uncle Pierre.

Uncle Pierre's eyes glistened, and Scott thought he could detect a wide smile behind his reserved demeanor. He was a formal man and offered the expected congratulations and embraces to Desirée and noted the beauty and health of the baby. He wanted to know the name and was not surprised that it was that of Desirée's childhood friend from Paris. As he and Scott went back into the hall, he said, "Perhaps it's not the time, but I hope your meeting with Sean MacAllister went well. It appears that somehow he rolled your membership through the process."

"Yes, he seems very efficient."

"I'm sure he has some ideas for you. It's probably time for you to find something more appropriate. After all, now you have an extra mouth to feed."

Uncle Pierre spoke with the face of a poker player. There was not a twitch of an eyelid, no hint of a smile or a grimace. He spoke as if he were presenting facts that he assumed would go unchallenged. Scott contested none of it, guessing his earlier question had been answered. Uncle Pierre might be in on the coup.

Back in the room with Desirée, Scott placed his hand on the back of their daughter's head and said, "She's beautiful, isn't she?"

"You know, you had a little something to do with it. It wasn't all me."

"The beautiful part is all you," he replied.

ON THE FIFTH DAY AFTER THE BIRTH, DR. PELZ RELEASED Desirée and Celine from the clinic, and they arrived back at the house overlooking the Lake of Geneva. It was a cold day, but still sunny, with traces of snow making a patchwork of white, brown, and green across the slope leading up to the house. Madame Francine Dubois, a professional nurse and the prospective nanny, was waiting for them at the front door along with Marie Claude, the cook, and Sybil, Desirée's maid. Scott saw too that Helena, Desirée's long-serving and trusted housekeeper from her chalet in Gstaad, had come down, and of course Madame de Bellecourt stood by as well.

Little Celine was the show. They all wanted to hold her, admire her, and tell Desirée what a beautiful baby she was. Madame de Bellecourt, puffed up in her grandmother role, agreed with and added to the many compliments that came the baby's way.

The nursery, which had been established in the bedroom next to Scott and Desirée's bedroom, was a cozy and cushioned world of pink and lilac. How had Desirée known it would be a girl? A beautiful white crib, along with various changing tables, a bassinet, a rocking chair, and various comfy armchairs furnished the room. The nanny's room was on the other side of the nursery. Celine could not coo without being heard. Madame de Bellecourt and Desirée had been busy.

Scott was going to have a tough time competing with all these women circling around Desirée and little Celine. But he had another preoccupation: MacAllister and company. What were their plans for him? He couldn't see how he could be useful to them.

Eleven

A NOTE WITHOUT FLOURISH FROM MACALLISTER, HIS sponsor, informed Scott that each Thursday morning he would take his fencing lesson and afterward would join him for lunch if MacAllister happened to be in the dining room. He wasn't consulted as to whether or not Thursday was convenient. He considered it his first order.

Wilhelm Kruger, master instructor, was waiting for him. First things first, Kruger made some adjustments to Scott's equipment, cinching here, loosening there. "I don't want to stick you in the wrong place," he said with a half-smile. It was a Helvetian attempt at humor.

He proceeded to show Scott the grip on his épée, the address of the sword, and his en garde, or ready, position. Then he asked Scott to move backward and forward, showing him how to advance and retreat without tripping and without losing his balance. Lose your balance or trip in this sport and metaphorically you were dead. As Scott had predicted, Kruger was unrelenting. There was little camaraderie and less compassion for a beginner. Kruger demanded that he perform the exercises over and over, faster and then faster still. All in all, Scott was surprised that he did as well as he had, but there would be no kudos from Kruger. As the hour ended, he saw MacAllister enter the instruction area. He ducked out quickly, but the message had been delivered. MacAllister would be in the dining room today. Scott guessed that meeting in plain sight was the best cover.

MacAllister was waiting for him at a table for four in the dining room of the club. Scott noticed that there were more members present than on previous occasions, all well-dressed men of the Swiss elite. MacAllister motioned for him to come over.

"So nice to see you," MacAllister said. "I hear from Herr Kruger that your first lesson went very well. You may have an undiscovered talent."

"I don't presume that a protest would do any good."

"Oh, I wouldn't protest. It might make you seem like a bad sport."

"I wouldn't want anyone to think badly of me."

"Just do your job, and we'll all do ours. That's the way it works out best. Are you hungry?"

"I'm always hungry."

MacAllister motioned for the waiter, but as the menu was offered, he interrupted, "How about we share a nice rare filet de boeuf with the vegetable bouquet and the Bérnaise sauce. You must be famished after that workout."

Scott noticed that MacAllister had placed a copy of his newspaper on one of the empty chairs, and that reminded him to ask, "I've been reading the *Tribune de Genève* every Wednesday, but I haven't seen any ads for Rolleiflexes."

"Can't help you with that. That's Wainwright's section. Just keep reading."

"And have you and Uncle Pierre found something more suitable for me?"

"Is Pierre de Bellecourt helping too? There are several ideas under consideration. That comes from higher up, way up. You'll be informed when it's official." MacAllister wouldn't be so easily tricked.

After lunch, Scott got into his Porsche and drove up the lake road a short distance. It was cold, but he got out of the car and sat on one of the benches. As he looked out over the water, the late afternoon light faded as the sun slipped below the peaks of the Alps in the south. The great body of water roiled a menacing gray, casting small bands of mist here and there. Absent their leaves, the hardwoods were mere sticks against the somber sky, and the pastures were the light tan of dead grass. He was in a real box. He couldn't think of anything except to cooperate; he had to, but deep down he was angry. They were messing up his life with Desirée.

When he first became enraptured with Desirée, she seemed an impossible dream, and then when she reciprocated his love, life seemed perfect. Then there was the problem of overcoming the objections to their marriage, the pregnancy, the Church, and all the rest. But who could have anticipated his problems with the draft and now his involvement with who knew what? Was it the CIA, the Defense Department, or U.S. Army Military Intelligence? No one was telling him anything, and he had zero leverage, because if he didn't cooperate, they could draft him, and perhaps out of pique send him to something far worse than what they had in mind for him now. They had him at a disadvantage. They were counting on his core beliefs, and they intended to use them to manipulate him. But this seemed to be a recruitment that might not have a termination, one that could go on indefinitely. And they, whoever they were, seemed to know almost everything about him, whereas he knew nothing about them. They wouldn't be receptive to any appeals to fairness.

YET SCOTT HAD TO PRETEND THAT ALL WAS NORMAL. Fortunately, Celine was a good baby, but even a good baby will keep her parents up at all hours. The nanny helped, particularly with the numerous diaper changes, but only Desirée could provide what the baby really needed and wanted. Out of his sense of participation, Scott was awake as much as Desirée. It was grueling but necessary. They had developed a routine and were looking forward to the time when Celine might sleep through the night.

Scott made sure he was the one who checked the mail every afternoon. If his information was correct, the letter changing his classification was due any day, and if he didn't intercept it, it would generate endless conversations of hypotheses regarding what they might expect. Desirée would fret and worry and search for answers where there were none.

Finally it came. The envelope was easily identifiable in the jumble of mail. He opened it in front of the mailbox, and as predicted and forewarned, he now had 1-A status. The letter didn't offer any appeals process or provide any other information other than the one-sentence notification.

He carried the envelope to their bedroom, where Desirée had just finished feeding the baby. He was sure his face betrayed his worry and anxiety. "What is it?" she said.

"They've changed my status to 1-A."

She was silent. He'd always admired her sense of knowing when her silence would make a stronger argument than anything she might say.

What could he say? He knew what she wanted him to do, and he knew what Wainwright and MacAllister and whoever else wanted him to do, but he wasn't sure he could do it.

After his next fencing lesson, he learned from MacAllister that the draft notice would be arriving in less than two weeks. His sponsor wanted to know if Scott had discussed the situation with Desirée and what her opinions were. Scott told him that he wasn't sure she had a good grasp of the labyrinth that was the American Selective Service System. MacAllister seemed certain that whether she understood or not, she certainly would not want him to leave her and the baby.

Like clockwork, his draft notice arrived two weeks later. He was to report to Fort Knox in Kentucky on June 1, some two months later. He wondered how Desirée would react when he told her. She had always been able to handle adversity with a certain grace and in some cases disdain, as if the difficulty was unworthy of her consideration. He reluctantly, but necessarily, gave her the bad news.

"Have you figured it out yet?" she asked.

"Figured out what?"

"Darling, if you remember from the early days of our courting, I can be as romantic as you, but I'm a lot more practical. Is it time to call David Blum?"

She was right. From the beginning, no matter the subject, she'd been a lot more practical than he. She was the one who didn't care who knew that she was dating a young man that others considered inappropriate. She was the one who insisted that they not be chased from Gstaad in fear of running into her ex-husband, and she had first announced to her friends that she was in love and that everyone needed to accommodate their attitudes to that fact. Perhaps there was a lesson in her pragmatism.

"Maybe. I'm thinking about it." He couldn't make it appear too easy. She knew he had been opposed. What she didn't know is that now he had no option, but he had to make it appear that he was more conscience-stricken than he was.

"Don't confuse patience with procrastination," she warned.

Twelve

A FEW DAYS DIDN'T HELP. HE WAS STILL TORN ON Thursday as he trudged to his fencing class. By now he had progressed to the point that Herr Kruger would engage him in slow-motion matches of lunge and parry. His demand for repetition with slight variations was endless, and his steely corrections incessant. Scott didn't know how well his fencing was coming along, but it was obvious to him that he was getting in the best physical condition of his life.

After his class, he went up to the dining room. He was not surprised to see MacAllister waiting for him. "You look a little glum, Scott," MacAllister said.

"And I'm sure you know why."

"Scott, grow up. This is an opportunity to serve your country, not betray it."

"That's not what my wife will think, nor my parents, nor my friends back in the United States, or those I've made here."

"You'll have to decide which is more important, appearances or reality."

"By the way," Scott asked, "how long must I keep up this charade?"

"That depends on how effective you are."

Uh-oh. In essence, the more *effective* he was, the longer this could go on. He had a lot of questions, but MacAllister wouldn't answer, and if he did answer, he might not be telling the truth. Scott decided to put him on the record anyway with a few questions. “The things you’ll be asking me to do, are they dangerous?”

“We’re not going to ask you to blow up any bridges or assassinate anyone. Your role will be subtle but just as necessary.”

“How will the other side view my activities? Will they consider me a threat and think about ending my activity?”

“I think you’ve been reading too many spy novels.”

“How many people on our side will know about me and my activities?”

“That’s a good question, and an astute one. Now you’re beginning to use the guile we know you have. Only two, Wainwright and myself. All others will know you by your code name.”

“I have a code name?”

“Yes, Absinthe.”

“Absinthe? Why that, and why do I need one?”

“It’s an aperitif traditionally made in the Jura between France and Switzerland. Clever, don’t you think? And you need the code name for our own purposes within the company. We can’t go bandying your name about.”

“My experience with absinthe is limited, but I know it’s an acquired taste.”

“Touché, my boy.”

“And speaking of secrecy, I can’t understand why you’re interested in me. I’m not famous per se, but if I’m known it’s for no other reason than being the countess’s husband. My ability to sneak around for you is very limited.”

“But that’s exactly the point. For what we have in mind your celebrity is only a plus. We want you to be high profile. It’s the perfect cover.”

WHEN SCOTT ARRIVED HOME FROM LUNCH, HE TOOK THE steps two at a time up to the second floor, where Desirée sat in a rocker with Celine. It was a pretty picture. The baby offered a soft giggle, then choked and coughed, having laughed a little too much. Desirée patted and hugged her, and a small burp was heard. He went to them, knelt beside the rocker, hugged his wife, and tenderly touched and kissed the baby's forehead.

"How was your fencing class?" Desirée asked.

"I think I'm getting a little better, but you wouldn't know it by listening to Kruger."

"You can't please Swiss Germans. They are maniacs about work. They would be a lot happier if they ate more croissants."

"Speaking of croissants, I think we should call Blum."

"What does Blum have to do with croissants?"

"Nothing, but we still need to call him."

Desirée easily arranged an appointment with David, who, Scott learned, was a specialist in the area of obtaining Swiss nationality, visas, and work permits, and handling other immigration matters. Uncle Pierre had recommended him for just what they had in mind. Uncle Pierre did get around.

Blum's office was not too far from MacAllister's. Scott would also meet with an attorney at the French consulate in Geneva and begin the process of naturalization to French citizenship at the same time. While it wasn't necessary for him to have dual citizenship, it was probably safer when he was in each country to be a citizen of that country.

As was his new habit, he read the classifieds in *Tribune de Genève* on Wednesdays. Three ads from the bottom of the column, he saw "Rolleiflex," the make and model and then the identifying, "Georges S., 22 44 51 19."

Trying to be as nonchalant as possible, he told Desirée that he wanted to go to Geneva and pick up a book at Payot. There was nothing unusual about this, so he didn't get any questions. That was a relief, because it meant he didn't have to lie.

He arrived at the bookstore a little after two in the afternoon. Since he had come to Geneva as a student over a year ago, the bookstore was one of his favorite places. It had been in the same location for decades and had a clientele of university and lycée students as well as bibliophiles of all ages. There were three floors; the first two were always bustling with both browsers and readers who sometimes sat for hours in the same chair, never moving, lest they lose their spot. There were tables, racks, and bookcases arranged in various configurations following the layout of the floor and the intervening support pillars of the construction. The lighting was dim, but adequate for young eyes.

Scott thought it was a good place for a message to be passed, since there were always so many people milling about without a real agenda. He too could meander, picking up books here and there, glancing around for anyone who looked suspicious, if he indeed would know what that looked like. At some point, he could drop in upstairs and roam around the English section, not an unusual activity for an English-speaking person. More importantly, the restroom where he could dispose of any message that he received was also on the second floor.

He knew where the Shakespeare poetry section was, but he didn't fall on it directly, taking instead a more serpentine approach. As he was instructed, he didn't look around trying to discern which one of the people on the second floor might be the one. He knew the person who would pick up his message of inquiry would have already identified him.

He took his time, picked up the book of sonnets, thumbed through it a couple of times, sat down to read a few, and then he turned to sonnet 119. A folded note lay against the binding. He closed the book, put it back on the shelf, and took another one down, thumbing through the pages, pausing here and there to read a few lines. After replacing this book and going back to the original one, he walked behind the bookcase and came out the other side with the message in his pocket. It read, "Wednesday, Grands Magasins, Men's Department, 12:30." He went directly to the restroom, waited on the outside for a moment, looked to see if he had been followed, and then entered and went into a toilet stall. He read the message again, silently tore it into small pieces, peed for good measure, and flushed.

Grands Magasins was not a place where Scott would have ever shopped, and after marrying Desirée, it was even less likely that he would buy anything there. It was a store of good quality but not luxury goods. Far from it. He settled on the idea that if he ran into someone he knew, he would say he was shopping for a tie for Gustav.

But his alibi wasn't needed. As he got off the escalator on the third floor, he saw Wainwright in the suits section. Wainwright approached him and said, "May I help you with something?"

Scott noticed he had a nametag pinned to his suit jacket that read, "Gilbert."

"Yes, I'm looking for a nice tie for an employee."

"We have an extensive selection just over here. Were you thinking of something in silk, perhaps a solid color or pattern?"

Wainwright was really playing it, but Scott tried to be as professional as he. "I'm not sure, can I just look around?"

There were no shoppers at the tie counter, and Wainwright informed him that he should have his attorney write the draft board and the American consulate in Geneva and in Paris, saying that he would not report to Fort Knox and was in the process of becoming a Swiss and French citizen by virtue of his wife's dual nationality and his opposition to the war.

Scott flinched. The American consul was a good friend of Desirée's and had been to their home several times, at least once since they had been married. Scott's decision to renounce his citizenship would circulate to the highest echelons of the diplomatic community. More serious, however, was the fact that the American ambassadors in both Bern and Paris were also friends of Desirée's. They were sure to gossip about him already renouncing his American citizenship. And the newspapers and paparazzi would relish the news.

"My being a draft resister will make all the papers. People will think I'm a coward."

"I know, but that's what will make the next steps convincing."

"What next steps?"

"All in due time. Let's get to it. Go tell your lawyer."

Scott wondered what they would do if he did not report to Fort Knox, renounced his citizenship, obtained the dual nationality, and then didn't cooperate. They had probably already thought of that possibility, and knew he'd think of it too. Would they mention it, and the consequences, just to reinforce his allegiance and resolve? They couldn't wait forever.

"And Scott, don't even think about double-crossing us. That's not an option. There are worse things than working for us. Make sure you don't find out what they are."

They read minds too. He would have to do what they wanted for the time being, but he would be working from day one to find a way to extricate himself safely from their hold. He wanted his passport back.

Thirteen

It was time to tell his parents. They resented always being the last to know. In the last year, they had learned about his involvement with the countess through a photo in *Life* magazine picturing them at the Cannes Film Festival. Next, he had surprised them by his proposal of marriage, and then his mother had guessed that the pregnancy was the reason. Now this. There was no way for them to participate in the decision, but they would surely suffer some of the consequences. Most parents would not want their son to go to war, but most would probably prefer that to seeing their son resist the draft, much less renounce his citizenship. Nevertheless, most young men were not in Scott's position, but his parents would not see these as extenuating circumstances, nor could he reveal the truth. This would be hard on them, and he couldn't help them with it, and he would necessarily appear callous to their pain. He was certain they would feel betrayed.

The next morning, he told Desirée about calling his parents right before lunch. "They'll blame me," she said.

"They'll blame both of us, but there's nothing that can be done about it."

Just after noon, he called. The telephone rang once, then twice, and his mother answered. "Good morning, mother," he said.

"Oh, Scott! How's our little Celine?"

"She's the best baby. She's sleeping the night through, and she eats like a little pig." He heard a click on the line and knew his father had picked up the phone in his study.

"I'm so happy for both of you," his mother said.

"How is Desirée?" his father asked.

"She's fine too, regaining her strength and her figure. Dr. Pelz has her working with a nutritionist and a gym instructor, doing some Far Eastern exercises. But there's another reason I'm calling." He waited for them to ask what it was, but they knew him too well. They waited. "A few weeks ago, after my status was changed to 1-A, I received an order from the army to report to Fort Knox, Kentucky, to join the U. S. Army on May 1."

His mother cried out, "No!"

"Yes, but hold on. Given the circumstances of being newly married and having a baby plus the unpopularity of the war, I have decided to remain in Switzerland and not report." He had worked on this presentation a lot. It sounded so much better than some other ways he could have explained it.

There was a moment of silence, and then his father spoke, "But Scott, wouldn't that mean that you would be a draft resister, and you couldn't come back to the United States without being prosecuted?"

"I'm afraid that's right, Dad, but I don't see many options."

"But just because you're drafted doesn't necessarily mean you would be sent to Vietnam," his father said. He could hear his mother weeping softly.

"I can't take that chance. I'm married now. And there's Celine. I can't just think of myself or even you and Mother."

"Son, I hope you understand that this means that the only way we can see you and the baby is to come to Europe."

"There's no way to soften the consequences," Scott said. "And there will be others. Your friends who have sons who have been drafted will not be understanding."

"I hope you've thought this through," his father said. "While this solves the immediate draft problem, for the long term you may be creating situations that are irreversible for us all."

"What are you saying? That I should obey the order?"

"I'm not sure. You don't want to be called a traitor."

"I had hoped that you would be behind me."

"I am. We are."

"But not all the way."

"Will you be safe in Switzerland?" his mother asked. "Can they make you come back?"

"I'll be granted asylum here. I'll be untouchable."

His father interjected, "I hope you know what you're doing. Isn't there some compromise? There may be things that you haven't thought of. Isn't there any way to appeal the classification of 1-A?

"No Dad, it's either report or seek asylum."

"What a mess," his mother added.

They insisted on dissecting every aspect, sometimes two or three times. They wanted to know things that were either unknowable or he didn't want to tell them. At the end of the conversation, he still hadn't told them about renouncing his citizenship. How much could he expect them to take in one session? He could only be truly disappointed if he had expected them to be totally supportive. His mother wanted him safe above all else, and his father did as well, but his father was thinking about his own position and how it might be affected. After he hung up and was reviewing what had been said, he concluded that it had gone about as well as it could. After all, what parent wants to hear the kinds of things he had just told them?

Fourteen

DESIRÉE WANTED TO COME WITH HIM TO THE LAWyer. Scott couldn't object, and he was certain that David Blum thought it a good idea. Monsieur Blum was a partner in one of Geneva's oldest law firms, Schmidt, Beltran, Fenster, and Blum, and as Desirée noted, he had been an acquaintance of her father and remained a confidant of Uncle Pierre. His office was in one of the venerable buildings on the Left Bank, overlooking the Lake of Geneva. The reception area resembled a club with all the accouterments one would expect, including large leather armchairs, dark wood paneling, and a reverential silence. A young receptionist made the call to Monsieur Blum on their arrival, and they were led to his office almost immediately.

They took the two chairs in front of his desk. Without speaking, M. Blum opened a file, quickly ran through a few pages, and said, "Scott, I presume that you have thought this over carefully, because once accomplished, it will be very difficult to reverse."

"Yes, I have not stopped thinking about it. It's a very important and wrenching decision, but we have decided that it's in our family's best interests to proceed."

"Normally, both for French and Swiss citizenship, it would be necessary to have been married a number of years, three and five to be precise, to become a citizen. But because of this draft situation, you will need to claim asylum status. The asylum classification will supersede the length of marriage requirement. Nevertheless, it may be difficult to prove that you need asylum."

"I have an idea about that," Scott said.

"And that is?" Monsieur Blum said.

"I would like for you to write the American consulate here advising them that I will not report as ordered, but I have decided to seek asylum."

"Well that would certainly accomplish the goal of your proof of the asylum status, but it may have consequences that you haven't considered."

"I know, and the most odious would be that someone in the consulate will probably leak this to some reporter who will in turn see the sensational aspect of the story as it pertains to the countess and her new husband."

"I see you have anticipated the consequences that I was thinking of. Are you and Desirée prepared for the negative consequences?"

"We're already hounded by the press but less now than before our marriage. Their interest is not about me of course, it's Desirée they're after. When we returned from our honeymoon, and particularly after the baby was born, they were always roaming about. I don't guess one more thing matters."

"I hadn't thought about it becoming so public," Desirée said. "But I believe Scott is right. It's the way to ensure the citizenship application."

"Of course, he's right, but I would have never suggested it," Monsieur Blum said.

Two weeks later, Desirée and Scott were having breakfast at the table in the bay window overlooking the lake. Scott wondered why the newspapers weren't already on the breakfast table as was the custom. He rang for Helena and inquired as to where the papers were. She sheepishly admitted that they were still in the foyer. Desirée interrupted and asked her to bring them. Shortly Helena returned, papers in hand. Desirée reached for *Le Figaro* and Scott *The*

Tribune de Genève and *The Herald Tribune*. The article in the Geneva paper, their local paper, appeared below the fold, and in the two Parisian papers, it was in the society section. The source must have been a wire service report, because all three reported the story of the countess's husband and his renouncement of his U.S. citizenship in much the same way. None of the papers could resist running old photos of the couple in various locales such as Cannes and Paris, looking gay, happy, and rich.

The telephone rang. Desirée answered it and immediately said, "Louise, you're calling early." There was a long pause, and then, "Yes, we're reading it now."

He was glad that the baby had come before all this started in earnest. They had begun to make love again, and their lovemaking was always a good barometer of the status of their relationship. At this time, the barometer readings were very positive, and they both needed that to get through the days ahead.

THURSDAYS HAD BECOME A DUTY RATHER THAN A PLEASURE AS Scott reported weekly to his fencing class with Herr Kruger. He faked enthusiasm to get through the endless drills and repetition, along with the embellished lectures on the history and attributes of fencing per his instructor. His stamina had improved, and he was challenged by the physicality of the sport as well as the strategy of the attacks and defenses. MacAllister had also instructed Kruger that some martial arts instruction would be helpful in addition to the fencing. The sport reminded Scott of fast chess and controlled mayhem.

About every other Thursday MacAllister would be there for lunch after his lesson. One Thursday, as Scott entered the dining room, MacAllister stood to greet him, and as soon as they had ordered lunch, he lowered his voice and said, "I saw the papers. You did a good job. How did you persuade the attorney to write the newspaper? I thought he might be against it. Attorneys don't usually seek notoriety for their clients."

"He didn't. He wrote the consulate, and it was leaked. He did initially oppose the idea, but I told him that it was a way to ensure my asylum."

"See, that's why we like you. You're sly. But don't be too sly."

"What do you mean?"

"It might enter your mind to think that now that you are a Swiss citizen and you've suffered the slings and arrows of being a draft dodger that you might not need us anymore."

"Wainwright explained rather well that quitting wasn't an option."

"I heard, but I wanted to reinforce the importance of our understanding. Am I clear?"

"Brutally so. And by the way, I hope my parents don't disown me. They're not happy with my decision."

"Sorry, but necessary. In any case, we're not really worried about you. You know where your best interests lie. And you're not a person to go back on your word anyway, nor are you not able to see the benefit to the country of your actions."

"Well I'm not seeing much yet."

"You will. And by the way, we want you to travel to Bern next week," MacAllister told him. "Tell your wife it's a job interview. A car will pick you up, drive you to Bern on Tuesday, and you'll be back in the afternoon."

"What kind of job interview? I've got to have some believable story for my wife."

"Tell her it's with *Le Point Opposé*, a small political and foreign affairs journal with offices in Bern and Paris."

"And I'm interviewing for what position?"

"Freelance journalist and editorialist."

"And spy extraordinaire? What do I know about journalism?"

"Don't be melodramatic, Scott. You know a lot more than you think."

Fifteen

When Scott arrived back at the house in the afternoon, he decided to wait to tell Desirée of the plan to go to Bern. The Bertrands had invited them and the Goosens to dinner at their home, and he didn't want to surprise her with this crazy idea and disrupt the evening. These two couples were among the first people Scott had met when he and Desirée began their relationship. In the beginning, they had been skeptical and protective of Desirée, but over time they had relented, particularly after the marriage and more certainly after Celine's birth.

Desirée and Scott had remained pretty much at home before and after the baby's birth, but now that Celine was sleeping through the night, they had decided to begin a more normal life, one they had enjoyed prior to their marriage.

Scott had attended a luncheon at the Bertrands' before he and Desirée were married. The property was situated on a small outcropping above the Lake of Geneva. A stream ran by the house, which originally had been a mill. Only a couple experienced and appreciative of design could have imagined the renovation. They were both French from Paris and, as Desirée told the story, they fell in love with this run-down property. They promptly engaged a famous architect from Amsterdam who had preserved the defining aspects of the structure from the exterior view while integrating a Nordic minimalism into the interiors. They, like many French, were into modern. The most imposing feature of the home was the original round castle keep where the water wheel of the old mill had once been attached to the grinding stone housed in its interior. The wheel was long gone, and the keep now functioned as an observatory for the lake and the heavens. A series of dams and sluices regulated the pond level as the water rushed past the house on its way to empty into the lake. The extensive renovations and additions to the original structure now included not only the luxurious living quarters but also a half-size Olympic indoor-outdoor pool and a gravel-floored, temperature-controlled wine cellar of enormous proportions. Yves and Jacqueline had two children, both in boarding school at Le Rosey, not far from Lausanne, less than thirty kilometers away.

The black Jaguar in front of the house informed them that Jon and Louise Goosens were already there. Yves, always debonair in a white turtleneck and Bordeaux velvet blazer, met them at the door with a bottle of Taittinger champagne and two glasses. The others joined them in the foyer. It had been a while. Yves was managing director of the French bank Paribas, and Jon an officer in a private Dutch investment bank.

"Should I offer a toast to the couple's coming out from the vestiges of being newly wed and new parents?" Yves asked.

"I think you should," Louise said. "My dear Desirée, we have missed you terribly. And you as well, Scott."

Scott and Desirée played along with their humor, all raising their glasses of champagne in the playful toast. Of course, they were all aware of the circumstances of Scott's recent appearance in the newspapers, and they all probably wanted to know the inside details, none more than Louise Goosens. Scott wondered how long it would take before she would find some way to ask. He was sure that it would be in an indirect way, but it would be interesting to see what she would come up with to camouflage her intense curiosity. She was the one who also maintained at least some connection to Desirée's former husband.

She waited until dinner. They were between courses of a sauté of shrimp and a tenderloin of beef, when she asked, "Well, Scott, given recent events, do you plan to continue at the university or are you thinking of something else?"

"I seem to have several options," he said. "I'm still in good standing at the university, and it is open for me to continue. My interest in politics and foreign affairs may offer some new horizons."

"That sounds interesting, but somewhat secretive," Jon said. "You know we're all interested in your and Desirée's happiness. We're not just being nosy."

"Of course, and . . . . we appreciate your concern," Scott said.

"I'm sure it would not be difficult to find a suitable position in finance or banking," Yves said. "Jon and I would be glad to make some inquiries."

"My dear friends, you are too kind," Desirée said.

"But I think I probably know more about international relations and politics than I do about banking," Scott said.

"It sounds as if you have something in mind," Louise said.

"Well it's really just an idea at this point, but I wouldn't turn down an opportunity to become a journalist or editorialist in the right milieu," he said.

"Are you thinking of something like *The Herald Tribune?*" Yves asked.

"No, something smaller, more scholarly, and with more point of view," Scott said.

"Be careful, some of those political journals are radical," Jon said.

The conversation on that subject at last arrived at a dead end. Scott knew that they had more questions now than when they had begun, but he wasn't going to say any more. And he couldn't tell them much more, because he had a lot of questions too, the first being how could he be of value to any publication, scholarly or otherwise, without any experience?

As they drove back home, Scott could feel the tension rising. "Where did all that come from? And what are you talking about?" Desirée asked.

"For the moment, it's just an idea I've been rolling around in my mind. Nothing decided or fixed at this point."

"Well I hope not. We should discuss it before you make any decisions. And I thought it was very nice of them to offer to find you a position, if that's what you want. Uncle Pierre could help too," she said.

"It was. But I think if I find something more or less on my own, then I might be happier."

THE NEXT DAY, MADAME DE BELLECOURT WAS COMING TO lunch, and Scott had begged off to go into Geneva to the library to do a little research. Desirée didn't seem to mind, and it would give her some time with her mother and the baby.

A student at the university, Scott had full access to both the university library and the cantonal one. Both were well stocked with books, periodicals, and revues, political and scholarly.

It didn't take him long to garner the facts about *Le Point Opposé.* It was a scholarly journal that originally had been the idea of Guillaume Peridot, a political science professor at the Sorbonne in Paris. Although left of center, Professor Peridot was equally content in skewering the left or right dependent on the positions taken. The name, *Le Point Opposé*, was appropriate, because the periodical opposed various positions taken by governments or political figures without regard to ideology. The circulation was only some three thousand, by subscription only. While the subscriber list was not available, it was thought that in all probability it was a mix of both left and right cognoscenti. The subscription rate was a hefty 700 Swiss Francs per year for twenty-six biweekly issues.

A few current copies were in the archives, and a quick overview revealed that, true to its original mission, it spared no group its disdain. It attacked ideas considered faulty and was even more sarcastic and ridiculing of political figures and governments.

In 1961, upon the death of Professor Peridot, the ownership and direction had been passed to a trust administered by the Union Bank of Switzerland and an anonymous board of directors. He wondered why the board wished to remain anonymous. Was it charitable reticence? Donor shyness? Ulterior motivation? Documents also indicated that circulation had declined around ten percent after the professor's death.

AT DINNER THAT NIGHT, HE DECIDED TO BROACH THE SUBject of his impending trip to Bern with Desirée. "So how is your mother?" he asked. "Did lunch go well?"

"She must be fine, because for the entire lunch, she proceeded to give me instructions on the care of Celine. How I needed to watch her weight, that her hair might need a little trim, that I shouldn't let her use a pacifier. On and on."

"Well I'm glad I wasn't around. I think she might have had some instructions about my hair."

"Oh no. She only thinks of Celine. I might as well not have been there. And you, well, my darling, you will always come in a distant third with my mother."

"When is she returning to Paris?" he asked.

"In three weeks, thank God."

"I was at the library today looking over some potential periodicals that I think might have merit. I found one that looks good and has all the right associations. They have offices up in Bern. I might go up and meet them," he said.

"What's it called?" she asked.

"*Le Point Opposé.*"

"I've never heard of it."

"No? It's very small, only a few thousand readers."

"Then this is not a money-making venture?"

"I don't know exactly," he said. "I'm trying to understand how I might make myself useful or attractive to them."

"I'm sure you'll come up with some idea."

"Would you like to come with me?"

He prayed a little as he proffered the invitation, but he knew she would decline because of the baby. It was best to give her the possibility in order to conceal the real purpose of his trip. And a little later she was surprised that he was using a hired car and driver rather than driving himself or asking Gustav to take him to Bern. He deflected this by saying he wanted to prepare for his meeting during the trip and that she might need Gustav. She seemed to accept this explanation.

Sixteen

Tuesday morning, a chauffeured black Mercedes pulled in front of the house. Desirée accompanied Scott to the front door with little Celine. He gave them both a kiss and Desirée a hug as well.

"My darling, I hope everything goes as you want it," she said.

"Don't worry. I'm sure it will be fine."

The chauffer got out to open his door, and he immediately recognized Wainwright. His uniform was a nice touch. "Good morning, sir. Phillipe at your service," Wainwright said.

"Good morning, thank you. You have the address?"

"Oh, yes sir," he said. "I know exactly where to go."

Scott waved goodbye as they started down the long drive. It was a little less than two hours to Bern. Though he had a lot of questions, he decided he would let Wainwright lead.

"The people you will be meeting with today run the review," Wainwright said. "There have been certain inquiries made on your behalf and your resume submitted, and these people know of the recent actions you've taken regarding your citizenship. They also know you're a student in the international relations program in Geneva, and it was embellished that you often write theses and reports on current events as a part of your university requirements. We actually had our pros write a few samples, which we turned over as your work for their review. They were really good, I thought. Your credentials may have been exaggerated here and there, but it's all for a good cause."

"Who's they?" Scott said.

"Those who want you to succeed in obtaining a position at the review."

"For what purpose?"

"*Le Point Opposé* is an important and serious journal that solicits and receives points of view and argument from all sorts of influential and well-placed people in politics, business, the arts, in fact from every important area of society, including various bureaus of information and intelligence services. In many cases, some of these people write, speak, and act indiscreetly, revealing secrets and anticipated policies and movements of their governments or their companies or societies and clubs to which they belong. Your job is to fit in, to become an accredited source, a like-minded individual, so that these others will want to cozy up. You will be a member of their little club. We'll supply you with the articles that will critique the war in Vietnam from an American perspective. We'll give you inside information that no one else has. You'll soon be the darling of the anti-American groups. Before you know it, they'll be asking you to speak at their conventions, attend their conferences, and with a little luck, you'll know them all."

"If I understand correctly, you're looking for me to insert myself into a position where I would in effect overhear or eavesdrop on these communications." Now it was becoming clear to Scott. He would be a pawn in their game of learning about the opposition.

"I wouldn't call it eavesdropping, just listening."

"And why would they trust an outsider? I mean why would they even hire me?"

"There are two reasons. First because your renouncement of your citizenship, your opposition to the war in Vietnam, and your taking of French and Swiss citizenship makes you a kind of celebrity, and second the trustees at the bank, the ones who hold title to the journal, receive funding from a trust account where we have influence. Besides, haven't you noticed that when you're with your wife, the paparazzi follow you two around like puppies? To some in this milieu, you're a hero of sorts. You've already got a following. Besides, we didn't learn until recently that you were editor of your high school newspaper and a reporter for your university paper. You're an old hand at all this. Plus Dr. Hochstadt must think the world of you."

How did they come up with all this information, some of it six or seven years old? Perhaps the *Le Point* people wouldn't like him or rather would find out that he had no qualifications to work there.

Arriving in Bern shortly before eleven, Wainwright pulled into the gated courtyard where a large townhouse stood. "We're here. Your appointment is for eleven. I'm sure they're expecting you. Good luck," Wainwright said. "And by the way, we told them you were the only American that had been accepted into your class at the Geneva program, and we also dug up some of those articles you wrote for your university paper back in the States. You know, the ones about banning the bomb. Good arguments, although incorrect."

Scott climbed the few steps and pushed the button of the large brass doorbell. He heard a click and knew by the click that the door had been electronically unlocked. Inside, a woman was sitting at a desk just beyond the foyer.

"Welcome, Mr. Stoddard, they're waiting for you."

She led him to a door, knocked, and they entered. Two men were sitting at the end of a conference table nearest the windows. The room décor resembled a London club. Bookshelves lined the walls, there was a large globe, and leather armchairs and sofas were scattered about.

They introduced themselves as Jean de la Haye, director and treasurer of *Le Point,* and his associate, Christian Delacourt, the editor.

"Mr. Stoddard, your representatives have provided us information regarding your experience and qualifications," Monsieur La Haye said. "You demonstrate some early promise, but I must admit we are a little puzzled as to your choice of our little enterprise. Just why would you be interested in *Le Point Opposé*? Why not one of the newspapers in Geneva or Paris?"

"I don't think they would give me a job. I don't have that much experience."

"So why should we?"

"Because there's little risk and a lot of potential. You would only pay me if you print what I write."

Monsieur Delacourt intervened. "We already have plenty of articles disapproving of the Vietnam War."

"True, but from what I've read, they are from the European point of view."

"And because you are—or were—American, you are suggesting your viewpoint might be different?" La Haye said.

"The articles you run are intellectual treatises. Mine would be more factual and, frankly, blunt. I would question the motives of those behind the war," Scott said.

"Can we get sued?" Delacourt asked.

"You can hope. If you want to increase readership then your readers must become more engaged. You can pass on any article your attorneys deem libelous, but I doubt any of the parties want additional publicity."

"Will your articles deal only with the Vietnam situation?" Delacourt asked.

"No. The issues that drive the anti-war movement are the same ones that are attached to the student and union movements in France and Germany. There's no shortage of subjects."

"And what do you get out of this, Mr. Stoddard?" La Haye asked.

"A prestigious platform, an intelligent audience, and a readership that is multilingual and multicultural. I can write in French or English, so it won't be a problem."

"Thank you for that," Delacourt added. "Anything else we need to know?"

"Yes. If for whatever reason you decide not to publish one of my articles, then I would be free to have them published elsewhere," Scott said.

"More often it's not an absolute rejection, but more a negotiation about edits to the article," Delacourt added.

"Then I guess it depends on the edits themselves."

"We couldn't pay you much," La Haye said.

"I had anticipated as much," Scott said.

"We'll need to discuss it further," La Haye said.

"Of course, but when might I have an answer?" Scott said.

"It shouldn't take too long, maybe by Friday," La Haye said. "And do you have something in mind for your first article?"

"It's already written."

"Does it have a title?"

"Not quite yet."

ALL IN ALL, THE INTERVIEW HAD TAKEN ABOUT AN HOUR AND a half. Wainwright opened the door to the car, and they were off. "Where's lunch?" Scott asked.

"There's a little inn I know about twenty minutes from here. It should be quiet."

A few miles off the main road, next to a large lake, the Inn of the Bear appeared. Wainwright was correct as it was almost one-thirty, and there were just a few people having lunch in a large dining room. They asked for a table in a corner near the windows.

"C'mon, Scott. How'd it go?"

"They said they needed to discuss it further. They'd let me know."

"You can stop worrying. They have a say, as long as they say yes."

"They didn't seem to like the idea regarding the fact that I didn't want any changes or edits made."

"Why would you do that?"

"I thought that's what you'd want."

"Let's not rub their face in it. They'll accept what you write, but let's leave them a little dignity."

"I'm not used to the role of lackey, Wainright."

SCOTT WAS BACK IN GENEVA BY NIGHTFALL. DESIRÉE WANTED to know how it went, and he downplayed the reality of the meeting but concocted a more plausible scenario in which he related how they had done most of the talking, asking him questions and making suggestions how he might fit in. She listened carefully and said that she was glad it had gone well. She still expressed some mild objections because she couldn't understand why he was even interested in pursuing a journalistic career. She had offered to intercede with her Uncle Pierre and find a position in banking, which no doubt she considered more appropriate. He was sure that she had more or less counted on him to take on his new nationalities and relax.

On Thursday he went to his weekly fencing lesson and afterward he wasn't surprised to see MacAllister waiting for him at lunch. Scott was certain that Wainwright had already communicated the gist of the Bern meeting to him, and this was MacAllister's opportunity to reinforce that acting as a journalist was going to be easier than he thought. "Think of it as being like an actor," he said. "Just play your part. It'll be easy once you get into it."

Already Scott noticed that it was easier to agree than protest. What would be next? Would he lose his power to think for himself? Like Scott, *Le Point* had no real say in the matter. And these were the same people so opposed to despotism.

With his tacit compliance, their conversation turned to fencing, the Geneva soccer team, and the currency markets. A few members dropped by to say hello to MacAllister, who introduced Scott as a new member—this after four months. The Swiss warmed up slowly.

Friday morning around ten o'clock, the telephone rang. Marie Claude came to the living room and told Scott that there was a call. It was Jean de La Haye. Scott had been waiting and hoping.

In effect, *Le Point* offered to review the articles that he had described on the terms he had proposed for a period of a few months. After that, they would decide whether a permanent byline should be offered. Scott thanked him and indicated that his first article was ready and that he would send it in the next few days.

He knew La Haye wanted to know the nature of the first offering, and Delacourt was probably standing right beside him, hoping to overhear the conversation. But Scott wasn't going to preview it for them. Besides, he didn't even have the first article. He was as curious as they were.

Seventeen

On Thursday, Scott went to his fencing lesson with Kruger. He had made a lot of progress and was in the best shape of his life. During one of their exercises, he saw MacAllister appear at the doorway. Apparently, he wanted to ensure that Scott was to join him for lunch.

In the dining room, Scott sat down with MacAllister and asked the waiter for a bottle of Badoit.

"I heard they hired you," MacAllister said.

"Yeah, I'm sure you're surprised."

"And what if I told you that we didn't have to resort to any pressure. They hired you on your own arguments."

"I wouldn't believe you."

"Where did we go so wrong?"

"Spilt milk. Where's this article I've supposedly written?"

"Scott, you seem upset. Remember, we're on the same side."

"Keep reminding me."

"I get the feeling you're always hiding something."

"You started it."

"There's an envelope containing your first article in the fold of the newspaper lying in the chair next to you."

"What's it about?"

"War and the protests."

"And what's the direction of the article?"

"I didn't write the article, Scott. Other people wrote it, in your style."

"You and Wainwright said that only he and you would know of my identity. Now you mention other people. How many know about me?"

"Only Wainwright and me, plus the director, and of course the author of the articles. He could easily figure it out, but he is a trusted veteran of the service. You don't need to worry."

"So far you haven't asked me to do anything illegal, which by the way, I won't do. But let me warn you, the people you want me to attract will not be satisfied with half measures regarding the war in Vietnam. Some of these people are Communists and many more are anarchists."

"I don't think you quite understand. We know this business pretty well. We write the articles, and you submit them. Then there will be no mistakes. Understand?"

"If you write them, and I don't believe in them, then I'll be no more than a ventriloquist's dummy."

"Our writers are professionals. Trust us."

THE FOLLOWING MONDAY EVENING, SCOTT RECEIVED A COPY of *Le Point Opposé* that would be on newsstands and in the hands of subscribers the next day. His first article, "Gulf of Tonkin, Grand Deceit?" questioned the reported facts of the incident that were used to leverage Congress into a continuing resolution whereby the president could pursue armed conflict in Vietnam without oversight. The article cited facts, including dates, reports, and news conferences that occurred at the time as well as the discrepancies in the accounts as reported by the American press. In fact, it pointed out that the American ship had not been attacked contrary to the reports that were being circulated in Washington. The article went on to intimate that there were probably sources within the government in Washington who knew that the facts as reported were incorrect, but they intended to whip the American public into a patriotic fury. The article affirmed that the war was a huge American folly.

After reading the article, Desirée said, "Scott, I didn't know you could write like this. But darling, don't you think you might be a little too frank? And how do you know some of these facts?"

"I presume the first part is a compliment. Thank you. And I believe it's the truth, so why not just say it? So far as the facts, I'm exaggerating a bit for the effect."

"Your opinions will be welcomed by some but won't make you any friends in other quarters."

"Are you telling me not to write, or not to write what I know and believe, or to be careful?"

"My darling, I'm just saying there will be consequences."

Desirée didn't know how prescient she was, and he couldn't confide in her. This was deeply disturbing because they had always been completely honest with each other through the hardest times. He felt he was betraying her, and it didn't feel good.

The next day, he received a call from La Haye.

"Mr. Stoddard, the response to your article is jamming our switchboard. We have those calling to applaud you and others that want to know where in the world you've come from."

"I guess that's good for a start, right?" Scott asked.

"It's chaotic. In general, our little review is mostly an intellectual endeavor. We're not accustomed to this much attention."

"Well, it could be good for circulation though."

"Indeed, but we'll just have to see how this works out. We're taking all the messages, which we'll send you directly. The American Embassy here in Bern called asking for a copy. I think someone must have told them about the article. They can't be pleased."

"I wouldn't think so."

THE NEXT MORNING, HE RECEIVED A LARGE ENVELOPE THAT contained telephone messages with the caller's name, date, time of call, and affiliation. In a few cases, someone, probably La Haye, had written in the margin a notation clearly identifying the caller. For example, one notation read, "Propagandist for liberal student newspaper, Berlin."

Scott looked at each one carefully, scrutinizing the names and affiliations. He had to admit that there would necessarily be a lot of study required to secure a working knowledge of the players. He typed a list of all the slips, including La Haye's annotations.

Next, he needed to signal Wainwright that he would be placing this list in a Bible at the Payot bookstore. The arranged communication wasn't difficult. He merely had to drive his Porsche into town on a Tuesday and park his car between ten and eleven o'clock in a square close to a wine store and a boutique for men. He would do a few errands, have a coffee, buy a couple of bottles of wine, and return to the car. Every week, every Tuesday, someone would be watching at the appointed time for this sign that a drop was to be made the next day at the bookstore.

Although the list was long, some sixty-five names, Scott had managed to type on both sides of a thin onionskin paper, which when folded, was a square of roughly two and a half inches. He could palm it and slip it into the Bible without reaching into his pocket.

Wednesday afternoon when he returned from having made the drop at the bookstore, he was certain that the list had probably already been picked up and was in Wainwright's eager hands.

Eighteen

MacAllister told him to check the newspaper classifieds for the signal that there was a drop for him at Payot. They were preparing a detailed study of the most interesting names. MacAllister also wanted to know if he had called any of them. Of course, he hadn't, though he was curious as to why they had called. Surely among the callers there were those who would object to his views and want to give him a good tongue-lashing. Then there were others who would probably applaud his point of view and his candor. The fact that his article lacked the prerequisite proof would not be an impediment to those who had an agenda to promote.

MacAllister indicated that two names held particular interest: Heinrich Steinhausen, the titular head of a leftist academic union with headquarters in Berlin, and Antoine LeFebre, a Parisian financier and supporter of organizations thought to be either socialist or communist. There were others as well, but these two would need to be contacted first. MacAllister also explained that he wanted Scott to meet with Wainwright the following Tuesday at their usual spot outside Geneva for lunch. MacAllister then turned to more important matters.

"The first article was well received, don't you think?" he asked.

"If you're happy, then I'm happy."

"When you get back to your car, you'll find the second article under the seat on the passenger side."

"And the subject of this one?"

"Civil wars and guerrilla tactics versus conventional forces."

"Have I become an expert on military tactics too?"

"Of course not, but we want to engage the suspicions and opinions of those who think you are."

"And what if someone questions me regarding some aspect that I know nothing about?"

"Did your parents have trouble with you? Can't you just follow orders?"

"My parents complained mostly, and they really complained about my giving up my citizenship. I don't like to be bossed around. Why don't you just fire me if you don't like what I'm doing?"

"Look. We're supposed to be a team. And we're not worried about you answering questions. We're not going to give you anything that you can't do. You're glib, but when you're not cooperative, then I'm the one who must report to the director. And that's not pleasant for me, and then I begin to take it out on people who cause me problems."

"Everyone has their own cross."

On Tuesday, Scott made the excuse that he was going to the university library to research his next article, which, as only he knew, he would be writing. He planned to substitute his article for the one MacAllister would supply. It would address the subject of how the war in Vietnam might be linked to the Cuban Bay of Pigs disaster. It was a hypothesis only, but it wouldn't matter to those of anti-American sentiment. They would take any criticism as gospel as long as it agreed with their politics. He was sure this subject would be celebrated by the anti-war factions and cause MacAllister and company indigestion. Maybe if he made them uncomfortable enough, then they would let him go, restore his citizenship, and leave him alone. This was probably wishful thinking, but he hated being their puppet.

To meet Wainwright, he drove toward Geneva but quickly took a back road and circled back toward the Auberge. He was on time, but Wainwright was already seated with his real estate brochures at their appointed table in a corner of the dining room overlooking the lake.

As Scott slid into his chair, Wainwright said, "Your articles are causing quite a ruckus. By the look of who's responding, you're attracting attention from the right places."

"Yes, I'm so pleased that you're happy."

Wainwright bristled a bit and said, "But not everyone is happy, some people in Washington, for example."

"Look, Wainwright, it's not my fault that it's not going so well over there."

"You're very cynical for someone your age."

"I'm cynical so I can be honest."

"Anyway, let's drop it," he said. "This meeting is to brief you on two names who have called you, and how we would like for you to handle the call back."

"Shoot."

Wainwright's first subject was Heinrich Steinhausen. He laid out a brief biographical sketch revealing that Steinhausen had been born in Gottingen in 1932 into a family of academics and intellectuals. His father was a university professor of philosophy, his mother a classical violinist and musicologist. He graduated from the University of Heidelberg and received his doctorate in political science. He had always been active in student politics and later as an advisor to political campaigns of those candidates left of center. He was a contributor to several left-wing magazines and newspapers and had published a political treatise on the advantages of Germany looking toward the East for more immediate solutions to the division of the country. It was thought that he was independent of Soviet clandestine influence, but it couldn't be categorically verified that he did not receive indirect intelligence to better inform and mold his opinions as well as camouflage his funding. It could be stated, however, that he held great sway in the organization of the SDS, the Socialist Democratic Party.

Then Wainwright turned to Antoine LeFebre, the Parisian banker. He was born in Paris in 1930 into a Jewish banking and academic family who had escaped the Nazi occupation of Paris by fleeing to London. Returning to France in 1947, Antoine entered the prestigious Political Science school of the Sorbonne and later stood for his doctorate. He helped organize political protests, particularly those that professed Marxist principles. It was undetermined exactly how far left his politics were, but he was probably more of a French communist than a Soviet-style universal communist. He was thought to be rich and well connected enough to be either a source of funding or an aggregator of funds for left-wing activists.

Wainwright indicated that the reason for their interest in Scott was not known, but both Steinhausen and LeFebre would appreciate any point of view that might oppose the United States. And it would be desirable if Scott could find out more about their associates, their future plans, and their funding.

"And, Scott, a word of warning. We don't know if either of these two persons has any direct links with enemy intelligence services. It would not be out of the realm of possibility that the KGB, or in the case of Steinhausen the East German intelligence service, the Stasi, could be lurking behind the scenes. Just be yourself and be careful. Obviously after you've spoken with either one or both, you will need to be debriefed."

Scott had plenty to think about on his drive back to Geneva. He would have thought that more would be known about the two activists if they were as interesting as Wainwright purported them to be. But maybe the available assets to track political opponents were thin, and political intrigue might be minor compared to military targets. He wondered if he should call right away as instructed or wait and see if the second article provoked either to call again. Patience is always an advantage, and he thought he might appear a little too eager if he called so soon. He decided, as a committee of one, to wait.

La Haye called him a few days later. "Your second article, 'Conventional Forces versus Guerrilla Tactics, A Fool's Errand,' has flooded our telephone and mailbox. I'll be sending you the messages and correspondence by expedited packet today. But I must tell you from the messages it seems you may be making more enemies than friends."

"Thank you, but do I detect a certain displeasure with the results?" Scott said.

"Not at all. We are very pleased, and subscriptions are up by fifteen percent. Fifteen percent in our category is a tidal wave of interest. We have also received some inquiries from other media outlets that would like to reprint the articles."

"I'm glad, but I don't want my articles to be used as propaganda."

"You are quite right in being sensitive to this issue, and among the requests, there are those that might be suspect for that very reason."

"I hadn't anticipated that my point of view might be in such demand."

"None of us did. But having read the first two articles, it seems to me that what might be driving the interest is your rather candid style and contrarian point of view."

THE NEXT AFTERNOON, HE RECEIVED THE EXPRESS PACKET from La Haye containing the letters and phone messages. In his study, he quickly sorted through them and found messages from both Steinhausen and LeFebre. He transferred the information from the messages onto a single sheet of thin paper that he would drop for Wainwright and company.

He was locking the packet in a desk drawer when Desirée came into the study with Celine in her arms. They were both radiant. He took Celine from her mother's arms and nestled her close to his chest. He made funny expressions and noises, and the baby laughed and grinned and cooed. He placed his other arm around Desirée's waist and pulled both of them in close.

"Darling somehow I wish we could just have a normal life like this rather than all this preoccupation that you have with your articles," Desirée said.

"I know, I'm sorry. I didn't know that the response would be so intense. But I must answer some of these people. My next article might be a dud that no one is interested in."

"I rather doubt that. But really, who could have known? Well, besides me. I know you can do anything."

"Your prejudice is much appreciated."

He couldn't see how his connection with MacAllister could end soon. Already MacAllister was pushing him to go full ahead, and this early success would only make him and his cohorts more demanding of his time. If he helped them accomplish their goals in this task, what would they think of for him to do next? Scott could foresee some sticky situations in the future with Desirée. When Celine was a little older, Desirée would begin to think again of her life before marriage, namely a series of parties, benefits, travels, and balls. And where would his university studies fit in this schedule? Realistically, his university career seemed further away than ever. And he knew that there wouldn't be any sympathy from MacAllister regarding his personal life. They owned him they thought. He had considered quitting more than once, but Wainwright's threat stuck in his mind. Would they hurt Desirée or Celine or his parents? He was certain that in their business they could always justify the means to accomplish the ends. He couldn't take the chance.

Management of his secret activity, the articles, Desirée, and MacAllister and company kept Scott vigilant, but a more pressing concern was how he might extricate himself from this situation. Paradoxically, his success in accessing the targeted people and organizations only increased his usefulness to the people he most wanted to lose. He was a victim of his own success. He was certain that they would not willingly let him quit, nor would they accept any singular success as payment to satisfy his obligation. He imagined that they would insist that he continue until he failed, was exposed, or worse. And all the while, he would need to distract them from his real intent—to get out. Blackmail was the coin of the realm they most believed in. But where would he find something that they would fear revealed?

Nineteen

LeFebre wasn't in when Scott called in the afternoon, so he left a message. Not ten minutes later, LeFebre called back. After an opening round of pleasantries, LeFebre congratulated Scott on both articles. He then asked an oblique question regarding how Scott had come up with some of his deductions. Scott knew that he wanted to know his sources. Scott was equivocal, citing research and media, but LeFebre was insistent that there was more there than one could obtain by reading, particularly the article on the guerrilla tactics.

"Well if you must know, there are a lot of disgruntled military out there, and they see me as a conduit for their opinions," Scott said.

"I knew you had to have inside information," LeFebre said. "It's just too on-target to be research." Then he got to the real reason for his call.

"Each month I hold a rather informal gathering at my home in Paris, a small dinner party of a half dozen or so individuals with a deep interest in the current events that impact our times. I'm sure you would recognize most of their names and their organizations, as they come from various sectors of academia, business, finance, and politics, even a few military types from time to time. We like to have fresh ideas from new people on the scene, and I thought you would be a provoking addition to our little soirée. Our next meeting is in three weeks in Paris. Would you be able to come?"

Scott thanked him for the invitation and promised to get back to him no later than Thursday or Friday. This delay would give him time to quiz La Haye as well as discuss the situation with MacAllister after his fencing lesson Thursday.

He then turned to Steinhausen and put in a call to a Berlin number. After several rings a woman answered, and soon he was on the phone with Herr Steinhausen. Whereas LeFebre had been of a nuanced and silky-smooth delivery, Steinhausen was blitzkrieg blunt. He applauded Scott's article on the Tonkin Gulf incident, casting it as an American-fabricated confrontation designed to dupe the public and the witless media. Then he asked if they could meet either in Berlin or in Munich. Scott deferred, telling him that he was very busy at the present moment, but perhaps at a later date. Steinhausen sweetened the offer by intimating that he thought Scott's articles should have a wider audience and that Scott had the credibility that an academic leftist would not have. He had in mind an association and syndication of the articles in the *Westdeutsche Zeitung,* the large Bavarian left-of-center newspaper, published in Munich.

"But why my articles?" Scott asked. "They're not that much different than other articles with a similar viewpoint."

"True, the viewpoint is familiar," Steinhausen said, "but the salient facts seem firsthand. I think you're holding out on us."

"I talk to a lot of people," Scott said.

"And not just anybody it seems."

Scott indicated that he was honored by the possibility, but although he was not under contract, he wanted to check with his publishers at *Le Point Opposé* as a courtesy. He really needed to check with MacAllister. Steinhausen countered saying that Scott's viewpoint and the resulting audience was too important to take the advice of some academics and their scholarly journal in Bern. It was not difficult to understand Steinhausen's position. He intimated he would come to Switzerland if Scott would meet him in Zurich. Scott promised he would get back to him by the following Monday. Steinhausen added that his preference still was Munich as there were a few people he would like him to meet, and if Scott would agree to Munich, his expenses would be covered.

On Thursday after an intense fencing class, Scott joined MacAllister in the dining room of the club for lunch. "The generals in Vietnam aren't happy with our latest," MacAllister said. "Perhaps they need a new strategist."

"They could do worse from what I've read."

"Have you been in touch with your two admirers?"

"I have, and one wants me to come to Paris and attend a salon of political thinkers. The other wants me to come to Munich and meet with some people, perhaps from the *Westdeutsche Zeitung.*"

"What did you tell them?"

"That I needed to check with Desirée."

"Smart fellow. I'm surprised you didn't accept without asking."

"The thought crossed my mind."

"Well, thank you. What do you think?"

"I'm inclined to say yes."

"It would be fine to go to Paris, but until your citizenship papers come through from Switzerland or France, you can't go to West Germany. You're a draft resister, remember?"

"You mean I wouldn't be safe in Germany?"

"Your risk in West Germany is not just from the American authorities. The country teems with intelligence services."

"I remember you joked in the beginning that you wouldn't ask me to kill anybody, but it seems like I'm the one at risk."

"There won't be any risk once your French or Swiss nationality conversion is official. We want you to have a passport and identity papers that are not connected to your previous affiliation. Besides the higher profile you have, the less vulnerable you become."

"*Previous affiliation.* That's rich. You mean as an American citizen, that before I was an American, and now I'm not."

"Stop complaining. Let me remind you it is for an excellent cause. You may be the only one who can pull this off."

"I don't quite see that what I'm doing is worth it."

"You will."

When he returned home after lunch, he found Desirée and Louise Goosens playing with Celine in the living room. Scott hadn't seen Louise in a few weeks, not since before his articles had appeared. Louise in her roundabout way mentioned that she had read both articles. He would have never believed that she would read an esoteric journal such as *Le Point Opposé*. He had assumed that the journal was less accessible than her reading tastes might indicate. Perhaps she and her husband, Jon, were interested in it merely as a novelty to see if he could write?

"I presume that these articles may offend some in certain circles where you may become a persona non grata," she said.

"It's possible. There are those who agree, and then there are those who disagree. It's hard to please everyone. I just do the research, and the articles write themselves."

"Jon tells me that at some business functions that he's attended you—well, your articles—are quite the story."

"I wouldn't have imagined that there would be that much interest."

"I think you underestimate the splash you've made since you and Desirée began courting last year. Everyone could tell that you were intelligent, particularly in an academic way, but we hardly imagined your capabilities to leverage your ideas into a larger forum."

"I'm basically an amateur with an opinion."

"Your opinions don't seem to be those of an amateur. I don't believe any of us knew how articulate you could be for such anti-establishment points of view."

"The establishment is not served well by ill-advised policies."

She left, wishing all three well and proposing they plan to have dinner in the near future. She indicated that she wanted Scott to meet a visiting lecturer at the University of Geneva from the University of Ghent. He was quite well known in the Netherlands and was a specialist in Southeast Asia. Scott said he would like to meet him and that she was kind to make the introduction.

"Oh darling, I'm so proud of you. Now my friends want to introduce you to experts," Desirée said after Louise had gone.

"Yes, probably to find out just how little I know."

"You couldn't know so little and write the articles you write."

Scott decided this was the appropriate moment to tell her of his impending trip to Paris to meet with LeFebre. She didn't like the idea, but when he proposed that the three of them go to Paris for a few weeks, maybe until just before Christmas, she acquiesced.

"Perhaps I should ask Uncle Pierre about Antoine LeFebre," she said. "It might be helpful if you knew more about him before your meeting."

"People generally don't like being investigated," he said. "Any snooping would need to be discreet."

"Dearest, remember, I'm French. Richelieu's blood courses through our veins."

THE NEXT MORNING, HE MADE THE CALL TO PARIS AND informed LeFebre that he would attend the dinner party on the twenty-fifth of the month. LeFebre gave him the particulars, including the address, which was in a desirable neighborhood in the 7th arrondissement on a street of some importance, the rue Grenelle, amidst a number of high-level government buildings. He asked Scott which hotel he would be staying in should he need to contact him, but Scott indicated that he had not decided. There was no need for the stranger to know that he and his wife lived in splendor on the posh l'avenue Foch.

Next was the call to Steinhausen in which he indicated that he would be able to meet him in Zurich in the next two weeks, but after that he was fully committed. Scott didn't mention the real reason for not considering Munich as a meeting site. There was no use in sharing his fear of traveling to West Germany with Steinhausen. It was a little early to share too much information with him. Far from deflecting his interest,

Steinhausen proposed the Wednesday two weeks hence. If Scott could arrange to stay at the Savoy Baur au Lac hotel, then they could lunch together, and if one or more of his associates could make the trip, they would all have dinner. Scott agreed, saying he would take an early train.

Desirée was not thrilled that his burgeoning journalism career seemed to dominate his time and interfere with their personal lives. She didn't complain outright—that wasn't her method. But the long sighs told him she was not entirely content. He apologized and said that the results were unexpected, that he was in the early stages of his career, and that the excitement around him was sure to level off in a few weeks. She rolled her eyes.

Two days later, while they were having lunch, Desirée mentioned that Uncle Pierre had gotten back to her regarding Antoine LeFebre. Primarily he confirmed what Scott already knew: the family in banking, the Sorbonne doctorate, the nationalist, the Communist. But there was one little piece of new information that Scott filed away; LeFebre was homosexual and kept his preference hidden. This fact made him subject to blackmail. In addition, Uncle Pierre's informants—just as MacAllister had said—were unclear where the money came from to support his political activities, since none of his political initiatives produced revenue. MacAllister would want him to find out who was financing them. To find out more, Scott would need to wait until Paris. He assumed the purpose of their meeting was more than a friendly chat.

Twenty

IN THE MEANTIME, THE THIRD ARTICLE APPEARED, THIS one authored by Scott. It was blatant speculation and over the line, but it would attract the attention of those more interested in ideology than facts. MacAllister's article followed the same line that the first two had. And although Scott expected MacAllister to be angry with the substitution, he felt it was worth the risk to achieve the sensationalism he believed the situation required. Based largely on conjecture and deduction and woefully absent substantiating facts, his piece proposed that the reason Kennedy had taken such a hard line in Vietnam—which was being continued by the Johnson administration—was because of the United States' embarrassment in respect to the Cuban fiasco at the Bay of Pigs. Not wanting to be considered weak and ineffectual, the Kennedy clan had doubled down on Vietnam, so as to not give the impression of losing another sphere of influence to the Communists. Johnson was continuing the bluster. Scott hoped his readers would make the connection that the United States was always butting in where they weren't wanted.

He could better imagine how this treatise was going to be viewed by the likes of Steinhausen and LeFebre than by his handlers. Those two would love it, factual or not. When he had submitted the article to *Le Point Opposé,* he had half-expected La Haye to counsel against running it or to ask him to soften some of its more unsubstantiated allegations. But to his surprise, nothing, not even a whimper. He guessed that with subscriptions, soaring economics overruled prudence.

MacAllister was another matter. When they met for lunch, he had apparently decided to blister Scott. While he smiled and didn't raise his voice so that any onlooker in the dining room would have thought they were discussing an innocuous subject like football, he said, "The director is not pleased, and he has told me to tell you not to write any more articles but to use the ones that we supply. Is that clear?"

"Or what?"

"Or there will be consequences."

"What consequences? I've figured out that there's not much you can do to me except fire me, and I've taken steps to chronicle everything in a diary, which is in a safe place just in case you get any other ideas."

"I told them you might be too smart."

"Look, the articles you give me try to walk a thin line that aims to not offend anyone. But they won't attract the people you're after. I'm cooperating, but you don't appreciate it."

"I don't think the director will buy it."

"Remember I'll be Swiss in a matter of days."

He also told MacAllister of the upcoming meetings with both Steinhausen and LeFebre. He was not surprised that MacAllister had a few pointers for the meetings. Scott was to mentally record the name, approximate age, and professional connections of each person in attendance. He was to listen carefully to each person's point of view and any disagreements that might surface during the conversations and to map the hierarchy of the group, specifically who was in charge. And he was to follow any line of conversation that might root out where the money comes from. MacAllister reiterated that these persons and groups were probably financed by entities that could be traced back to one of several clandestine services, the KGB being the number one suspect. It might even be possible that the principals could believe that the funding came from a legitimate source while in reality the origin of funds might be more circuitous than they imagined. If these suspicions could be verified, then ultimately the sources of funds could be exposed, and the legitimacy and impartiality of the principals could be undermined.

"Wouldn't they be able to trace any intel back to me?"

"We wouldn't divulge it immediately, and we would find another plausible source to reveal it to us, probably through some sort of blackmail. Unless you know the correct answer, you can't ask the right question. You are going to provide us with the answers, so that we can ask the right questions of others who will only unwittingly verify what we already know."

Scott was finally beginning to understand his role. His prima facie information gleaned from listening and infiltrating these groups wouldn't be used directly, but indirectly. He was in effect a bloodhound, picking up the scent. Others would see to it that the suspects were brought to ground through some elaborate and deflecting chase of sorts.

With that revelation, he realized he would need to devise a strategy that would further distance him from any information that might inadvertently be revealed either through impatience or carelessness. For many reasons, he didn't trust Wainwright, MacAllister, and whomever the hell else was handling him. He was going to be very democratic. He would treat them all the same—with suspicion and a certain disdain.

Scott hated to be pessimistic, but he failed to see how from a dinner conversation alone he would be able to deliver on parts of his task. Oh, the names and all that he could do easily, but when it came to funding, wouldn't they be a little stingy with these facts? And wouldn't they be trying to figure him out as well? He didn't mention it to MacAllister, but he continued to mull over how he might learn more than they would be prepared to tell him. The bait would need to be irresistible. When in doubt, always be the ingénue.

Scott decided to travel to Zurich on Tuesday, the day before his meeting with Steinhausen. Desirée and Celine accompanied him, Gustav driving, to the Geneva airport. It was early in the day, yet the paparazzi were up to the task. But when Scott and family reached the airport, their pursuers were soon disappointed because

Scott quickly grabbed his bag and disappeared into the terminal, where the photographers weren't welcome. Still, they got their shots of Desirée and Celine and the embraces of goodbye. At least they wouldn't know where he was going.

He checked into the Savoy Baur au Lac in the late afternoon. Around seven he crossed the bridge over into the old town to have dinner at Kronenhalle, one of the city's oldest and most prestigious restaurants. Desirée introduced him to it when they traveled to Saint Moritz before they were married. Those had been great times of excitement and romance so unlike the secrecy that now enmeshed his life. As he dined on beef Stroganov in the main room, where hung a most notable collection of expensive art—including a Modigliani, a Georges de la Tour, and others—he felt melancholy as his thoughts turned to his wife and child. Would they ever return to their carefree life of before? Would these men of resolute beliefs and little humor ever allow him to escape their designs on his usefulness to them and their cause? There had to be a way. He just needed to recognize it when it came.

The next morning, he checked in with Desirée and told her about his dinner at Kronenhalle. She feigned a little jealousy that he had enjoyed this without her. He wondered when they would have a day or two off from the baby and his journalistic duties to reconnect.

At lunch, practically no one was in the hotel dining room, and that was probably how Herr Steinhausen had planned it. In his mid-thirties, he was as tall as Scott and quite handsome, with an athletic build and blond hair. Herr Steinhausen's French was not too good, and Scott's German was limited to tourist babble. Due to the American and British occupation of West Germany, English had become a second language for many Germans. They decided it would be their lingua franca. With the formalities attended to, they ordered, Steinhausen the Wiener schnitzel, and Scott the dorade.

"I'm pleased to meet you and see who's behind these very candid articles," Steinhausen said. "I must congratulate you on the latest one about the Kennedy and Johnson paranoia of losing ground to the Communists."

"It seems to have resonated in a number of ways, from the response I've received."

"By the way, we will be joined this evening for dinner by Ian Broder, a friend and associate of mine from Munich. He is a political editor of the *Westdeutsche Zeitung*. Do you know it?

"I know of it, but my German is weak, so I'm not a subscriber."

"It's a very influential paper, read by many Germans not only in Bavaria but throughout the country and abroad. They also sponsor a number of symposiums where important discussions take place regarding politics and policy. Ian suggested that we have dinner at Kronenhalle. It's a very fine restaurant, very well known."

Scott didn't mention that he knew it well, and he presumed the restaurant staff would be discreet enough not to mention his attendance the previous evening.

"I was interested in how you decided on a journalistic career and how you selected *Le Point Opposé*."

Scott realized that this would need to be a convincing answer, one that was ironclad and buttressed with the force of syllogistic logic. "Perhaps you are aware that as a result of my opposition to the war, it was necessary for me to take not only a public stand but the resulting draconian step of seeking asylum and ultimately renouncing my American citizenship. I decided that I needed a public platform to profess my opposition. The choice of *Le Point* appealed to me because it was serious and directed toward a readership that would carefully weigh my opinions. I did not believe that a more mainstream outlet would audition a novice journalist."

"Given your situation, I would have expected you to express more anger and frustration, but these are not the emotions that seem to drive your articles."

"In your opinion, what does?"

"The tone of your articles is one of cold objectivity even when the facts are somewhat sketchy. You don't equivocate. But there is also an undercurrent of an intolerance of stupidity."

"As an experienced journalist, what advice do you have for me?"

"Keep writing. But you really need a wider audience than *Le Point* can provide. And a wider audience deserves to read what you think. The fact that you are an American, a young American who was subject to being involved in the war, and let's face it, a person who has been more associated with society and frivolous issues, gives you a novelty that most critics of the war don't have. I predict that as more people become aware of the issues in Vietnam, the protests will grow. You're early to the game, and that's good. Most detractors are tainted with previous associations or agendas that infect their objectivity. And let's be clear, they are not American, not young, and unknown out of political circles. I would presume that some of the more conservative types in your milieu are not pleased that one of their own is somehow so liberal."

"I hadn't thought of that."

"Ian and I have discussed it. There's a lot that you can do. Do you have more articles ready for publication?"

"I have a number in draft form, and an even larger inventory of ideas that I'm researching."

"Can I have a little preview?"

"I don't preview my articles with anyone prior to publication. What did you mean when you said there's a lot that I can do?"

"Most of the voices against the war or ones challenging the policies of the governments in place are activists: students, professors, people with a preexisting agenda. You, on the other hand, have no obvious background in these matters. Moreover, you're a journalist, which implies impartiality, and you were an American citizen. I can see that with a wider exposure, you could be the darling of some of these factions, and they may in turn provide you with even more information than you have presently."

"I think you're being too optimistic, although I appreciate the inferred compliment."

"And I think you underestimate the impact of these articles. But a word of caution: I don't know who your sources are, but there would be those more interested in where you get your material than me."

Twenty-one

They arrived by taxi just as Ian Broder was walking up the sidewalk to Kronenhalle. Perhaps he was staying somewhere nearby in the old town. He was well dressed in a charcoal gray suit, white shirt, and dark blue tie. In general, Germans were not known for their sartorial chic, but Scott could tell that his suit was well-tailored and his cuff links were discreet but expensive. He appeared to be around forty.

They were shown to a table in the front dining room. Scott was right, the Swiss staff was too diplomatic to reveal that he had been there the night before. Apparently, Herr Broder was a regular as the maître d' subtly patronized him.

"I'm glad we are able to meet," Herr Broder said, "but I wish that it could have been in Munich, because some of my colleagues would have welcomed the opportunity to meet the person writing these articles that are so exasperating to certain people."

"Thank you," Scott said. "Maybe next time."

"Do you have any idea how much trouble you are stirring up?"

"Only slightly. I've been at this just a few weeks," Scott answered.

"Well, I can tell you. You're saying what everyone is thinking, but no one else is quite so blunt. Our sources tell us that the Americans are furious with your suggestion regarding Kennedy and the Bay of Pigs, not to mention these innuendos that the American public is being deceived. If you join us, we can help protect you." Broder said.

"Protect me from what?"

"Well, they might plant some derogatory stories with their own set of sympathetic journalists."

"Derogatory, like what?" Scott asked.

"Oh, they don't have to be true, they just have to undermine your credibility."

"Then why haven't they already done it?"

"Because you're only with this little journal in Switzerland."

"What are you proposing?"

"I might as well be straightforward and tell you what interests I represent," Broder said. "The *Westdeutsche Zeitung* and its affiliates would very much like to syndicate your articles and provide opportunities for you to promote yourself and attract like-minded people to your cause. I notice that sometimes you write in French and other times English. I can promise you accurate translations of your work into German if that is a concern."

"I hadn't thought of myself leading a cause," Scott said.

"Perhaps not," Broder said. "The U.S.'s escalation of the war in August is not well understood at this point. But others, including you, see this as only the beginning. I believe that the opposition will grow substantially if the current policies are followed."

"There are a lot of people out there who agree with you," Steinhausen said, "but you're not going to reach them through a journal of such paltry circulation."

"*Le Point* did give me an opportunity when no one else would, and I'm not going to renege because a new situation comes up."

"You won't have to. They can have a day or two head start, and then we will publish your work as quickly as the translations can be done. You'll have a national—even an international—readership," Broder said.

"There is the financial consideration as well," Steinhausen said.

They seemed to be either unaware of or ignoring Scott's financial position. But what no one could understand was that just because his wife was rich didn't mean that he was rich. His father was rich, but Scott wasn't. He was dependent. A little income of your own is not anything to cavalierly dismiss.

Ian pushed an envelope across the table, indicating that inside the financial arrangements were contained in greater detail. Depending on how his articles might be received in Germany, Ian speculated that he could foresee syndication remuneration, even speaking fees, and expenses for travel. Even a proposal for a book recounting his transformation from American citizen to draft resister and asylum seeker was not out of the question.

"I'm quite surprised and complimented, but I will need to study the offer and speak with the principals at *Le Point Opposé* as well as my attorney," Scott said.

"Do you think it possible that we could have your answer in a week?" Broder asked.

"I would like to have an answer for you quickly, but it is impossible to arrive at a decision prior to the end of September. If that is too long, I will understand if you would like to rescind your offer even before I've read it."

"I was hoping we could at least go over it and see if you have any questions," Broder said.

"Under the circumstances, I think it is best for me to review the offer in private, but if you can't wait until the end of September—"

"No, it's fine, take your time. We want you to feel comfortable in your decision, and we don't want to get started badly by putting too much pressure on you," Broder reassured.

Scott caught the early train to Geneva, and by noon he was back at home. He had reread the offer on the train. It appeared appropriate for a novice, but MacAllister's and his articles were in high demand for those opposed to anything American. Scott guessed that the reason MacAllister and his team were willing to expose inside facts within the articles was to make Scott attractive to the more radical elements. He would bet that MacAllister wasn't fishing for the known anti-Americans but those who were working behind the scenes, maybe even undercover. If those hardliners were attracted to his articles and ultimately contacted him, then MacAllister would discover who they were. At the same time, Scott understood that it could be dangerous for him if one of these types discovered his duplicity. Naturally MacAllister had left this possibility out of the discussion.

THE SYNDICATION FEE WAS MODEST IN THE BEGINNING WITH some upside, performance-based incentives. A speaking honorarium based on a sliding scale was commensurate with the prestige of the institution and the number of participants. Expenses, meals, and travel were also in the mix.

As Scott put his bag down in the foyer, Desirée descended the steps, beautiful as usual. She threw her arms around him. She was dressed head to toe in soft, blue cashmere. A gold link Cartier belt graced her pre-baby waist. "Did you miss me?" she said.

"I always miss you when I'm away from you for more than a moment."

"That's the right answer. How did it go?"

He handed her the proposal. She sat down and carefully read it, maybe more than once. "Is this incredible or what?" she said.

"Pretty unbelievable, I would say."

"Did you accept?"

"No, I told them I needed to wait until after Paris."

"Didn't that make them mad? Won't they know you will be considering another offer?"

"Yes, I think they do."

SCOTT RELATED TO MACALLISTER HIS CONVERSATION WITH Steinhausen and the dinner and Broder's proposal. MacAllister was surprised that Broder himself was there and grudgingly grunted his approval since it signified that Scott was taking steps to being accepted into the ranks of the target audience, but Scott understood that he was ambivalent about his success, particularly since it was achieved through his stinging criticism of the policies of the United States. But there was no other way, no half-measures, no mild reproach that would have had the same result.

"Isn't this fencing cover and meeting you weekly becoming a little thin? People must wonder what we're discussing so intently each week. I imagine your role isn't known, but can you vouch for everyone here in the club, including the visitors?"

"I don't think there would be much risk, but I'll inquire and see if we can come up with an alternative."

"You know, we're going to Paris next week, probably for a couple of months, so I don't imagine that you or Wainwright can be appearing there very often."

"Let's get one thing straight. From now on we've got to have more than a few days warning of approaching travel plans. Even better, why don't you ask me rather than tell me."

"Don't be so grouchy. Our life is returning to normal, so I can't appear to let this journalism thing get out of hand. My wife is intuitive, more so than men normally accord women, and she'll become suspicious if it becomes more than a kind of pastime. And if you're thinking that I should have a new contact in Paris, another person involved, well, it makes me nervous."

MacAllister nodded.

What would they conjure up now? They didn't have long. They finished up their conversation with MacAllister encouraging him to accept the Broder offer. Scott said that he was thinking about it, but he wanted to see what LeFebre was going to venture. MacAllister cautioned not to offend the Germans by waiting too long or shopping their offer around. In any case, Germany and Berlin and Munich, in particular, were laced with spies, double agents, handlers, diplomatic fronts, and influence peddlers of every variety. He indicated the Germans were more interested in this area than the French, whom he dismissed as simply French nationalists, their arrogance persuading them that they were on the forefront of saving mankind.

Twenty-two

WHEN SCOTT AND DESIRÉE ARRIVED AT ORLY AIRport in Paris, Gustav, who had been sent a few days earlier, and the paparazzi were waiting for them. The photographers in Geneva had alerted their compatriots in Paris of the couple's travel plans. The usual crush ensued. Scott was glad that they had shipped several large steamer trunks ahead. They wouldn't be delayed at baggage claim.

From mid-September on was the ideal time weather-wise to be in the city, and it coincided with the grand *rentrée,* the period when Parisians returned home from their August vacations. The sun setting deep in the southwest cast a warm and golden glow on the grand avenues, monuments, and building façades. The leaves of the enormous plane were beginning to yellow and brown, and some dropped on the cobblestoned streets. Fall was nigh.

Desirée had stayed on the telephone constantly during the previous two weeks, lining up their calendar and checking in with her extended entourage. Just the thought of Paris brought her to life, the chance to show off Celine to her friends and shop in the elite fashion houses. Scott couldn't have been prouder or more joyful to see both his girls in such high spirits. And lest he forget, Desirée's mother, Madame de Bellecourt, had already insisted that they join her for an early dinner. He was quite certain that little Celine was the primary motive for the dinner invitation. It had been over a month since Madame had seen her granddaughter, which as she expressed to Desirée, was much too long.

When they disappeared into the apartment, the photographers hung on for a while, but then perhaps thinking that the couple wouldn't reemerge, gave in and left. After situating the nanny, Desirée suggested that since they wouldn't be hounded, perhaps they could walk to her mother's apartment only three blocks away. They placed Celine in her stroller, a gift from Madame de Bellecourt, manufactured by one of the oldest baby carriage makers in Paris. It was a coach destined for a princess: large, chrome-spoked wheels with shock absorbers, padded crib, a cashmere blanket, and a dark blue convertible top with various protective weather sheaths.

It was still light as they paraded down l'avenue Foch as many couples must have done over the centuries. They left the carriage in the care of the building's concierge and took the elevator to Desirée's mother's apartment, which occupied the entire fifth floor. When the elevator stopped, they stepped into the apartment. Madame de Bellecourt was there to meet them, and she launched into a very uncharacteristic singsong of baby talk, reiterating how she had missed Celine, how beautiful she was, and how her grandmother loved her. She also pulled Desirée close, the three Rosier girls. She even found a moment to nod approvingly at Scott.

Celine was an excellent baby. As long as Scott or Desirée cradled her, she was content to allow them to dawdle after dinner to chat with Madame. And Madame never missed an opportunity to steer them toward the best of whatever Celine might need. She inquired about her appetite, her diet, and her sleep regimen—nothing went unchecked. Desirée was patient with her mother, recognizing her supervision of the situation for what it was, a genuine love and interest in her granddaughter's welfare. But Madame was in tune on many fronts. Like her daughter, she was always synchronized to the world around her. Neither missed many opportunities to let it be known that very little escaped their gaze.

"Scott, from what I've read and what I've heard, your articles are creating something of a tempest. At a luncheon I attended two days ago, there were a number of diplomats—I won't mention any names—but they are friends of mine and Desirée's as well. They didn't ask me directly, but I overheard them wondering aloud exactly what had become of that nice American that Desirée had married. And if they are saying these kinds of things in public, then what might they be saying in private? I think that everyone in our circle is disappointed that you seem to have such a gift to upset them.

Was she waiting for a response brimming with modesty, or one with defiance? Whatever he responded she would have a rejoinder that would elicit another response. It would be difficult to have the last word, if not impossible.

"My job is to write."

"So it seems. I hope you are prepared that with such decided opinions, it is probable that you—and by extension Desiree and Celine—will not be popular with many people who may heretofore have been her friends and yours."

"To date, I have not been confronted with this condition, but now that you mention it, I can see how that might occur."

"As long as you know what you're doing."

"Do we ever know?"

"Maman, it's not like he isn't writing the truth," Desirée said.

"Of course not, my darling, but sometimes the truth hurts, and sometimes the truth is better left unsaid, unless its revelation makes an enormous difference. Will it make such a difference, Scott?"

"It would be presumptuous for me to say yes, but I hope so. Many lives are at stake as a result of these errant policies."

In her opinion, he was wrong. She left it alone after that. They gathered up Celine, said their cordial goodnights, and returned to their apartment to put the baby to bed. Desirée joined him after a time and folded easily into his arms. They hadn't been in their Paris bed since before their wedding some fourteen months earlier. Scott let it be known in some not-too-subtle ways that they needed to re-christen the bed. She must have had the same idea as she made it easy for him to wrap his body around her. Soon the soft moans and tremors of passion consumed them.

Twenty-three

SCOTT WAS GLAD TO BE BACK IN PARIS. HE HAD AN IDEA for an article, but it needed firsthand reporting, eyewitness accounts, and those experiences could only be obtained from Vietnamese refugees who had recently immigrated to the city. He had by this time become familiar with the demographics of most of Paris, and he was aware that a large population of Vietnamese congregated in the 13th arrondissement. A flood of Vietnamese had arrived after the French were forced to give Vietnam its independence in the 1950s, and now with the new war, more were fleeing to France if they had connections. These people had the stories he wanted, if they could be persuaded to share them.

The Vietnamese, like many immigrants, didn't assimilate into the French culture when they arrived in Paris. Most acquired only enough French to get by and continued to live in dense pockets where they established their own shops, restaurants, and grocery stores catering uniquely to themselves and other Asians. It was similar to the situation that happened in Manhattan when early Italian immigrants established Little Italy.

Fortunately for Scott's purposes, many of these immigrants, particularly the new arrivals, were Catholic. And through Monsignor Bonfait, the priest who had married Scott and Desirée, he was soon in touch with Monsignor Pasquait at the Saint Rosalie Church. When Scott explained what he was after, the priest indicated that he would check around and see what he could do. A few days later, he called and said that a Monsieur Dao reluctantly agreed to meet Scott as a favor to the monsignor. Father Pasquait explained that Monsieur Dao was one of the patriarchs of the Vietnamese community. He owned boarding houses where some of the more recent refugees temporarily landed. Little happened in this closed community without his knowledge.

Fortunately, Desirée had left the apartment before him, dredging the reporters with her. As a result, it was unnecessary for Scott to take precautions against being followed. He met Monsieur Dao as arranged in the late afternoon in a Vietnamese restaurant just off la Place d'Italie. The establishment was more or less empty, and a young woman accompanied him from the entrance through a set of beaded curtains to a small office in the rear, where a stooped man in a black Mao-style suit sat staring at some papers. The light was dim, and the walls were without decoration. One chair sat directly across the table from Monsieur Dao. He looked up, rose, bowed, and gestured for Scott to sit down.

"I agreed to meet with you, but I'm not able to assist you," Monsieur Dao said.

"I understand your reluctance," Scott said, "but I believe what I have in mind could very well generate some sympathy and a better understanding as to what is taking place in Vietnam."

"It's too late for sympathy."

"But it's never too late to stop the war."

"There's not much hope for that."

"I brought a few of my articles," Scott said. "They're in this envelope. Would you read them and then call me if you can help me?"

Dao's response was a reluctant nod. It was better than an outright no, but Scott didn't have much hope that the articles would convince him since he seemed foursquare against changing his mind.

After a few days, a woman called and fixed an appointment with Dao two days later. She informed Scott that some families would be made available for his interviews and explained that she and Monsieur Dao would serve as interpreters. On the agreed-upon afternoon, the address wasn't hard to locate on rue de Pouy. The woman was waiting for him at the entrance. She introduced herself as Ly Dang. They climbed the stairs to the second floor, where three families and Monsieur Dao were gathered in a modest apartment.

Meager would insufficiently describe the impoverished conditions of their dress and the furnishings of their accommodations. The room smelled of cooked noodles, and the furniture consisted of a series of interlocking mats, some made of rattan and others of cloth. No chairs, tables, or beds were in sight. Scott met eight adults, three sets of parents and two older persons, probably grandparents, and seven children who appeared to be under the age of twelve. The children gathered tightly around their respective mothers much as goslings would cling to a mother goose.

Was the look on their faces one of shyness or stoicism? Were their blank stares due to shock or malnutrition? Scott reeled when one of the children, a little boy, turned his head, revealing the disfigured skin of a bad burn. The skin was smooth like plastic. He dreaded to discover the source of this maiming.

He asked Monsieur Dao to assure them of the confidentiality of their information and their identities. He didn't want to know their names, but he did want to hear their stories. He quickly figured out that Monsieur Dao had selected these families precisely because they had survived a bombing of their village and by a miracle had been able to emigrate because they had relatives in Lille. They planned to join them as soon as their papers were finalized.

Monsieur Dao spent several minutes speaking in Vietnamese and then turned toward him and asked what questions he wanted to ask.

"I would like to know the region they're from, the dates of the attacks on their village and what happened, and when they arrived in Paris.

Ly Dang took the baton, and in a staccato and lengthy soliloquy she apparently asked his questions. The Vietnamese looked at each other, a few words were exchanged, and one of the men began to speak in clipped bursts, pausing then continuing.

"He says that they are from a village south of Saigon in the Mekong Delta. He says that they came to Paris only a month ago after a forty-day freighter voyage that landed at Le Havre on the

Normandy coast in France. He doesn't know the exact date of the attack on their village. It was late last year. He was told afterward that Viet Cong were thought to be in their village. He hadn't seen any. And American soldiers had been in the area."

"Was the attack from planes or helicopters or gunfire, like artillery?" Scott asked.

Ly Dang translated. The same man, the designated speaker for the group, answered after a brief confab with two others.

Ms. Dang gave Scott the gist of his response. "It was airplanes. We didn't see them. They must have been too high. But we did run. I grabbed one of my children, my wife grabbed another, and we ran. We almost ran into some bombs. They were exploding in front of us, behind us. We huddled in a ditch until it was over."

"How long did the attack last?" Scott asked.

"It seemed like a long time. Probably only ten or fifteen minutes passed, but the noise and the fire seemed to go on forever. We were terrified. Our little boy was burned badly." He pointed to the child Scott had noticed earlier. "We're lucky he lived."

"What about your neighbors?" Scott asked.

A new man moved in front. "My parents and two of my children were killed. At least half of the village was dead, and there were many wounded, some badly. Our animals were killed or scattered. The sticky fire burned long after the attack. We all walked around in a daze. My children, the three who escaped, have nightmares when they sleep." He turned and found a small bag and gave Scott three photographs that supported his claims. Scott knew that the sticky fire he talked about was napalm.

The women's eyes glistened with emotion. They held their children tightly. Scott felt bad. He had just asked them to relive a painful and grisly experience. He listened to the tragedy of what had happened to these simple people who didn't have a refrigerator, a telephone, electricity, or indoor plumbing, yet had been subjected to the ravages of what the most advanced technology of arms could visit on them. Their eyes remained stoic throughout the interview. Scott had to believe there were just no more tears.

THE NEXT DAY, SCOTT HAD INVITED HIS TWO NEWSPAPER friends from *Le Figaro*, Andre and Leon, to join him for lunch. Desirée was meeting a few of her confidants for lunch, including her best friend, Celine, for whom the baby was named. He wouldn't be missed.

They met at their usual haunt, Epoque, a brasserie on the Champs-Elysées. As was their habit, they were already at the table when he arrived. He hadn't seen them since the wedding.

"Scott, my boy! You look well. Congratulations on being a papa," Andre said, with Leon echoing his sentiments. "But we should be mad. Now you have decided to be a journalist. You know that's our job."

"I don't believe you have anything to fear," Scott said. "My writing is just for a few people interested in politics. I'm a little surprised you know it at all."

"Everyone who knows you or the countess knows about and has probably read the articles."

"But it's such a small journal with a minuscule circulation."

"Dynamite comes in small packages. I would have guessed that you were more conservative, although you are a student in the international program," Andre said. Scott noticed that Leon was letting Andre do the talking.

"What could be more conservative than questioning the validity of the United States, uninvited, unrequested, and at odds with the Paris agreements of 1954, interloping into a country's internal politics and bombing this indigenous people, 99 percent of whom are agrarian peasants, with a murderous firepower that is used without mercy? It's barbaric and inhumane, not worthy of the principles and values upon which the United States was founded."

"Don't get ruffled, Scott. We and most French agree with you. But you're our friend, and we don't want to see you get hurt."

"No, we don't," Leon said.

"It's going to get worse before it gets any better," Scott said.

"What are you planning?"

"There's a possibility I could be writing for a larger audience."

"We knew that was coming. You can't write what you're writing and not become someone's favorite. But that's the danger. You'll attract a lot more attention, some pro, but a lot con. You know a journalist for a Paris paper disappeared in Berlin last year. He was never found. He wasn't writing about the war, but he must have been annoying someone important. What you're writing now is confined to a few readers, important ones, but once you have a wider audience, then—"

"I know there are risks."

"Just remember that one side likes what you write a lot better than the other side. You're a fresh voice, somewhat independent, and lest we forget, you are the husband of the former Countess de Rovere."

"I'm sure no one will allow me to forget."

Scott believed that they were genuinely concerned for his welfare. They didn't say that he should start checking under his car, but they raised the possibility of the displeasure and discomfort his articles might cause should they suddenly become more widespread. There might be more discussion about them in the press, and he might develop a notoriety that could be dangerous.

He could tell they were eager to know more. They always were, but he couldn't reveal what he was thinking or what his next steps might be. For that matter, he wasn't sure himself.

Twenty-four

SCOTT LOOKED OUT THE FRONT WINDOW AND SPOTTED two photographers pacing back and forth on the sidewalk. It was the twenty-fifth and dinner at LeFebre's. He was glad that he had asked Gustav to pick him up in the alley, at the service entrance to the building. They arrived at the LeFebres a little late, about ten minutes after seven. Gustav let him out at the corner and said he would be waiting for him at the same spot in a couple of hours. Scott said it wasn't necessary, but Gustav informed him that Desirée had deemed otherwise.

There was only one apartment at the address, a four-story limestone structure flush against the sidewalk with a porte cochère, an interior courtyard, and an imposing double door at the top of three wide stairs. It was unnecessary to knock, because two other men were arriving in separate cars at the same time. A butler greeted them, and Monsieur LeFebre made the introductions. Several of the guests were already there, and with the addition of two other late arrivals, it seemed to Scott that the company was complete. The conversation turned mainly on summer vacations, the weather, and, of course, some de Gaulle guffaws.

Scott listened more than he spoke. The conversation was in French, a French as spoken by learned and accomplished men, men of letters, men of finance, and men of power. There was little doubt as to who he was, but either through courtesy or instruction, no one mentioned his writing or even questioned his reason for being there. Scott assumed that would come later.

Nevertheless, he began from the first introduction to remember the names and occupations: Monsieur Phillipe Boisfeulliet, president of the Socialist Newspapers France, SA; Monsieur Jean Carriot, professor of political science at the Sorbonne; Monsieur Jerome Beaupais, journalist for *Le Canard Enchaîné*; Senator Maurice le Grand, an attorney from Rouen; Monsieur Robert Grenier, otherwise unidentified except he was from Brussels; Monsieur Edouard Clement, a leader of the Socialist party in France; LeFebre; and Scott. They were eight for dinner, which was served in an elaborate dining room on the second floor.

The waiters were in and out of the room, serving the various courses, so the conversation stayed fairly mainstream. It was not a working dinner by American standards; it was as elaborate and as gourmet as any multi-starred restaurant one might find in Paris. They were served a shrimp remoulade to begin, and a delicious crown lamb carré with a gratin of potatoes and braised fennel. Afterward, a platter of cheeses and a soufflé dessert of Grand Marnier, all accompanied by vintage burgundies and Bordeaux. When dinner was over, they retired to the confines of the massive library, where bookcases loomed two stories tall, where cognac—Rémy Martin and Hors d'Age—and Cuban cigars, including Churchill's favorite, Montecristos 2, were offered. *Some proletariat*, Scott thought.

LeFebre took charge. "I'm so glad that all of you were able to come this evening and meet Mr. Scott Stoddard. I know that you have read his articles in *Le Point*. It is important for him to know that many of us share his opinions, and I and others here with whom I have conferred agree that his viewpoint needs the force of syndication and the publicity beyond what he can currently expect."

At that point, the mystery man from Brussels, Monsieur Robert Grenier, said, "From my read of your first three articles, and how you might go forward, I agree with Monsieur LeFebre. But if we are to support your efforts both ideologically and financially, how can we be assured that you won't begin to waiver or perhaps even buckle under pressure you might receive from certain sources?"

"I am unaware of any request that I have made for support," Scott said. "And it has not been necessary up to this point that I make any commitment to anyone. I simply formulate ideas, do the appropriate research, write the article, submit it to *Le Point*, and shortly thereafter it appears in print. I seem to be fortunate to have a surfeit of ideas as well as the time, the interest, and the freedom to pursue them."

Monsieur LeFebre was quick to interject. "Quite right, Mr. Stoddard. We appreciate your independence, and it is an aspect that makes you all the more valuable, but one of the reasons for inviting you here this evening was to allow a few of the leading members of our little group to meet you. Your viewpoint could be quite synergistic with our own efforts. We would like to propose an arrangement by which we can work together."

"Monsieur LeFebre, you and your associates have been very welcoming and hospitable," Scott said, "and I have enjoyed the conversation immensely this evening, but I can't promise anything more than to listen."

"Fair enough," Monsieur LeFebre said. "With your permission, Senator Le Grand and I would like to present our proposal to you tomorrow afternoon in his office, also on rue de Grenelle, conveniently near here."

Scott made a gesture of checking in his *annuaire,* a small calendar and address book from Cassegrain, the stationery store on rue du Faubourg Saint-Honoré. Every French man and woman carried a version of this thin little book printed on onion skin paper with a calfskin cover and the current year stamped in gold. Of course, Scott didn't need to consult his little black book to know that he was available the next afternoon, but he studied it for a moment and said, "I believe I can reschedule a prior commitment to accommodate you."

As he left, several of the guests offered to give him a lift, but he said that the walk would do him good. As he turned at the first corner, Gustav followed him in the car while he walked another block. When he was certain no one was looking, he quickly slid into the back seat of the Mercedes. Back at the apartment, Desirée was waiting, although the hour was late. She began quizzing him on the events of the evening, the identity of the attendees, and the topics of conversation. He informed her of the impending offer for the next afternoon, recited the names of about half of the group, not wanting to admit that he had committed all the names to memory, and averted her curiosity by minimizing the topics of conversation to some hackneyed political discussion available in every newspaper and newscast.

She appeared to know practically all the people whose names he mentioned, if not well, at least enough to know some of their history and their current occupations. He was not surprised. Although her family for generations were more of the conservative—even royalist—persuasion, if you were involved in charitable activities, then it was necessary to deal with all comers who could assist your efforts. Desirée was no novice when it came to practicality.

THE NEXT AFTERNOON, HE TOOK A TAXI TO HIS APPOINTMENT, and the driver was able to lose the reporters in the traffic around the Arc de Triomphe. When he arrived, he was immediately ushered into a conference room where LeFebre was seated. Senator Le Grand soon joined them. After the briefest of cordialities, Le Grand got right to the point. "Monsieur Stoddard, we haven't prepared a legal document of engagement, but rather a letter of intent, which you will undoubtedly want to review with your attorney. I believe you will find that it anticipates all the requirements."

Before Scott could answer, LeFebre joined in. "Not wanting to be gauche, I think it would be fair to mention that we are aware that compensation is not the issue for you that it might be for some. Nevertheless, your work is valuable, and it demands remuneration commensurate with its value."

"You're very kind, but if I don't seem to be motivated by monetary motives, it is to preserve my independence. I'm sure it's trite, but I actually believe in what I'm writing."

"Nevertheless," Senator Le Grand said, "I implore you to review our offer and give us a positive answer as soon as possible."

Scott was glad he escaped, if that's the word, without a time limit being imposed. He caught a taxi at the intersection of rue de Grenelle and rue de Bac and was back on l'avenue Foch in less than twenty minutes. He and Desirée read the conditions of the offer, and in truth it was a little more generous than that of Steinhausen and Broder, but not appreciably so. The real question and one unknown to Desirée was that MacAllister would need to have a hand in this. But so far, no new arrangement for contact had been formulated. Perhaps they were working on it.

Twenty-five

THE NEXT MORNING, SCOTT RECEIVED AN EXPRESS envelope from Geneva in an unmarked envelope. It had to be from MacAllister. The note inside told him to go the following day to the law offices of Monsieur Jacques de Beauvoir. Scott could confirm Monsieur Beauvoir's identity if he mentioned the inn where his real estate agent and he had lunched.

He would tell Desirée that he was going to the library at the Sorbonne. He was becoming unduly practiced at making up plausible scenarios to conceal his real actions. This dishonesty weighed on Scott. He loved Desirée, and he didn't like to deceive her, but it couldn't be avoided and was likely to become more frequent as it became more complicated.

The next day he took a taxi to the Champs-Elysées, asking the driver to drop him across the wide thoroughfare from a drugstore. He crossed the eight lanes to the wide sidewalk on the other side, went in, reviewed a few magazines in the drugstore's book shop, quickly went up to the restrooms on the second floor, waited a few minutes, then proceeded toward the front door. When he reached the entrance, he did an about-face and walked directly toward the back of the store through the pharmacy. He exited on the rue Marceau side, immediately stepped into a taxi and gave an address in the 4th arrondissement not far from the office of Monsieur Jacques de Beauvoir.

Scott didn't actually think he was being followed or monitored, but how would he know, anyway? In some ways, his familiarization with dodging the paparazzi was good practice for evading anyone interested in monitoring his movements. Several times since he had been back in Paris, he thought he had seen suspicious characters, but he couldn't be sure. He was jumpy, particularly after his meeting with Andre and Leon. The reporters were easy to spot; they made no secret of their intent, but the others, potential spies and the like, would be more cagey.

De Beauvoir would be a new contact, and the longer he could keep his existence secret, the better. It was good practice for him to play hide and seek. Sure, Wainwright had given him a few pointers, but there was no way he could be trained like the graduates of the CIA schools. He was an amateur at best. And amateurs in general get exposed, caught, or killed.

DE BEAUVOIR WAS, AS HIS NAME SUGGESTED, DEBONAIR. SCOTT guessed he was around fifty. He shook Scott's hand and said, "I really love that little inn outside Geneva, Auberge des Chasseurs. There was one dish I especially liked, but I can't recall what it was. I think it was one of their specialties."

"Veal with morel sauce," Scott said.

"Exactly, thank you for reminding me. I used to take delight in sitting on their terrace overlooking the lake and enjoying an absinthe. Do you know it?"

"Yes. I think it's an acquired taste."

With that exchange, they each were assured they were speaking with the right person. De Beauvoir went to a closet in his office and came out with a large suitcase and a tube that appeared to be a carrying case for a fishing rod, but of course, Scott quickly realized, it was his épée and his other fencing equipment. Were the fencing studios the home of the CIA in Europe?

"Monsieur, I don't know your name or anything about you, other than I am to give you this envelope. I have been instructed that you need to read its contents, commit it to memory, and then burn it in this ashtray."

The unopened letter was addressed to Edward Townsend c/o de Beauvoir. MacAllister was prudent. Scott liked that. He silently read the instructions twice, though their meaning was clear on the first read. He struck a match, lit the piece of paper, and held it by the opposite end as the fire spread up the page. He dropped the remaining corner into the ashtray and watched it burn. He then extracted a letter opener from a holder on De Beauvoir's desk and tapped the ashes into a fine powder.

As he reached for the suitcase and tube, De Beauvoir said, "Any time you need information transferred, you can call my office and leave a message that Gaston will arrive on the Trans Europe Express at 15:00 from Nice. This will be my cue to meet you the next afternoon at 14:00 at the bookstore La Haine in St Germain. Make sure you are not followed, and I will do the same."

Scott thanked him and left the building. He had arranged for Gustav to meet him at a nearby corner. Placing the suitcase in the trunk along with the tube, he gave Gustav the address taken from the instructions he had just received. They went to the SCUF, the Sporting Club of the University of France, in the 17th arrondissement, very close to their apartment in the 16th. The note had also advised him to contact Emile Vincent at Editions Tuileries, one of the oldest literary Parisian publishers located in the 7th arrondissement.

The appointment with Monsieur Vincent was immediate. Scott had called the day after receiving the note, and the next day he was in Vincent's office, which was filled with bookcases and scattered piles of books and manuscripts. Vincent was in his mid-forties. He was impeccably dressed, and each item of his wardrobe had been carefully selected for his elegant frame. Everything about him spoke of quality and taste. It was a good look for a man of letters.

M. Vincent and Scott exchanged the required polite gestures, as Vincent invited him to a sitting area in the corner of his office. He motioned for Scott to take the couch while he took a place in a side chair facing him. He must have signaled his secretary, and when she entered, Vincent asked Scott if he would like tea. The secretary quickly returned with the tea and then left them quite alone.

"M. Stoddard, my instructions are that we will be proceeding on a binary track. On one hand, I am to be your contact here in Paris, but I should tell you that I am more a messenger than a person of operations. Your friends in Geneva are quite jealous of their operatives in the field. And the other track will be to consult with you on a book regarding your recent sparrings with the U.S. government. We can meet regularly without drawing any suspicion ostensibly to discuss your book. During those times we will be able to help you keep abreast of other issues as well."

"Thank you, and I am honored to work with you and your firm. Nevertheless, I am concerned that my identity is becoming more widely known than makes me comfortable."

"Originally it was planned that only three people would know of your existence, but your sudden splash and the decisions that must be made demand that we work together to achieve the desired ends. I hope you understand and agree."

"Do I have a choice? It seems you know a lot about me, while I know nothing about you other than the obvious. How do you fit into the picture?"

"Although you may not appreciate it now, there could be a time when not knowing is a benefit. But let's deal with the present matter of importance. You have two offers, both generous, similar in terms, conditions, and compensation. From your meetings, do you have a preference for either one, or more succinctly, which one can you develop the most completely in your opinion?"

"Don't forget that so far as the German contingent is concerned, I only met two principals while the French group included seven people. I've been thinking about it, and I'm wondering why I could not work with both given that they serve different markets but may share similar aims."

"I'm not sure they would accept your working with them both. We are unsure as to their aims and backers. There's a list of unknowns. But they are probably jealous and exclusive."

"The real question is would they rather share than not have any access at all?"

"If there were more history, I believe you would have more leverage, but to be honest, you only have three articles at this point."

"True, but I believe the series that will begin to appear early next week may strengthen my hand."

"What series? MacAllister didn't say anything about any series."

"I've been interviewing Vietnamese refugees and political asylum seekers in Geneva and Paris from both North and South Vietnam. These firsthand stories are quite believable and at the same time harrowing and, more importantly, diametrically at odds with what is being reported in the American press. Some of the refugees are simple peasants, but others among the political refugees can corroborate a distinct pattern of subterfuge and intrigue in the political life of Southeast Asia right down to the village level."

"You're correct that neither one would want to be left behind, but I must warn you that articles of this kind will generate many outright opponents and even more manipulative propagandists. And there could be real danger to you. Outside of the three or four people on our side, everyone else sees you as a threat, and we can't protect you unless we undermine the very secrecy that will promote your success. And on the other side, they very well could try to do more than influence you. They might try to directly recruit you."

"But isn't that what you've been trying to have happen?" Scott asked. "In effect, don't you want me on the inside?"

"It's ideal, but dangerous. You've had no training at this. You know nothing of their techniques and don't know what to watch out for."

Scott proposed that he stall both parties until after the first article of the series appeared early the next week. At that point, if they called, he would tell them that he didn't want to limit his exposure to one market. If they demanded exclusivity, he would indicate that he must decline their offer in favor of another direction. Vincent was doubtful that they would accept such a condition. Still, Scott would be able to take one of the offers, if he couldn't manage to manipulate two. Vincent also reminded him that he couldn't travel in Germany until after his French citizenship was official, and Swiss citizenship was preferable as it would be even more inviolate. And he reminded

Scott that if he were to travel to Germany, he should not be surprised if he were approached by an American intelligence service, if for no other reason than to scare him.

Twenty-six

THE SOCIAL SEASON WOULD BEGIN IN EARNEST THE first week in October and continue right up to the Christmas holidays, when it would go into hiatus for a month. It would restart in mid-January, after everyone had returned from ski vacations and beach holidays in locales such as the French Alps and Morocco, and run through the first of March. Desirée, and by extension Scott, was in high demand. Since Celine was older now, Scott knew that Desirée was excited to get back to their normal participation on the charity circuit in Paris.

As soon as he entered the apartment after his meeting with Vincent, Desirée offered him a glass of champagne and engaged him in discussing their upcoming calendar of events, which included several benefits: two opera galas, a ballet opening, and numerous cocktail and dinner parties. She was disappointed when he reminded her that he would not be able to attend the annual Thanksgiving celebration at the American Embassy. He didn't want to risk being arrested just to share a turkey dinner. Having not thought about the implications of his new status, she didn't think it was as funny as he did, because she'd attended the function for years.

The article "Clusters, Napalm, Defoliants" appeared in *Le Point's* subscribers' mailboxes on the Tuesday after Scott's meeting with Vincent. It reported graphic and pitiless accounts of entire South Vietnamese villages being systematically decimated through the use of modern weaponry against defenseless peasants. Scott didn't leave much out, describing the noise and terror of the attacks, then the immediate and dazing aftermath, as well as the dead, the maimed, and the mutilated, and worst of all, the orphans. Either fortunately or unfortunately, dependent on your viewpoint, *Le Point* never ran photographs with their articles, but it was footnoted in the story that such photographs had been used as prima facie evidence of the stories of the refugees along with the dates and other circumstances. Those footnotes were to underline the authenticity of the articles.

Scott dreaded MacAllister's reaction to the article. It was a real indictment of the U.S. actions in Vietnam and would provide immense propaganda opportunities for those interested in penalizing the U.S. Scott recognized that in some respects he was getting back at the people he thought were mistreating him.

La Haye called him that afternoon at the apartment and indicated that the office was besieged with calls, and Steinhausen and LeFebre were asking to be called as soon as possible. Scott and La Haye had already agreed that these two would be the most acceptable syndicators and partners of Scott's articles from *Le Point*'s perspective, although La Haye graciously reiterated that he understood that his approval was not necessary under Scott's contract.

Scott called LeFebre first, judging him to be more malleable and more desperate. He assumed that LeFebre's failure to mention the latest article was a tactical maneuver that wasn't going to work. Instead LeFebre adroitly inquired if Scott had been able to reach a decision. Scott told him he had made a decision, and he hoped LeFebre and his associates would consider it, because he believed his proposal would strengthen the position of all parties. He then dropped the bomb that he wanted to work with both LeFebre's group and another interested party that included the *Westdeutsche Zeitung*. In addition, he had begun working on a book with an editor at Editions Tuileries.

There was a protracted silence, but LeFebre recovered and said, "I'm quite surprised. We expected to compete for your services, but we never imagined working with anyone else. I'm not sure that there will be any willingness at all for this direction."

"I completely understand," Scott said. "My interest is in getting the message out to the widest audience, and it is difficult for me to engage in agreements that by their very nature restrict the exposure."

LeFebre dug deep, obviously trying to be nice, but Scott could sense that he wasn't happy. He indicated it might take a few days. Scott said that the sooner the better. LeFebre also couldn't hang up without asking what the Germans thought about the idea of sharing. Scott said that he thought they too found it to be not exactly to their liking, but he hoped that they would see the mutual benefits in his arrangement. It wasn't a complete lie. Steinhausen was the next call, and Scott was only anticipating his reaction by a few minutes.

Steinhausen answered on the first ring, "Steinhausen *hier*!"

Scott proceeded to lay out the same parameters for an agreement that he had just proposed to LeFebre, and there was the same long silence. Then the accusation and associated veiled anger broke through: "I'm disappointed. I think you exposed our offer. I'm rather surprised."

"On the contrary, I was contacted by both parties at the same time, after the very first article. I did not share the contents of your offer or the names of the principals involved. There may be no way to convince you of this, but the fact remains the truth whether believed or not."

"All right, it's just a surprise, and I know that the *Westdeutsche Zeitung* and its principals will not go for this at all."

"I understood that possibility when I proposed it."

"What do the French say?"

"I'm not authorized to reveal their decision. I will say that at the outset they were not pleased either."

"But they came around, right?"

"You're making it very difficult for me to maintain my honest broker status. Let's just say that I don't think they would be disappointed if your group refused."

Before he rang off, Steinhausen too inquired as to the timing. Scott indicated that everyone wanted to move forward as soon as possible. News is perishable and imitators would possibly be on the scene quickly if they hesitated. Steinhausen agreed that time was of the essence, but he would need to travel to Munich. This was too delicate to be broached by telephone. Scott deferred, saying that Steinhausen knew his associates best.

On the third day, Desirée mentioned that Scott seemed nervous. He admitted he was. He'd hoped to hear from one or both parties during the day. She was nice not to mention that perhaps he had overplayed his hand and demanded too much. But she reminded him that the end of WWII was only some twenty years earlier and that the French had not yet forgiven the Germans, and the Germans themselves were still cowed with guilt and shame, sometimes ambivalent about present motives. Asking these two parties to work together was demanding a lot, maybe too much. He freely agreed that she was right, but he reasoned that if there was a way that they could come to terms, then it could be a good start.

He guessed that their strategy was not to call him before the end of the third day, the agreed-upon time limit. He was young and inexperienced, and maybe they thought that they could make him sweat a little. Nevertheless, he was surprised that both would use the same tactic.

The call from LeFebre came late in the afternoon on the fourth day. He offered a reluctant apology for the tardiness, explaining that the negotiations on the revised terms had been difficult to resolve. He revealed that the political members of his group were more positive than those controlling the funds. He drifted all over the place, in effect renegotiating the proposal from all angles, not with Scott, but with himself and his absent cohorts. Scott wasn't one to beat around the bush, rather he always wanted to know the price first and the particulars after. He wondered what the whole point of LeFebre's dissertation was. At last the answer became apparent even before the revelation of the decision. LeFebre wanted to be dramatic and wanted the credit of having persuaded the others. Reluctantly it sallied forth; they would share the syndication rights with the Germans. But they would require that the timing of the release of the articles be simultaneous. They didn't want to be scooped by the Germans. And there was little likelihood of this transpiring as the Germans would be hurrying to translate the documents just to keep pace. And there would be a requirement of an equal time provision regarding Scott's participation in any symposiums, seminars, or speaking engagements. Scott halfway expected that there would be a demand of some adjustment to the remuneration, but it never came. He speculated that LeFebre's report of dissension between the two factions in his camp was only invented to dramatize the decision and his part in resolving it.

At the end of the conversation, Scott saw by his watch that they had been talking for forty-five minutes. Naturally, LeFebre couldn't let him go without knowing the status of the Germans. This was a subject that Scott had wanted to avoid, but he thought he couldn't. Prudence would dictate a lie, but he was too fastidious to lie outright. He much preferred oblique equivocation.

"There's a sticking point. I don't know just how important it is, but I'm to hear something tomorrow. If it proves to be an issue that cannot be overcome, then we might be working alone." He hadn't really said anything, but LeFebre made some agreeable noises of understanding on his end of the phone. Scott promised that he would get back to him as soon as the decision was final.

THE NEXT MORNING, HE HAD HIS FIRST MEETING AND LESSON with Monsieur Jean Montand, his new fencing instructor, only recently—very recently—employed by the club to satisfy the burgeoning interest in fencing. Since Scott was a new member, he would be assigned to the new instructor. Apparently Montand liked to begin early because his suggestion was that they meet at 8:30 in the morning at the club. Scott had had Gustav drop his equipment off at the club some days before, so when he arrived, he already had a locker and all the other accessories of membership.

Upon their first meeting, Montand intimated that he had already checked in with Wilhelm Kruger in Geneva to ascertain Scott's level of expertise, his training, his conditioning, his areas of strength and also his weaknesses. MacAllister had also added to Scott's curriculum vitae by suggesting areas requiring particular concentration. He was to learn that MacAllister was especially concerned with his physical conditioning, stamina, strength, and reflexes.

He was surprised when Montand, within the first five minutes, suggested that they go across the street to a small café to enjoy, as he said, a coffee of his choice. Thank God he was unlike Kruger.

Once they were seated at a corner table, Montand said, "Monsieur Stoddard, I'm to instruct you on the finer points of fencing, but also you are to receive an intense course on clandestine techniques. The first of which is how not to be followed. Have you ever worn any disguises?

"I've been to quite a few masquerade balls," Scott said. "Does that count?"

"No, that doesn't count. We'll work on all of it, but we'll need some time. Next week, you will meet me in Neuilly at this address, where you will learn the finesse of the Beretta."

"Italian isn't it?" Scott asked.

"Yes, but it's not just any gun; it's light, automatic, accurate, and ostensibly foolproof. Do you have any experience with guns?"

"None. And I'm wondering why I need any."

"I just follow orders," Montand said.

"Me too, but not over a cliff."

WHEN SCOTT RETURNED TO L'AVENUE FOCH, HE WAS GIVEN A note that Herr Steinhausen had called. Desirée was out, no doubt at lunch with one of her many friends who without much prompting could deliver on what was happening in tout Paris.

He closed the door, sat down at his desk, and dialed, anticipating what the answer might be.

When Steinhausen answered, Scott said, "I was surprised to see that you had called. I had guessed since you hadn't called that the deal was off."

"No, it's not that at all. No, we just needed some time. And I'm sorry it took longer than anticipated. I called to tell you that we agree. We accept to work with your other associates. But it was intense."

Twelve days later, he received the call from his attor-ney, David Blum. It was done, he said, indicating that it had not been a lengthy negotiation. He also told Scott he should be encouraged by the outcome.

Two days later, he had hardly had time to read the final documents and put them in his safe before both LeFebre and Steinhausen were calling asking for the previously published articles and when they could expect a new one. Steinhausen also extended an invitation to Scott to speak at a conference being held in Berlin at the end of November for students and academics from Western Europe and some of the countries in the Soviet sphere. He explained that it was a unique opportunity, and Scott's views would be much in demand. Scott gave him his tentative approval, since he was to receive his Swiss nationality and passport before the end of October.

LeFebre had his own demands based on his association with both student groups and other organizations with left leanings. He too wanted Scott to attend a seminar, maybe participate in a few discussions and add a few off-the-cuff remarks. He pleaded that it would be a great favor to him. Scott agreed. He wanted to appear accessible, so there was no point in refusing the first requests they made.

In the meantime, he met regularly with Montand, sometimes at the fencing club but more often at the gun club in Neuilly. Who would have guessed that an establishment of this avocation would be on one of the tree-shaded avenues of this peaceful *banlieu* of Paris?

The club itself was housed in a nondescript structure set between two office buildings that were surrounded by stores and shops on either side of the street. When Scott and Montand arrived the first time, his instructor opened the entrance door with a key, which indicated to Scott that he was a member. The environment inside the club contrasted drastically with the outside. Off the main corridor, various clubrooms appeared, their décor laced with mahogany paneling and furniture, leather couches, and large armchairs.

Most of the members were avid gun enthusiasts and used the facility to hone their skills at target practice or to lounge around and endlessly discuss the various makes of firearms, their specifications and rarity, and brag about their costs. These were the collectors of hand-engraved Holland & Holland shotguns, men who traipse across continents in search of elusive and exotic game that will ultimately wind up on some wall decorating a château.

Another room farther down the hall, in the back of the building, housed the gun store. Here, in a well-lighted and immaculate space, were cases and racks of rifles, shotguns, and handguns. Montand introduced Scott to his instructor, Patrick Corso, a former French Foreign Legion soldier who was originally from Corsica. He spoke in French laced with the grunt acquired on an embattled island where words were sparse but choice. He and Montand seemed to be old chums, and Scott detected their dismissal of his prospects. Montand had placed all the burden of being a novice on Scott, telling Corso that he wanted to learn something about guns in addition to fencing.

Corso already had a gun resting on a velvet cloth—like a piece of jewelry. Scott's choice of firearm had been made for him. This came as no surprise as he had anticipated that the CIA would indicate when he could breathe, if he would let them. Corso got right to the point. He picked up the Beretta with practiced hands.

"Never point the gun at anything unless you plan to shoot it," Corso said.

"Sounds reasonable," Scott said.

Not amused, Corso said, "It's not a joke."

Scott decided he needed to be deathly serious, because Corso was not a man to be trifled with. Soon Corso settled into his regular exposition of the safety requirements of the Beretta, followed by a long list of how-tos: the correct posture when firing the gun, how to load the gun, how to replenish the magazine, how to sight a target, how to release the safety, how to clean it, and on and on.

"Always grip the gun like this," he said, "with both hands, and keep your thumbs away from the hammer. Otherwise you'll cut yourself."

The only appropriate responses were, "Yes, sir" and "Yes, sir."

It wasn't until his third visit that Scott finally was allowed to fire the gun. He was certain that Corso had made him wait to build drama and suggest the importance of the ceremony to make his position seem more important. They descended a staircase into the basement of the facility. Scott had wondered where the firing range was, particularly since he had never heard the report of gunfire. The noise from the Beretta Scott was using was almost imperceptible given that it was equipped with a silencer.

In mid-morning, however, they seemed to be the only ones around. Corso selected a firing station at the extreme end of the range. Scott's Beretta lay on the counter that separated the stand from the targets. Some targets were animals, some the traditional concentric circles, but Scott noticed his target was the silhouette of a man some thirty to forty feet away.

Corso gave him the Beretta and said, "Let's see what you've learned."

Scott took the grip and stock of the gun with both hands, lined up the sights, and fired. He heard the puncture of the paper target in the distance and an unobtrusive sound from the barrel.

"Never fire just once when you're trying to kill somebody," Corso said. "Make sure they are dead."

Scott fired a few more rounds. With a pair of small binoculars that Corso handed him, after first taking a look for himself, he could see there were four punctures on the surface of the target. Not bad.

"You would have slowed him up, but unless you hit him in the head, he might be able to get off a couple of rounds at you," Corso said. "Keep it in mind."

"A head shot is a hard shot, isn't it?"

"Yes. That's why you need to practice."

Scott's discomfort was amusing to Montand. No doubt it would be reported to MacAllister.

Twenty-seven

LeFebre's seminar, Students United, held the last week of October, was more important than he had indicated. In reality, it couldn't be called a seminar. It was more like a meeting or conference of left-leaning organizations. Even a contingent from the American Students for a Democratic Society was in attendance. Scott served as a panelist on several of the special sessions dedicated to particular subjects that would fit his expertise. His forte was obviously his opposition to the Vietnam War, but there were other subjects included, such as student rights, anti-capitalism, anti-colonialism, and disarmament.

In this homogeneous group of leftists, he proved to be somewhat of a celebrity. From the lack of reaction among the Americans attending the conference, it appeared that his articles were not as known in the U.S. as in Europe, but as they became informed of his opinions, they were approving. Nevertheless, he noticed that among these radicals, you could detect the same egotism and desire for power that was evident in more mainstream politics and even business. Jockeying for position, compromising of ideals, and fudging the facts were as everyday an occurrence in this milieu as they were in every other organization with which he was familiar. Scott was young, but not exactly unsophisticated. He wondered what these firebrands would do with power if they could achieve it. He wasn't optimistic, but he regurgitated his polemics, made all the acceptable criticisms, and let his voice rise in indignation at precisely the right moments.

Nevertheless, there were some—well, one in particular that he became aware of—who found him, for whatever reason, objectionable. At the very first session, he and three other panelists discussed American policies in respect to Vietnam and the support that Germany was giving the United States. The two men—one French, the other German—were amenable, but the woman, Brigitte Fischer, a German activist from the Free University of Berlin, seemed to be combative in spite of their agreement on most points. Her ire, not apparent at first, grew as the discussion progressed. And how did he know? Well, she said so.

After one of his fairly lengthy expositions of his stand on using American firepower on such unsuspecting farmers and peasants in Vietnam, she remarked, "Mr. Stoddard, you are a new convert to our cause, and with your circumstances, it is difficult to understand your empathy."

"And are there circumstances that would preclude one human being from identifying with the plight of another?" Scott asked.

"Preclude might be excessive; hinder might be appropriate."

He didn't offer any response. After the session, he asked who she was, and LeFebre informed him that she was a real firebrand in the German student movement. He warned Scott to be careful, because she was a confidant of the leaders and saw herself as a guardian of the purity of the movement. He took LeFebre's admonition seriously, because soon he would find himself in Berlin, and Fräulein Fischer would undoubtedly be in attendance. He would need to find a way to delicately convince her of his authenticity. It was obvious that she had no use for Americans, and her comment demonstrated that she had done some research on him beyond what was available in the thumbnail profile in the conference program.

THE NEXT MORNING, PRIOR TO ATTENDING THE FINAL DAY OF the conference, Scott called Steinhausen in Berlin. "I'm surprised you aren't here in Paris at the Students United Conference," he said.

"I had planned to be there, but your French friends indicated that this was their territory, so I obliged."

"It's new for me, to take part in these panels. Yesterday, I ran into one of your countrymen, a Brigitte Fischer—"

"Ran into or was run over by? She's a steamroller, just loves Americans. Did you notice?"

"Yes, all those. But what's really bothering her? What's her main issue?"

"That's easy. She knows that members of the National Socialists, the Nazis, are still active in Germany, holding government positions of real authority. And the Americans support this charade."

"How widespread is this opinion?"

"Rampant."

"Why aren't they exposed?"

"Because somehow the slate has been wiped clean. Can't tell who's who."

LATER IN THE DAY, THE MEETING OF STUDENTS UNITED closed with a farewell luncheon where all hundred and fifty attendees gathered. Scott made it his business to sit at the same table where Fräulein Fischer was already settled in with a man and a woman. He approached the table and said, "Mind if I join you?"

Fräulein Fischer was silent, but the other two answered that, of course, he was welcome. The other two places were filled shortly thereafter. The man accompanying Brigitte said, "Mr. Stoddard, I enjoyed hearing your ideas in person on the new colonialism of the United States in Vietnam. I have read some of your articles in *Le Point*."

"Thank you, but something tells me that in certain quarters, my opinions are not dynamic enough."

One of the women broke in, "Oh, I don't think so. Your viewpoint is very valid because you are an American. It's much easier to have your view if you're not American."

"You're very kind. But I can tell you that I'm not totally ignorant of the political pressure brought by the United States on its West European allies in its conduct of the war. Plus, it's not only political, but also economic and strategic from the NATO perspective. There may even be support of political leaders who are pro American even at the expense and to the consternation of citizens within those sovereign countries."

"You don't know the half of it," Fräulein Fischer said.

"Perhaps I need some instruction. I'm a fast learner."

"I'm not volunteering," she said.

"I wouldn't presume so, but maybe you could advise me of who might."

"Try Heinrich Steinhausen. I believe you know him."

What a den of thieves. Fischer had done her homework. Did Scott detect a bit of rivalry here? Was this an internecine squabble, jealousy, or envy, or all three? No direct answer would come from Brigitte, and he wouldn't be able to expect much from Heinrich either, but LeFebre would know.

After the luncheon he tracked down LeFebre, who was in the hotel bar with the more visible academics attending the conference. LeFebre was in his element, holding court and elegantly dressed in a three-piece dark blue suit of well-tailored proportions. While he wasn't a large man, his voice and his scholarly French easily enraptured his audience, which resembled little birds waiting to be fed. As LeFebre wound down, Scott asked to have his impressions of how the conference had gone. LeFebre was enthusiastic, as were his listeners, some of whom Scott recognized.

Then, taking him to the side, Scott thanked him again for inviting him and indicated that he was developing an article centered on the idea that America's Western allies were being pressured in various ways to support a war in Southeast Asia that was very unpopular with the public at large in those countries.

"If you're going to bring up subjects like that, I guess you're looking at West Germany primarily. You're now a French and Swiss citizen, so I think it's safe to speak out on the subject. And in the recent past, there have been a few innuendos in the press along those lines, but no direct accusations. It's a natural progression, but it's also one that could anger some who are not accustomed to being criticized. I like the direction, but I'd be careful."

The next two articles featured in *Le Point,* followed by their syndication in *Westdeutsche Zeitung* and several Socialist and left-leaning newspapers in France, indeed dealt with West Germany's apparent support of Washington's aims while public opinion in West Germany, particularly among the activist student groups, was opposed. The second article even raised the specter that perhaps some West German officials with National Socialist backgrounds had been allowed to progress to positions of real authority in the West German government with the approval of the American government. And by extrapolation, these same officials were in no position to object to the foreign policy of the United States.

At Scott's regular biweekly meeting with Emile Vincent at Editions Tuileries, Vincent reported that MacAllister was not happy with Scott's latest critique of West German government officials.

"Well, it's not as if I accused anyone specifically," Scott said.

"Thank God. But it's not me you need to argue with. MacAllister will be in the Paris day after tomorrow, or as he said, 'Before another article can be submitted.'"

"Maybe he's come to fire me."

"He'll be staying at the Bristol Hotel on rue du Faubourg Saint-Honoré. I'm sure you know it. At eleven in the morning on Thursday, take one of the three elevators in the lobby down to the lower level where the restrooms and some shops are. In the men's lavatory, you will find a key to his room taped underneath the right-hand sink. Come up to his room. Make certain you are not followed."

The spy business or whatever he was engaged in was taking a lot more time than Scott had originally guessed. He had to admit that there was a certain satisfaction in having people read what one writes and react to it. And there was a kind of expert status that he was being accorded that he had not anticipated. In the beginning he had used the first two articles supplied by Mac, but as he got more involved, he began putting his own take on the situation. The normal progression had been that in the end, he was relying on his own opinions partly because he agreed with the criticism of the war and partly because he wanted to get back at Mac. He suspected that the only reason MacAllister didn't complain more or order him to stop was that the articles were exposing the people MacAllister was looking for.

Meanwhile, back at l'avenue Foch, Desirée was not enjoying his newfound profession as much as he was. And there were more and more absences that had to be explained in a kind of contortionist's style to conceal the real reasons for his comings and goings. He was nervous at the prospect of concocting these excuses, and she was becoming suspicious.

On Thursday morning, when he was to meet MacAllister at the Bristol, he found Desirée at her desk writing a letter.

"Darling, I'm going to meet Andre for lunch. I thought I might get his opinion on an article I'm thinking of writing."

"I'm going out myself, and I had hoped you would be at home and have some time with Celine."

"I wish you had told me."

"I shouldn't have to tell you. This thing you're doing has taken over our lives, and I never know what you're doing or what you're thinking. It's really frustrating. You're always somewhere else."

"What can I say, but I'm sorry. You're right, it is all-consuming, and it's unfair to you and Celine. I promise I will do better."

But he knew the instant he said it that it was untrue. How could he do better? He could only do what he had been doing only more. And he knew Desirée would be monitoring his promise. His only refuge would be deceit, telling her one thing and doing another. He never felt quite so guilty.

"Alright. I know you want to succeed at this," she said, "but remember that you're not in this alone."

As he left the building, he spotted a man in a dark gray overcoat and a brimmed black hat on a bench across the street, reading a newspaper and smoking a cigarette. Three blocks later, at la Place du Venezuela, he noticed the man was behind him. He quickly engaged the only taxi there and proceeded to the Hotel Plaza-Athénée, where he gave the driver the fare but told him to circle the block, come back on the other side of the hotel, and pick him up on the l'avenue Tremoille in five minutes. If he did as he was instructed, he would receive a fifty-franc note for his trouble.

Scott went through the entrance of the hotel, proceeded to the lower level, walked the length of the building, came up the stairs on the other end, walked through the opposite doors, then up the street, and took a left onto l'avenue Tremoille, where his taxi was waiting. He gave the driver a new destination, and soon he was within walking distance of the Bristol. He stopped, he started, he turned around and retraced his steps, he crossed the street, he looked for reflections in store vitrines, but it didn't appear that he was being followed.

When he reached the hotel, he said that a friend from Geneva was thinking of staying there and wondered if he could inspect a room. The reservation clerk took him up to a suite on the fifth floor. Scott said that it would do nicely, and as they descended on the elevator back to the lobby, he pretended not to know the location of the restrooms and was directed to the lower level. He remained on the elevator as the reservation clerk exited on the lobby floor. Once in the restroom, he made certain no one was around, reached under the sink, and found the waiting key. He went back to the elevator and took it to the fourth floor, room 423. He used the key to open the door. MacAllister was waiting.

"You don't slum when you come to Paris," Scott said.

"I did it for you. I thought you might feel more at home."

"And I do."

"I'm getting a lot of heat because of your articles targeting certain of our allies. People are unhappy. I'm unhappy."

"I would be too, if it were me."

"Look, be reasonable. You're right in the position we want you in, but we're paying a hell of a price for you to get there."

"I think we've been over this before. You can fire me if you want to."

"Don't start. There's no quitting now. Got it? I don't think you know who you're messing with. First, these people don't know you're working for the good guys. Second, they wouldn't care. They can't afford for you to go around blabbing about their pasts."

"Then I've got to have some say-so."

"You're hardheaded and dangerous to all of us. We do and don't know what some of these people are hiding or how far they would go to shut you up. You're ruffling some pretty big feathers. Let's write about something else, shall we?"

"I'm really close to getting inside the German network of left-wing students. I can't be just a one-issue journalist. They'll only accept me if I can help them fight their cause."

"There must be some other way than creating a firestorm."

"I think a couple more articles will do it."

"I'm warning you to back off!"

"By the way, I think I was followed, but I lost him. Who do you think it was?"

"There's never just one, Scott. And the tail was ours. We didn't try to hide it from you, but we wanted to see your reaction. Don't be overconfident."

MacAllister wasn't all criticism. He thanked Scott for the names, organization affiliations, and personality traits of their associates that he had been routinely passing along through Vincent. Steinhausen and LeFebre facilitated his insight into their groups as both had relaxed their guard a bit, allowing him a peek into the inner workings of their groups. He still wasn't able to pinpoint the source of funds of either group, but he would bide his time and wait for the proper moment. He did have an idea as to how that might be flushed out.

From their conversation, Scott realized that he was close to the quick. MacAllister seemed unnerved, which likely meant the higher-ups were as nervous or more. Could he make it so uncomfortable for them that they would turn him loose? Perhaps, but to make them that nervous, he'd be making the other side even more nervous—maybe murderous. How to turn the key to the point where the highest note can be played without breaking the string?

Twenty-eight

THE NEXT MORNING, DESIRÉE AND SCOTT WERE HAVING breakfast when she began to quiz him about his lunch with Andre. Was there an alternative but to lie? She didn't pursue her line of questioning, but instead switched and asked casually, "Are you aware that a man followed you yesterday?"

"Someone followed me? You must be joking."

"I saw from the windows on the front overlooking the street. A man in a gray overcoat and a black hat was sitting on a bench pretending to read a newspaper. When you passed, he got up and followed you, and when you turned toward la Place du Venezuela, so did he. And why did you go that way instead of going toward the Etoile, the shorter way?"

"I didn't see him. It was cooler than I had expected, so I grabbed a taxi."

"I'm sure he was following you."

"Why would anyone follow me?"

"Maybe somebody doesn't like the articles you're writing. I'm really worried. You can't count on Steinhausen or LeFebre to warn you that you're going too far. They won't mind if it helps them sell newspapers and achieve their goals."

"Oh, be reasonable. I'm a little fish. Many journalists these days are asking questions."

"But I'm frightened. I spoke with Rheiner Honig yesterday. You remember him from Gstaad? He said that you were stepping on some important feet."

"Of course, he's the Radio Free Europe journalist in Berlin. He was the one who questioned me about de Gaulle at the first dinner party I attended at your chalet in Gstaad."

"I told him you would be in Berlin at a conference in another week. He knew about the event and asked me if I knew how leftist it was. He scared me, darling."

"I think you're putting too many things together and coming up with scenarios that fit your fear."

"But the fact remains, the man was following you."

The last thing that Scott needed was to have Desirée's considerable curiosity aroused. He was playing cat and mouse with a number of people, and Desirée knew him well enough that she might guess the truth if she continued to gather information.

His next article was directed at the West German government's budget reductions to higher education, particularly the universities. This action was to both punish the students who were becoming defiant of their elders and also to reduce the services provided by the universities, putting the squeeze on the students. Of course, Scott wrote the article in a way that compared these tactics to the reactionary forces present during the revolutions of 1848, and his article predicted that this strategy of siege against the students would ultimately fail.

After the article appeared, La Haye called him from Bern, telling him that a German woman, Fräulein Brigitte Fischer, had left a message for him to call her. "Do you know her?" Scott asked.

"I know of her. She's a powerful actor in the student movement in West Germany. I presume she would approve of the last few articles you've posted. But, Scott, be careful. She's very intelligent, but very manipulative for her own ends."

Scott returned her call the next day. She answered after one ring.

"I wanted to tell you how accurately your articles depict the situation here in West Germany. Did you write these articles because of what was said in Paris a few weeks ago?"

There was no reason to lie, so he told her the truth. "Yes, I did a little asking around and read a few pieces. The articles came from my learning about the situation in West Germany and realizing how the two issues are linked."

"You said you were a fast learner."

"I'm sure I know less than I think I do, but I'm willing to learn more."

"The last time we spoke, I indicated I was not open to helping you."

"I remember something to that effect."

"Would you refuse if I offered to give you some firsthand information?"

"I'm smarter than that."

"Where are you staying in Berlin? Maybe we could get together before the conference begins."

"The Hotel Savoy."

"Not exactly a hotel of the proletariat."

"Fräulein Fischer, I don't pretend."

They set a date.

Through Vincent, Steinhausen, LeFebre, and MacAllister were all prepping Scott after their own designs for the impending conference in Berlin, and he imagined that Brigitte had the same intent in mind. And it wasn't that he couldn't accommodate them all; he could. But his real interest lay in finding a way out of where all this was heading. He longed for a return to his life with Desirée, their child, their friends, their travels, a time prior to ever really thinking about Vietnam. Senator Morse from Oregon's comment, "Vietnam is not worth one American boy's life," rang in his ears. But how to get out. They made it clear in the beginning that he and his family were at risk if he dared double-cross them, if he abandoned his mission. The obvious way out was to fail, but even then, they might come up with something new for him to do. No, blackmail was the ticket. He had to blackmail them. That was what they would understand best.

Desirée let it be known before he left for Berlin that when he returned, they would take some time off and go to Gstaad before Christmas. It would be quiet in early December, and Helga, their housekeeper in Gstaad, would enjoy seeing Celine, as would Father Kohler. Scott promised they would go, and he meant it. He only hoped that circumstances wouldn't force him to alter their plans.

The Hotel Savoy in Berlin was a little out of the city center where the conference was to be held, but Scott thought it was better to be at a distance rather than be too accessible to the attendees. And even better, it had been restored to its prewar splendor. Situated on a street with a park in the middle, it was one of several seven-story buildings with modest architecture similar to the brownstones in New York. He entered the lobby, and his immediate impression was one of scarlet fabrics, inlaid parquet floors in large square patterns, and imposing black Doric columns. He could imagine Marlene Deitrich sitting in the lobby reading the *Frankfurter Allgemeine Zeitung* and smoking a cigarette with a long cigarette holder. The furnishings in his room followed the lead of the lobby, a little heavy with fabrics and circumstance, but everything was well appointed in its own way.

As prearranged, Fräulein Fischer joined him for lunch in the dining room of the hotel. She'd asked if she could bring along one of her associates, Fräulein Helga Schoen. They were shown to a table for four against the windows that looked out on a garden terrace.

Brigitte began by asking him to call her by her first name, a good indication that they were not to be enemies. If he worked hard, maybe they would become allies. "I hope that in your speech you will be addressing some of the issues raised and explained so clearly in your most recent articles," she said.

"German student concerns have a prominent place, but I don't want to preview my presentation by specifying exactly my point of view," Scott said. "I believe you will be pleased with the content and find that it addresses some of the issues that concern you."

God, these Germans were so different than the French. The French would wait until they had plied you with a little food and wine before they brought up anything of consequence, and it was more likely that the main topic of conversation wouldn't take place until the cream had been added to the coffee.

Scott noticed that there was something different about Brigitte. Her countenance was softer, and there seemed to be fewer lines emanating from her grimace. Her dress was more relaxed as well, still professional, but less dark. Berliners seemed to be addicted to black. Even her tone of voice indicated that she might be trying to be liked.

Fräulein Schoen, on the other hand, only listened and watched as Brigitte broached her plan. Scott learned later that she was an attorney assigned to review Brigitte's writing and maybe to keep her in check. Brigitte's primary request was revealed at the outset, but she had other ideas as well. He knew she would push and push until stopped.

"We were hoping to get an advance copy of your speech."

"I'm sorry, but I speak from an outline and notes that I've prepared. I like my speech to be as off-the-cuff as possible, as I believe it lends credibility." This seemed to appease Brigitte, and he assumed Helga would go along if Brigitte would.

"Is Ian Broder staying here at the hotel?" Brigitte asked.

"I believe he is," Scott said. "Do you know him?"

"I know him," she said, "but I'm not sure he knows me."

"I'll be pleased to introduce you and Fräulein Schoen some time."

"I presume Heinrich will be floating around too," Brigitte said.

"Then you know Steinhausen?" Scott said.

"Yes, but Heinrich wants his own way about everything. At times we disagree on strategy."

"In what way?" he asked.

"He favors a less confrontational initiative, as does Broder. But Broder is looking out for the *Westdeutsche Zeitung* first. They think that they are paying a little to everybody. So naturally they demand to have their say."

"Just for the record, I am paid syndication rights for my articles by the newspapers that run them, but no one is directing or editing what I write."

"I wondered."

"I knew you had."

Fräulein Schoen was remarkable in how little she said. If she were there primarily to keep track and rein in Brigitte, Scott couldn't quite understand why Brigitte was so unguarded in her speech. She of all people must realize that no one in her organization could be trusted not to share information with a plethora of parties. Helga was Buddha-like—stoic, conscious, attentive—and if he were Brigitte, she would be at the top of the list of suspects.

As they were leaving, he saw Rheiner Honig, Desirée's journalist friend who worked for Radio Free Europe, coming toward him in the lobby. She had insisted that they get together while he was in Berlin, and since the schedule was packed, Scott had asked if he would do him a favor and come to the hotel. He hadn't planned on this impromptu crossing of paths in the lobby, but the meeting with Brigitte had gone a little longer than anticipated. As Steinhausen had warned, Brigitte was always certain to map out her entire program as well as have the last word. There was no ducking Rheiner, so Scott introduced them. It seemed they had met before.

Scott and Rheiner went into the bar where it was quiet in the early afternoon, and over tea Rheiner said, "I guess Desirée told you that I had called and had told her what a splash you were making on the international news and commentary scene."

"Yes, she did mention it. Thank you."

"Did she also tell you that I warned you to be careful?"

"She did, and I can't understand all the fuss. These are just my opinions. Aren't people allowed to express their opinions?"

"Of course, but if the opinions you express encourage people to start digging around in the unpleasant past, then someone is going to blame the guy with the shovel."

"I know you write for Radio Free Europe, which is not exactly a paragon of impartiality."

"We don't purport to be even-handed, and, certainly, we're not questioning members of the West German government. Our mission is against the Soviets."

"Speaking of which, I'm close to something, perhaps an indication of how the Soviets might be influencing the students in West Germany and the labor unions in France. I'm not sure exactly what it is, but it could be a mole."

"I'm sure the people in the West German government would be grateful if you turned your attention somewhere else, anywhere else," he said with a laugh.

"But I'm a little stuck," Scott said. "My sources are limited when it comes to the Eastern Bloc."

"I don't know what your schedule is like, but if you're interested, my uncle, Fritz Honig, is a professor at Humboldt University in the East sector of Berlin. He could give you some real facts regarding the kinds of things you are writing. In general, he's an objective person, but he's always under a lot of pressure to tow the party line. And I must warn you. At times he's watched. He has a somewhat checkered past with the East German authorities. It's understandable, he's a professor, an intellectual. He's entirely impractical but lovable. You're a Swiss citizen, so you wouldn't have any trouble getting through to the other side and to the university. An hour or two with him might give you an indication of where to look for what you're missing."

"I thought Desirée said that your family had managed to escape East Berlin before the wall went up."

"We did. He wouldn't come with us."

"Why not?"

"Because his wife wouldn't leave her parents. They were too infirm to make the trip."

"What a choice."

"Yes, and now he's alone and not well. His beloved Heidi died two years ago. I worry about him. So does my father. Fritz is his only brother."

"I have my speech tomorrow, but there's a window the next day from noon on. Do you think he could meet with me then?"

"I'll see what I can do. I can take you to Checkpoint Charlie, where you cross over, but after that I can't come with you."

"Perhaps it's better we aren't seen together right now. I can find the crossing point, if you organize the meeting."

Scott returned to his room and found that a note had been slipped under the door. It was a phone message from Brigitte to call her. He had a feeling that he knew what the subject of the call would be.

"How do you know Rheiner Honig?" she asked.

"He's a friend of my wife."

"Do you know who he is and what he does?"

"Yes."

"I presume you know that he is in effect an employee of the very people that oppose our activities?"

"Brigitte, besides you, who else is keeping tabs on me?"

"Get used to it, Scott. In Berlin, everyone is suspicious."

"Lovely vacation spot."

"I mean it. Somehow the government knows everything we are doing. Just yesterday, two of our members were arrested for no reason. They had been at the printers and had picked up flyers that we were going to use at the conference. The students were held overnight, and the flyers confiscated. Now it's too late to print new ones."

"Well, obviously you have a leak somewhere, but I hope you're not suggesting—"

"Of course not. I'm just telling you to be careful who you talk to."

Everyone was so concerned about his safety. He wouldn't tell anybody about the little excursion he was planning into the Soviet-occupied East Berlin, but he could predict that MacAllister would disapprove, and Desirée would kill him. But this was an opportunity not to be missed. He was certain that what he needed would not be found at the library. The archives had been wiped clean. Still someone, in all likelihood, was holding something for a rainy day.

The next day, he took a taxi to the conference center long before he was to give his speech so he would have time to meet as many attendees as he could. As his taxi approached his destination, the driver pulled over because the police were redirecting traffic. Scott paid the taxi fare and walked the last two blocks. As he got nearer, he began to hear a loud commotion that was part shouts and screams and part police whistles and the tramping of feet. A handful of young toughs chased by police barreled through the crowd, crashing into demonstrators carrying signs protesting the government. Although the troublemakers seemed to get away, the police took advantage of the melee to roust a number of the attendees, throwing some to the ground and arresting others indiscriminately.

Looking more like a businessperson than an attendee, Scott avoided the confusion and the police by walking around the corner and using a side entrance. Once inside the grand hall of the conference center, he and Brigitte Fischer saw each other at the same moment.

"Someone's cut the electricity in the auditorium," she said. "It's pitch black. And they've arrested Rudi Deitweiler, our chairman."

"On what grounds?"

"They don't give a reason. They don't need one. They're more aggressive each time."

They took the stairs up to the second floor of the grand lobby. From there they could look out over the plaza in front of the building. Outside a brigade of police rounded up anyone carrying a sign. Brigitte cried out the names of several of her friends whom she could see being accosted, but she couldn't help them, and they couldn't hear her. The attendees already in the hall were safe, but those on the outside weren't so lucky. Finally, the lights came back up. Scott learned it was his turn.

His speech, an hour late, was given before a boisterous crowd of some seven hundred and fifty activists, students, journalists, and other political professionals. He opened with, "They can cut the electricity, but they can't cut the power."

This enlivened the crowd, and they chanted their resolve. By the end of his presentation, he could tell the crowd was with him. Some were chanting slogans, others waving banners, and at the end, he received a long and loud applause. Steinhausen and LeFebre were both sitting on the front row, but in different sections. They looked satisfied.

Afterward, behind the stage, Brigitte greeted him and chattered incoherently. She looked as if she were in a state of shock. She told him and anyone within earshot that Deitweiler had been released without being charged. When she had calmed a bit, she congratulated Scott with an unexpected hug and introduced him to a number of her colleagues from the university and a couple of local journalists supportive of the students.

Around noon the next day the weather was cool and an appropriate Berlin gray. He took a private car to the crossing point, Checkpoint Charlie. The approach to the border was a two-lane road with multiple signs in three languages warning that one was leaving the American sector and entering the Soviet sector. There was an impressive array of barbed wire strung along the demarcation line. Scott went into the small white hut on the American side, presented his passport, and stated the reason for his crossing, who he would see, and the length of his visit. This was the easy part. As he exited the hut and walked across the border, he approached the guardhouse for the Soviet sector. He purposely had only brought his passport, wallet, and a pen. He was visiting a professor of history and philosophy at Humboldt University as a student at the University of Geneva and a sometimes journalist. Whether through actual scrutiny or through a policy of creating necessary theater, the East German border guards were unsmiling, even foreboding, slow, and deliberate in their questioning and inspection of his documents. After about thirty minutes, his passport was stamped, and he was out of the custom booth and into the streets of East Berlin.

It was about a fifteen-minute walk to the university where Dr. Honig waited. Scott noticed as he marched along that it was very quiet in the streets, just the shuffling of shoe leather on pavement. There were few cars on this side of the wall, and most of the ones that were here were old and damaged. The buildings reconstructed after the war had the appearance of functionality rather than some compromise between utility and aesthetics. He assumed they were government offices since they brandished the red star emblematic of communism and the Soviet presence. Rubble filled the streets in front of buildings that had either fallen in on themselves or had been left over from the bombing. Most alleys between buildings and sewer access had been sealed off with huge steel grates. This was prison on a large scale.

He knew from the map Rheiner had given him where the professor's office was, and he knew enough German to ask directions if he got lost. He easily found the building, another foreboding, ramshackle three-story affair. He could see how the building had once stood along with others in a kind of quadrangle typical of university architecture and layout. Now it appeared that only a few of the buildings were occupied. A window or two was out in several places, and the façade was like most buildings in this sector, a dingy, grimy gray. When he asked how to get to Rheiner's office, a young woman in the drafty entrance hall pointed to the staircase, and he took the creaking steps to the second floor. As he walked down the hall, he read the names of professors on the doors. He stopped in front of the one labeled "Honig" and knocked. He heard, "*Eintreten.*"

Scott entered as Doctor Honig was rising from behind his desk. "Mr. Stoddard, it's nice of you to come. Rheiner wrote some nice things about you." Thank God he spoke English.

He was a gentlemanly, older man with the look of professorial tenure. On his desk were stacks of musty books and dog-eared papers, a row of pencils and a fountain pen, and a small reading lamp with a shade shedding strands of silk. The professor seemed tentative as he spoke, and Scott knew if his interview proceeded in this manner, he would learn nothing. He wondered if the office was bugged.

"Mr. Stoddard, Rheiner said you might want to see the book I wrote some years ago, before the war. My thesis was based on it. At the time I was very concerned that Goethe might be the last truly educated man."

Rheiner hadn't mentioned any book, but he would play along. "My German is mediocre, but I would love to see it."

"I wish I could offer you a copy, but this one is the last of only a few. It wasn't a best seller." He smiled and gave Scott the book.

It was a large-format book, about twice the size of a standard letter. He turned it over to see the front cover and binding in honey tan calfskin leather. There were discolored splotches here and there where the oils from a person's fingers had stained the leather. It wasn't a new book, but on the front cover set within an oval embossed frame, was a line engraving of Goethe's profile. The title of the book was stamped in gold foil, *An Illustrated Biography of Johann Wolfgang von Goethe*. It easily opened to page 121. Trapped in the center against the binding was a teabag with a message written on the paper wrapper: "Can't talk. Have documents you need in West Berlin." Scott turned the page, quietly reviewed the contents page, some of the footnotes, and gave it back to the professor.

"I really wish that I had more time to read it."

"Would you like a cup of tea?" Honig asked.

"Yes, thank you."

The professor turned to a table behind him where there was a hotplate, a kettle, and two teacups. He took the teabag from the book and another from a box and begin preparing the tea. He tore both paper wrappers into small pieces.

As they drank their tea, Scott asked the professor about his health, explaining that Rheiner would want to know, and they discussed Scott's international studies at the University of Geneva.

"I should probably be getting back," Scott said after a while.

He thanked Honig for his time and for letting him see the book. A glance up from his desk revealed the forlorn countenance of someone without hope. Perhaps this is what Rheiner wanted Scott to see. Maybe there were larger issues than student grievances at the university. They bade each other farewell in a kind of melancholy scene, and Scott wondered if there would be another time that they would see each other. Before leaving, he looked straight into the eyes of Uncle Fritz and gave him a slight wink.

As Scott reached the first floor to exit the building, a man standing outside an office door said in perfect English, "Mr. Stoddard, may I have a word with you?" He asked Scott to step into his office and offered him a comfortable, upholstered chair next to a fireplace. The atmosphere was warm and cozy, a welcome relief from the professor's cold and utilitarian room. The man sat across from him. "Doctor Honig is one of our most venerable professors. I know he must have enjoyed meeting someone who is so much in the forefront of the journalistic endeavors that point out situations that concern us all."

"I enjoyed meeting him. But we didn't discuss my journalistic career."

"It's a pity, because you're quite accomplished."

"And may I inquire with whom I have the pleasure of speaking?"

"For the moment, let's agree that I am a friend, even a supporter of those who seek the truth about the forces that undermine the rights of individuals."

"That's a high calling. You must be busy."

"You're right, it is demanding, and it requires a lot of help."

"I'm not sure why you're telling me all this."

"Because you have proved that you understand and that you are in a position to help."

"What do you want from me?"

"You are like your articles, you get straight to the point, Mr. Stoddard." He proceeded to tell Scott that his name was Karl Koch. He intimated that he too was in the business of disseminating information through various channels whereby the people could be better informed in all of Germany. He revealed that he could provide Scott with all kinds of privileged information regarding politicians and other personages in positions of influence and power in West Germany. This information could be persuasive in some of the efforts toward greater participation of the population in democracy. Through a predetermined system that they would establish, he could have background material that he could use to either persuade or coax leaders in the West German government.

"Why don't you coax them yourself?" Scott asked.

"I think you already know why not, but I will confirm it for you. Because if it were to come from a source identified as less than objective, it would be dismissed."

"Maybe I like digging around on my own."

"And that is what we're concerned about. We don't want you digging in the wrong patch."

"I'm not sure I understand your meaning."

"But I think you do, Mr. Stoddard."

"Perhaps you need to make it clear. I hate misunderstandings."

"Then we're already in accord. So do I. Your exact interests and intentions are clear in regard to the situation in West Germany. But you will need assistance to explore the issues that you want to write about. And without some guidance, you may stumble into areas that could embarrass you or, worse, be dangerous."

"Are you a spy, Herr Koch?"

"I am a source, a source of the kind of information you need, if you can be persuaded that some situations are off limits."

"Are you trying to bribe me or threaten me?"

"Have I offered you any money?"

"No, and why not? I like money."

"Mr. Stoddard, I'm not unfamiliar with your situation."

"And what's in it for me?"

"Access that you'll never have without my help."

"Before I buy anything, I like to know the price. It sounds high."

"I'll be in Paris in five days at the brasserie Bofinger. Do you know it?"

"Yes, quite well. Excellent oysters and choucroute."

"I'll be there at 13:00 at a corner table. I hope to see you. There's a car outside that will take you back to the crossing point."

The car returned him to Checkpoint Charlie where he reentered West Berlin smoothly, the trip undoubtedly greased because of his association with Herr Koch.

As for the balance of the conference, the sessions and discussions were anticlimactic for Scott. Outwardly, he maintained his enthusiasm and interest level. He was able to placate the various parties vying for his interest: Brigitte, Steinhausen, and LeFebre. He had a farewell drink with Rheiner and gave him a report on his uncle. Of course, Scott didn't tell him about the note or the book or, certainly, about Koch. But he did tell Rheiner that his impression was that his uncle was losing ground to depression and asked if he had tried to extricate him from his situation. Rheiner assured Scott that there was no way to get him out. The Stasi didn't forget or forgive affronts, no matter how long ago. His uncle had been resistant to the authorities right after the war. They had tried multiple times without success.

"But it isn't like he's a threat of any kind," Scott said.

"True. And before the wall, he was able to come sometimes to this side. I know he hoped to get back, because he intimated that he had some funds in the West sector that he could live on. He's crafty and secretive. Probably has a safe deposit box somewhere around here," Rheiner said.

You can bet that he has a safe deposit box, Scott told himself. That's where the documents are. All Scott needed to do was to get him out. The stories he could tell. And Rheiner was right. Old Fritz was crafty. He had enlisted Scott on their first meeting.

Twenty-nine

When Scott returned to Paris, his first priority was reconnecting with Desirée. He took her to Maxim's. Guillaume, the maître d', showed them to her favorite table, which had a commanding view of the center tables as well as the orchestra. She was back in form, her slim figure hugged by a silver-sequined sheath, with blazing diamonds in a necklace that rested against her chest. They dined on foie gras and filet de boeuf and drank Krug champagne, and they laughed and stole kisses. They danced and danced until well after midnight. Back at the apartment, they made love as they had before the baby—tender, passionate, and long. Sex was always the prime indicator of the health of their relationship. If they could enjoy sex with abandon, it meant that there was no suppressed resentment. Hesitancy and withdrawal meant that there was trouble in paradise. The next morning, they planned their escape to Gstaad. Scott told Desirée that he needed just a few more days in Paris to complete a few tasks.

Around ten the next day, he went to his regularly scheduled meeting with Emile Vincent, his literary editor. He didn't need to worry about being followed or otherwise observed when going to Vincent's office. He was writing a book, a perfectly logical and benign endeavor. There was no reason to keep it a secret.

He must have gained status in Vincent's eyes, because for the first time, Vincent showed him into an adjoining office, a small library that was part sitting room and part conference room filled with books, probably most, if not all, editions originated by Tuileries. The room was impeccably furnished in an art deco style of light woods, black marble, and glass.

Vincent was most interested in how everything had gone in Berlin. Specifically, he asked questions about the attendees, the subjects discussed, and any surprises. And he indicated that from press reports it appeared that Scott had handled himself quite well.

"MacAllister is concerned about what you have in mind for the next articles."

"MacAllister must come to Paris tomorrow," Scott replied.

"But why? He'll want to know."

"I can only tell him in person, and it must be tomorrow, no later than the day after tomorrow."

"Stay here. I have another telephone in a private office downstairs."

While he waited, Scott looked around at the manuscripts sprawled across every surface and then picked up *Le Figaro* off Vincent's desk and read the headlines. It was about twenty minutes before Vincent returned. "MacAllister said okay, but it better be good." He will be at the Hôtel de Crillon. A car will pick you up at l'avenue Kleber and the Etoile at ten o'clock and drop you off near the hotel."

THE NEXT MORNING SCOTT LEFT THE APARTMENT AT NINE o'clock. It was too early for any reporters since they knew the countess never appeared before ten. But two other people without cameras began following him. Over the next half hour, he backtracked and crossed the streets from side to side and took a few short taxi rides until he lost them. At least he hoped he had lost them. He settled into a small café next to the appointed spot on l'avenue Kleber and hid there until the ten o'clock pickup. The driver of the limousine gave him the key to the room at the Crillon and let him out on the side street of the hotel that faces the American Embassy. Scott took the stairs up to the mezzanine level and then caught an elevator to the fifth floor.

"This better be good," MacAllister said when they met.

"Do you know of an East German named Karl Koch?"

"And how did you meet him, may I ask?"

"I met him at Humboldt University, day before yesterday."

"Humboldt is in the Soviet sector of Berlin. What were you doing there?"

"I was seeing a friend, a professor."

"What did he want?"

"The professor or Koch?"

"Koch, of course. This isn't the time to be flippant."

"He's trying to recruit me."

"Karl Koch is an alias. His real name is Dimitri Rostov. He's a Soviet, a colonel high up in the KGB, and his cover here in Paris is cultural attaché at the Soviet embassy. He has diplomatic immunity. His specialty is counterespionage. We have lost several men to this brute. Who gave you permission to go to East Berlin? Do you know how risky that was?"

"No. If I'd known, I wouldn't have gone."

"You could have asked."

"There wasn't time. He'll be back in Paris in three days, and he'll want an answer."

"Jesus Christ, Scott. Well, by God, he'll have to wait."

"He won't wait. He wants to know if I'll cooperate or not."

"What does he want you to do, and what's in it for you?"

Scott explained that Karl—or Dimitri, if he preferred—would feed him secret information, probably the lowest kind of dirt, on the politicians in the West German government. Scott could use these revelations as he saw fit to expose and embarrass the men in power. The Soviets would be pleased if this would contribute to disruption of the political climate in West Germany. He left out the fact that Koch wanted him to leave certain politicians alone, no doubt the ones in league with the Soviet agenda.

"No matter what information he gives you, there are certain politicians who must be left alone. I'm not sure you can be trusted with this kind of information. You're not great at following orders."

Where had Scott heard that line before, "certain politicians"? Each side had those they needed to protect.

"There are?"

"This guy is out of your league. It's not what we planned."

"I want to make a deal with you."

"What kind of deal?"

"I'll do what you want me to do, but then I want out."

"But Scott, you could be really good at this."

"I was good at what I was doing before we met. I'm not kidding, Mac."

"We'll tell you when you can quit, and it's not now."

Finally, they agreed that he should meet with Herr Koch at the appointed time and listen to the proposal. MacAllister wanted to populate the restaurant with surveillance personnel of various stripes, but Scott argued that if Karl Koch was as professional as MacAllister had said, he would no doubt spot the team and quit the meeting. MacAllister had to admit that he was right, but he still didn't like Scott going in there naked. At least he should be wired. Scott refused that as well. MacAllister reminded him that the colonel would be wired, recording the conversation, to either confirm Scott's participation or use whatever he said as blackmail if he didn't cooperate. Scott joked that maybe he should change the meeting to a Turkish bath where they would both be naked. MacAllister was not amused.

In the end, MacAllister relented, but he had a list of instructions for Scott. First, never say anything that could be remotely used against him. Second, listen more than talk. Third, don't agree but plead for more time to think about it. Fourth, remember verbatim everything that was said. Scott nodded. The meeting would take place.

Bofinger is located in the 4th arrondissement of Paris, near la Place de la Bastille, where the Revolution of 1789 began with the freeing of the prisoners from the Bastille, the notorious prison where political prisoners were held. It wasn't exactly a restaurant where one would expect clandestine conversations would take place, but maybe that's what Koch had in mind. Decorated in the style of the Belle Epoque, with ample gold and red ornate brocades and sparkling chandeliers, the restaurant was one of the most famous in Paris. Scott loved the place, and he and Desirée would often have lunch there on Saturdays, enjoying the fresh shellfish for which it was known and afterward promenading through the avenues and small shops in the neighborhood.

When he arrived, he could see that Karl Koch was already seated at a generous table in the preferred corner of the restaurant. The maître d' led him to the table. Herr Koch rose and greeted him, and they exchanged pleasantries much the way two businessmen might inaugurate an important luncheon.

After Scott was poured a glass of champagne, his lunch partner cited the merits of the restaurant and noted the miserable weather. Scott took the first of a series of pieces of paper from his inside breast pocket, carefully unfolded it, and held it by its sides in both hands, turning the handwritten message toward Herr Koch for him to read. It said, "I'm sure you are wearing a recording device. Remove it, put it on the table, and turn it off. Otherwise you will lunch alone."

A few moments passed with Koch seemingly reading the note again, but of course he wasn't reading it at all, but stalling for time to decide what to do. It was an eternity before he reached inside the breast pocket of his suit jacket and extracted a small tape recorder about the size of a cigarette packet. He pulled the plug connecting the microphone and shut off the power switch, extinguishing the small flashing yellow light.

"Does that make you more comfortable, Mr. Stoddard?"

"Infinitely," Scott said.

"The reason I wanted to record our conversation is so that there would be no mistakes in remembering what we discuss. I hope you understand."

"Of course, but I'm sure you will be able to remember the important points. And by the way, I'm not clear on what you want."

"It's very simple. You write articles about Vietnam, and lately you have expanded your opposition to institutions in West Germany that limit student participation in the curriculum of the university and their criticism of policies of the West German government. I am in a unique position to give you deep background material on many of these reactionary leaders in the West German government as well as the origin and reasons behind the United States' support of these politicians. You could, as you say, dig on your own, but you would never be able to excavate what I can give you, a much more efficient use of your time, shall we say?"

"And exactly why would you do that?" Scott asked. "Why am I so fortunate? There are many journalists who would jump at this opportunity."

"Because most are hacks or already compromised by their associations. You are new, a tabula rasa, plus your circumstances attest to the fact that you can't be bought."

"But isn't that exactly what you're trying to do?"

"No, not at all. I want to provide you with the truth, that's all. I haven't offered any money."

"But you will be editing the truth you give me, protecting the ones you favor, and damning those you dislike."

"As you say in your country, sometimes half a loaf is better than nothing."

Scott presumed that Koch had concluded that he could not possibly decline this offer. And he was probably correct about dredging up the information. He would never uncover what Koch could so easily provide, information that would be carefully curated to send Scott marching in the direction they wanted. A little game of misdirection was next. It was time to set the trap.

As the colonel waxed on about the advantages of such an association, the merits of the exposure of certain characters to be named later, he also proudly revealed a scheme, a simple but foolproof system, as he termed it, of communication, and more importantly, drops. Koch had done his homework.

They either already had someone inside the premium dry cleaners on l'avenue Francois Premier that Desirée and her family had used for years, or they had placed someone there. Her family rarely wore any garment more than once before it went to the cleaners to be "refreshed," as they termed it. Desirée's designer clothes required special care, and Scott's handmade shirts and bespoke suits had to be pressed by hand.

To procure information, Scott would send his black Charvet blazer to the cleaners. Someone on the inside—Koch didn't say if it were an employee—would sew a small cloth sack, the same fabric and color of the lining, inside the breast pocket, where a silk handkerchief would normally be placed. The sack, so insignificant that it could easily be overlooked, would contain a roll of film with the information of consequence. With a magnifying glass and a lampshade as a backlight, he would be able to read the film. If he sent the blazer in without a button on the left-hand sleeve, it would mean he wanted to see Koch. They would meet the next day in the wine tasting room at Fauchon, a specialty food and spirits emporium on la Place de la Madelaine.

Koch seemed a little smug as he wrapped up the particulars, no doubt believing that he had anticipated every possibility and celebrating his recruitment of a rookie. The rookie part was right, but this particular rookie was willing to risk failure to achieve his ends. Now Koch was waiting for Scott's response, because during his exposition, Scott had not interrupted even once.

"I hope you are not looking for an answer today," Scott said.

"Actually, yes. Do you have any questions or comments?"

"No, a request."

"Tell me what it is, and if it will help conclude the agreement, I'll do what I can."

"Place a personals ad in *Le Figaro*. The ad should read, 'One is a lonely number,' with a telephone number, the last four digits of which should indicate the date when it will occur."

"What will occur, what date?"

"The date Professor Honig will cross over into West Berlin."

"I can't do that. He has a past, you know."

"Then we have nothing more to discuss. Thank you for lunch. It's probably for the best anyway."

Koch stared at him, his expression somewhere between incredulity and doubt. He was trying to measure whether Scott was bluffing or not. "If you change your mind, then—"

"I won't," Scott interrupted. "But I will read *Le Figaro* every day for the next two weeks. It's almost Christmas, you know."

THE NEXT MORNING SCOTT PLEADED WITH DESIRÉE FOR ONE more day before they left for Gstaad. He still had the Hôtel de Crillon key, and by previous arrangement, he was to meet MacAllister that morning. He asked Gustav to drop him off at Fauchon, where he picked up some chocolates and tinned cookies for Mac, then crossed the street, descended into the underground parking, and crossed the open garage to the other stairwell next to the rue Royale. After crossing the street, he circled the block, going in and out of stores, and finally arrived at the Crillon, where he went into the bar and ordered a coffee. The bar was virtually empty, with the exception of a threesome, two American women and an American man. He left 10 French francs on the bar and found the restroom on the lower level. He waited, he listened; he was not followed. He took the elevator up to MacAllister's room.

MacAllister asked if he would like something to drink. "Just water," Scott said, and then he laid out the entire conversation, verbatim except the parts about the drops and the message exchanges and the last few negotiating points.

"He's waiting on you to give him a response?"

"Not exactly. I'm waiting on him."

"I thought you told him you needed more time. That was good."

"No, he must decide."

"Decide what?"

"Decide to arrange for Professor Honig to cross over into West Berlin."

"He'll never do it."

"That's what he said. I believe he thinks I'm bluffing."

"He probably does."

"Then it's his mistake to make."

"I didn't realize you were such a humanitarian. Why Honig?"

"There's lots you don't know about me, Mac."

"I think you're in for a surprise. I repeat, he won't do it."

Maybe they both were, but Scott didn't say it. He told MacAllister that he believed Koch would come around, just to make him feel better.

"We have more at stake with Koch than this old professor," MacAllister said.

"You're so empathic," Scott said.

"I'm not paid to be empathic. I'm paid for results," MacAllister said. "You're not letting your wife's friendship with Rheiner get in the way, are you?"

"Don't be silly," Scott said. But he was glad that he thought that.

"They'll be following you now."

"Yeah, it could get crowded."

Thirty

THE NEXT MORNING, DECEMBER 14, SCOTT, DESIRÉE, and Celine flew to Geneva. A car met them for the drive up to Gstaad. Desirée, her cheeks aglow, had decked herself out in white chinchilla and their cuddly Celine in a fur-trimmed romper. This was life in the luxury lane far from the grim underbelly of the clandestine world. Scott so missed the luxury of being worry free.

The nanny, Christine, and Gustav had left the day before and would be at the chalet when they arrived. Christine was quite a find. She was an English girl from Dorset, but her mother was French, and she had been educated in Catholic girls' schools in Aix-en-Provence. Desirée wanted Celine to be fluent from the beginning in both French and English, and one could never be truly fluent if a language were learned after the age of two. Christine could accomplish a lot in that respect since she was with Celine most of the time and spoke both languages without accent.

They arrived in the early afternoon. Celine was tired and irritable given the length of the trip. When they rolled up in front of the chalet, Helena was the first person to greet them. She immediately swooped up the colicky Celine, and in no time the baby was giggling and cooing.

Scott had made a reservation at The Chesery, the gourmet restaurant where they had their first date. The regulars, the international jet set, would be arriving for the Christmas and the New Year's extravaganzas a day or two before the holidays, and then they would be in and out of Gstaad for the entire season, which lasted until mid-March. But there were some early arrivals, like Scott and Desirée. The restaurant as well as the entire village was already decorated. Wreaths and garlands, red ribbons, large cowbells, and tiny white lights reflecting off the fresh snow made everything glisten.

After dinner they went up to the Palace Hotel and its nightclub, the Greengo, where they had danced together for the first time nearly two years ago. They ordered a bottle of Krug, danced, and romantically reminisced about those early days. "Were you already in love with me when you came up to Gstaad that first time?" she asked.

"Not really."

"Oh, that's mean."

"But I was in love with you after my second night here. Remember, you said you were giving me a reason to stay."

"You would remember that."

"It worked."

They loved to tease each other and play hard to get, though both of them were pushovers for each other. Life would be perfect if he could rid himself of these interlopers into their idyllic life. If only they would release Professor Honig, one piece of the puzzle would be in place.

Scott had told his editors that he was taking three weeks off from writing articles. He needed a break, and he wanted to devote time to his family over the holidays. Steinhausen, LeFebre, and La Haye reluctantly agreed, after reminding him that the public has a short memory and that he had attracted a loyal audience, and while he might need a break, his readers might not. They might be looking for or expecting more. He said he understood, but in reality he didn't care.

He was very diligent about reading *Le Figaro* every morning. He had to go into the village to a small tobacco shop to pick up the papers, and one morning he had a start, because when he finally got around to going into town, the newspaper was sold out. Don't panic, he told himself. He went up to the Palace and obtained a copy from the concierge. There was no news. Well, not the news he was looking for. Koch had eight more days to signal him. Maybe MacAllister was right this time. Maybe he had asked for too much.

The next day, he picked up the paper early and went into a small café, ordered a cappuccino, and opened the pages to the personals. Halfway down he saw it, and he could hardly contain himself: "*Un est un numero tout seul. Tel: 45 24 12 23.*" The twenty-third was the day after tomorrow.

DECEMBER TWENTY-SECOND WAS ONE OF THE LONGEST DAYS of Scott's life, and he couldn't reveal his emotions. He couldn't share his inestimable happiness and joy with anyone, not even his wife, whom he adored. He guessed that the news of the Honig's arrival in the West would not be in the papers until Christmas Eve. Although Professor Honig was a little past his prime, anyone granted exit status would be big news. The part that worried Scott was that reporters and others would be snooping around from sources on both sides of the Wall wondering exactly why this elderly professor had been released and who was responsible.

Although he would be happy that the professor was reunited with his family, he was counting on the professor's teabag message that he had information that would expose the duplicity of both sides. If Scott could use it correctly, it might get him his freedom back. He did wonder, though, whether the old man hadn't been bragging or delirious. A few days would undoubtedly provide the answer.

THE NEXT AFTERNOON—THE DAY—HE AND DESIRÉE WERE downstairs in the great room, having coffee after lunch, talking and watching a fresh snowfall coat the valley below when the telephone rang. Helga soon entered and announced that Desirée had a call. She picked up the receiver. "Oh, Rheiner, what a surprise! Merry Christmas! It's so nice to hear from you. When are you coming to Gstaad?" She went silent, and as she listened, her eyes began to well up. Soon she was sobbing into the sleeve of her sweater. Finally she said, "Rheiner, I'm so happy." She handed Scott the phone.

"Rheiner, what's happened? I can't tell whether Desirée is happy or sad." He listened as Rheiner explained that Fritz had been released into West Berlin. "Oh, I see. What incredibly good news. I'm so happy for your family. How did it happen?"

"Thank you, Scott," Rheiner said, the phone line humming. "I don't know how you did it. I don't want to know."

Scott hung up the phone, dreading the inquisition.

"I wonder why he called us," Desirée said.

"I imagine he's calling everyone."

"He did say that you went over and met his uncle in East Berlin. That was dangerous, wasn't it?"

"Not really, not with a Swiss passport. I'm sorry I didn't tell you about the East Berlin visit. I didn't want to worry you."

"But why?"

"Rheiner said he might have some good tips for me, but he didn't. He looked sick. That's probably why they let him leave."

It was plausible on the spur of the moment, but she was still curious. Desirée was no novice at intrigue, and just a little suspicion would whet her deductive instincts. Over the next few hours, she would think of something. She continued to ask questions and associate various details such as the articles he was writing and his success in this journalism career, all to prove that there was something going on. And she reminded him of the incident in Paris when she had noticed he was being followed. As she laid out her case, she watched his eyes intently. He was certain that if he lied, she would know. She apparently didn't see anything because she didn't say anything. He must have passed, this time anyway. But now she would be more watchful than ever.

THE NEXT DAY, DESIRÉE READ EVERY LINE ABOUT HONIG'S release in *Le Monde,* the leading political newspaper in France. The real story in that paper as well as all the others was the speculation on what had precipitated this action. There seemed to be no diplomatic maneuver, no reciprocal release of any Soviet person or persons. The reporters and wire services were stumped, and from the mood reflected in the press, they didn't like being on the outside and not in the know. They knew that someone knew, and they were going to find out whom.

These newspaper stories only made Desirée ask more questions. This predicament was the unexpected result of what Scott had considered a good deed. He hadn't considered all the speculation as to who might have caused the professor's release. And Rheiner's call just increased the focus. He meant well, but there were the unintended consequences of Desirée's curiosity and that of the press. Scott had a real decision to make. Should he tell her? Would she be angry? Would she ask or even demand that he stop? Then what? He couldn't stop now. They wouldn't let him anyway. They had made that clear. If he had just waited another six months, he probably could have gotten out of this mess without her knowing anything. But then Honig appeared. He couldn't very well pass that up. He was clear on that. He had done the right thing, but it could be a frosty winter.

HE WAS GLAD THAT THE HOLIDAYS INTERVENED TO TAKE THE attention off the Honig situation and his possible participation in it. Christmas is a time for children, but Celine, only ten months old, couldn't fully understand the fuss. Madame de Bellecourt, although not a fan of the mountains and cold, made the trip from Cannes up to the chalet in Gstaad to stay for the week between Christmas and the New Year.

As was her custom, Desirée had her preferred florist in Gstaad decorate the house, including the placement of two evergreen trees of nearly three meters, one in the foyer and the other in the great room. The one in the great room had white lights and real candles that were lit on Christmas Eve. Helena and extra help prepared the dishes traditional for the holiday feasts, of which there were many.

The Stoddard chalet, better known as the countess's chalet, had once again become the scene of any number of dinners and parties. And now Desirée had Celine to show off to those who had not already been introduced. As Desirée floated from one guest to another, the perfect hostess having just the right comment for each person, Scott could tell that she was regaining her form, the one that he knew and loved so much.

One evening they invited Jon and Louise Goosens, Yves and Jacqueline Bertrand, and Madame de Rosier for dinner. Just as they were *à table,* the first course was being served when Louise asked, "Desirée, I was surprised to hear from Rheiner Honig a couple of days ago. He said he had spoken to you and Scott, but he wanted to let me know personally of the excellent news."

"Yes, we're so happy for him," Desirée said. "Apparently it was quite unexpected."

"Very unexpected," Louise said. "We are all wondering how it happened."

At that point, Jon piped up: "Rheiner said that you had been to see his uncle in East Berlin just ten days ago. I got the impression that Rheiner thinks you had something to do with his release."

Scott glanced at Desirée. She was transfixed to hear his response and watch his expression. He was steel. "No, I was there, and he looked in ill health. Maybe that's why they let him go," Scott said.

Madame de Bellecourt said, "Scott wouldn't tell you if he had anything to do with it."

Thirty-one

After New Year's Day, Desirée and Scott decided to return to Paris for a few weeks. He reminded her that he had work to do, and he couldn't do it from Gstaad. There were people he needed to interview and background material that could only be found at the Sorbonne Library. And he had to send his blazer to be cleaned to signal Koch that they had a deal. Although it wasn't what she wanted to do, she agreed, but she exacted the promise that they would return to Gstaad for the entire month of February. What could he do but acquiesce?

They returned to their Paris apartment to the usual stack of mail and packages. Most of it was for Desirée, but one package, with a West German postmark, was for Scott. He took it to his desk in the library. The package was wrapped in brown paper and secured with a natural twine, knotted in a few places and pulled taut. He cut the string, tore off the paper, and saw the Goethe book he had seen in Franz Honig's office in East Berlin. An accompanying note had been inserted behind the cover: "As one who loves antiquarian books, I'm sure you will appreciate the fine binding and elaborate illumination of this edition." There was no signature, but a tiny label inscribed, "Marga Schoeller Bücherstube" gave some evidence of its origin. Scott recognized the name of the oldest bookseller in West Berlin. Retrieving the brown paper from the waste can, he verified that the package had made it through customs without duty and without being opened. This was probably thanks to the rush of the holidays. The mailing label indicated the sender as the bookstore. Now who would be so thoughtful to send him this elaborate gift? It could only be one person.

Desirée came in and saw him looking at the book. "Who's that from?"

"It's from a bookstore that I visited when I was in Berlin."

She began looking at it. "This is a really old one, but beautiful. I know you admire Goethe. It's too bad the back cover is a little loose."

"It's over fifty years old. I'll probably have a few things coming loose by then." She smiled. He still had most of the books he had ever read, but this one would forever be special.

Inadvertently, she had revealed the secret of the book. At last, she left, saying she had calls to make. They were having dinner at Allard at seven-thirty, she reminded him.

He examined the back cover of the book and noticed that the end paper looked as if it had been recently re-glued. When he passed a razor blade between the end paper and the leather, the layers separated to reveal a letter-size envelope, which he extracted from its hiding place. An old photograph had been tucked inside, featuring three men standing in front of an official-looking building. All wore uniforms complete with the chevrons of rank of the Stasi, the secret police of East Germany. Scott didn't recognize the men or the building, but someone had penciled an arrow over the man in the middle with the added note, "Kleinst, 1946."

He had no doubt as to the provenance of the photograph. He supposed that the sender had to take into account that the package might be intercepted, thus it appeared to originate from the bookstore. The photograph had been taken as a candid shot, not one that was planned or posed. The men in the photograph probably had not even been aware that a photo had been captured. Scott guessed from the sliver of a reflection of a hand in the lower foreground of the picture that the photographer was stationed in a car in front of the building, perhaps waiting for something or someone. The image in the reflection was fuzzy, but still revealing to someone with a clue. He would need to do a little detective work to learn what the photograph pictured and why it was important. A visit to the Sorbonne library was his next stop. He pasted the end paper back in place and left the book on his desk. The photo he placed into a file behind his desk entitled "Questions."

Koch had done his part freeing Dr. Honig. Now Scott was interested in how he would follow up. The blazer would be back from the cleaners shortly. He felt it was important that he operate with a business-as-usual air. He resumed his weekly lessons with Antoine at the SNCU, which, in addition to fencing, now included other techniques of spy craft, such as disguises and detecting shadows. And he met weekly with Emile Vincent at his office, although his book was a backburner project. Once they were alone in his office, Vincent said, "MacAllister wants to know what's next, now that Honig has been released."

"I'm waiting on Koch."

"MacAllister is impatient. He feels that you're acting alone."

"He worries more than my mother."

"I'll tell him what you've said. He wants to know how you and Koch plan to communicate."

"We are communicating. I'll have something for him soon."

"He won't be happy."

"He's never happy."

After their meeting, Scott went to the library of the Sorbonne. It was as much art gallery as library although it housed some five hundred thousand books. From the reading room, he could solicit volumes from the archives upon the presumption of research. He picked one of the community tables with the small individual lamps in the vast hall where a large painting of early academicians dominated the front of the room and frescoes decorated the domed ceiling much in the fashion of a cloister. The location was away from most of the students. Here on this hallowed ground, the students were serious. Most were transfixed by their work, and they spent long hours in the library, which was probably more conducive to study than the cramped and cold lodgings where most of them lived.

Scott requested several volumes regarding landmark buildings in the Soviet sector of East Berlin. Next, he asked for books dealing with government officials of the West German government since 1950. And for good measure, he sought out university yearbooks particularly from the elite German universities now in the Eastern Sector.

A half an hour later he was summoned to the information desk and was given a stack of musty volumes. He was glad that his university studies had required so much sleuthing and cross-referencing. He quickly got into the flow of identifying Kleinst as a man of fifty-two and secretary to the defense minister of West Germany. Other than some sketchy information about earlier positions in the government, it was as if Kleinst's early years never happened. Who were his parents? Where was he born?

Scott had brought along a magnifying glass with a Zeiss lens, 4x, from his office for the anticipated task of examining the hundreds of tiny heads looking back at him from these yearbook pages. He was determined to find Herr Kleinst. It was all a matter of ticking off the pages one by one. Finally, in year 1933, he found him in the University of Leipzig yearbook. There was no doubt when he compared the face in the photo from 1946 to the one in the yearbook of Kleinst posing with members of his swim team. The boys were gathered around the edge of the pool, two rows of seven young men each, and there on the second row, second from the right, was Kleinst. But his name wasn't Kleinst; it was Ott, Günther von Ott. With the name, Scott was able to find him several more times, but nothing about his family. Ample documentation existed, however, for his participation in the Hitler youth movement, his elevation to colonel in the Wehrmacht, and, finally, after the war, his enlistment into Stasi. But from 1947 on, it was as if he had disappeared. He simply ceased to exist, but that was not a surprise as public information on officers in the Stasi was suppressed. His change of identity and navigation to his current position as secretary to the West German defense minister obviously had been carefully buried. The fact that Kleinst had never been found out testified as to how secret and how important his position was. Perhaps MacAllister could help.

The building in the photograph was easy to find. The portico design of the entrance made its identification unmistakable. It was pictured over and over in the books Scott had requested. It was the infamous Stasi headquarters and prison in Hohenschönhausen, an East Berlin suburb. Every photo caption for this building spoke of the terror it incited.

Next, he reviewed the uniforms of the three men in the photograph. The stripe down the trousers leg, probably red, and the shoulder boards confirmed that Kleinst was a major. Kleinst would have some explaining to do at some point.

Suddenly, it was all clear. The peccadillos of student unrest and infiltration of foreign interests into student affairs paled by comparison to what this photograph and the dual identity of Kleinst meant. A spy, a Stasi/KGB mole, was lodged at the nerve center of West German and Allied defenses of Europe. This information was radioactive, and Scott couldn't allow anyone to know of his discovery. Obviously one other person knew, but Scott didn't worry about him talking. Scott had been hunting a mole and had bagged an elephant. This was going to require a big gun. It was just what he was looking for.

Thirty-two

THE NEXT DAY, SCOTT MET WITH VINCENT AT EDITIONS Tuileries and asked that he get a message to MacAllister. He wanted to know if there was information available regarding a Günther von Ott, German, Leipzig University, born between 1912 and 1916. Vincent performed his role very well from Scott's perspective. He didn't ask why, who, or how much.

On schedule, the blazer came back from the dry cleaner midweek. When he arrived at the apartment, Sybil, Desirée's maid, had already placed it in his closet after taking off and disposing of the protective wrapper. Scott reached inside the designated pocket, and felt the sack containing the microfilm. He left it where it was until he could steal some time alone to read its secrets.

The next morning, Desirée left the apartment early for a coiffeur appointment and then lunch with her best friend, Celine. He took a pair of small snippers into the closet, closed the door, and extracted the film from the pocket. He then carried the roll to the library, closed the door, grabbed his large magnifying glass from the desk drawer, placed the film against the light shade, and read a list of ten names, their positions in the National Socialist Party pre-1945, and their positions in the current government of West Germany. He immediately realized that most of the persons included on the list were lower level, not the bigwigs that he'd expected. He'd once heard someone explain that all Germans have a past, but after the war, the Allies had to have someone to run the government. The fact that the information revealed was of such modest importance alerted Scott that Koch was going to be stingy with meaningful facts and was probably testing his patience. He wouldn't disappoint. He assumed the message was intentionally cryptic, a test to see what he could figure out. He had a plan.

He wasn't back in Paris a week before La Haye, Steinhausen, LeFebre, and even Broder telephoned, wondering when the next article would be available. Scott promised something for the next week. Keeping his promise, he sent the finished article to La Haye at *Le Point Opposé* on Friday. It would print over the weekend and be in their subscribers' hands by Tuesday. The socialist and leftist papers in France and the *Westdeutsche Zeitung* would run it on Wednesday.

The reaction was entirely expected. When La Haye and the editor of *Le Point*, Christian Delacourt, received the draft, they called immediately, trying to protest in a diplomatic way the format of the article, namely that it was a crossword puzzle and in English no less, and they had no idea how they would be able to translate it. Scott admitted it was a bit unusual, but he had his reasons. And he reassured them that so far as the crossword being in English, he was certain that the target audience for this article either spoke English or had access to translation resources. He reminded them that they had the right to pass on publishing it, but of course he knew and they knew that they weren't going to risk losing an opportunity even if was a bit unusual. They dropped their protestations, and Scott assumed that the next day he would receive his copy by express mail.

By Wednesday evening, the article had been published in the mainstream media. The wire services had picked up his column, not the article itself but the conundrum it posed. One of the first calls was from Brigitte Fischer. "And who's idea was this?" she asked.

"Mine," Scott said.

"It's brilliant. It's even more effective than simply naming names."

"And this is just the appetizer."

"How did you figure all this out?" she asked.

"Research."

"Then your library must have better sources than mine."

"Different sources. Have you made any headway on the leak?" Scott asked.

"None. But three students, leaders in our movement, were expelled yesterday from the university."

"Brigitte, maybe you're the one who needs to be careful."

"I know. Maybe they'll leave me alone because of my ties to the press."

"I hope so."

She wanted more information, and she continued to probe and nip, tease and cajole, which was hardly her forte, but he maintained a state of normalcy and an impenetrable one at that. She finally gave up, asking him to stay in touch. And if there was any information that he needed, then he could call on her. He thanked her.

Later, Andre, his friend at *Le Figaro,* called. "Scott, *mon garçon,* I did not realize you were so clever with *les mots croisés,* crossword puzzles." The clues of the puzzle, if guessed correctly and placed into the appropriate spaces on the grid, would yield answers that, while still veiled, could be either guessed or would stoke innuendo and suspicion. Scott had used initials rather than names, acronyms rather than organizations, and abbreviations and nicknames rather than positions or jobs. All in all, it was quite cagey. He had come upon the idea one morning while waiting for Antoine. He was reading the paper and saw the crossword and thought it could be a good way to hint but not directly expose. Of course, the principals involved, "The Ten" as Scott named the puzzle, would be able to solve the puzzle easily, at least for their own name. In all probability, only a few would be able to break the code in its entirety, and this was by design. Other than the names, all the other clues for the puzzle were immaterial to the main message, but easily solved. For the most part, these were low-level officials but still within the public eye. Those with something more incriminating to hide were already worrying about who might be next.

"I'm not that good at crosswords," Scott said.

"There are those who would disagree with you. My boy, I'm worried about you. Please be careful. You are treading on some sensitive toes."

Andre's worry was the consensus opinion. At first, Desirée, along with others, didn't understand the import of the puzzle, but over the first few days in circulation, conjecture increased regarding the answers, and it received more and more interest in the general press. It wasn't long before journalists were playing the game, saying that they had unlocked the code of the grid. The Ten, although unnamed, became the objects of mounting derision. For politicians, scandal is preferable to ridicule. Without accusing anyone directly, Scott had let mere suggestion fuel the insatiable curiosity of the public and the press.

IT WAS TIME TO MEET WITH KOCH, WHO WAS PLAYING SCOTT. He needed to be called on it. Scott sent the black blazer back to the laundry with Gustav, commissioning him to mention that the button on the left sleeve had come off. He supplied the button, but he needed it resewn.

The following day, as it was prearranged, he would make his way to Fauchon, the premier food emporium offering the most extensive wine inventory in Paris and attracting commensurate oenophiles, and Scott's destination, the multichambered wine-tasting facility. As he left the l'avenue Foch apartment, he spotted in the distance a woman with a briefcase in her left hand, the agreed-upon indication that MacAllister's people were on the job. But as he walked along the avenue and purposefully sped up and slowed down, going in and out of shops as if undecided about his whims, he also caught a glimpse of a man who appeared to be a street cleaner. He was dressed in the traditional blue uniform and held a broom at the ready. Scott figured that he was probably not alone, probably followed by at least three or four people.

He decided the Galeries Lafayette would provide some exercise for his pursuers, so he took a taxi to the great department store behind the Paris Opera. The store was always filled with a mass of people of every stripe. He was carrying a small duffel bag, and after he entered the store, he went to one of the elevators and pressed the fourth-floor button. He saw that at least two of his shadows had made the elevator with him. They didn't press any button. The full elevator stopped at each floor, and when it reached the third floor, women's lingerie, several of the women exited the elevator as more got on. Scott hugged the position next to the door, and as the door was closing he quickly slipped out at the last possible second. His pursuers were blocked in the back by those getting on the elevator. He would be alone, but for only minutes. He quickly entered one of the women's fitting cubicles, and from his duffel bag he extracted a long black coat, a heavy scarf, and a Russian fur hat, a *papahka.* To his disguise he added a pencil thin moustache and clouded gray wire rim glasses. He stuffed his own clothes into his duffel bag. It took all of five minutes. He took the escalator to the first floor and found a taxi near the Opera. No one seemed to be interested in his movements.

He was only three minutes late to Fauchon. Surely Koch could forgive three minutes. He scrubbed the moustache from his face with a white handkerchief as he crossed the threshold into the store, then he left the obtrusive elements of his disguise at the coat check. As was their signal, he told the master sommelier that he was most interested in the vintage Bordeaux, particularly those from the Rothschild properties. He indicated he was to meet with a wine consultant to discuss possible wine acquisitions. He was informed that the wine consultant was already in one of the wine-tasting rooms and had ordered several selections to be tasted. He was shown down into the lower levels, which were as quiet as a tomb.

Koch was waiting for him, standing in a private room at one of the elaborate tables with several wine bottles that had been opened so the wine could breathe. A number of Baccarat crystal glasses in the Bordeaux shape were waiting for the right moment.

Scott shook his hand and asked permission to pat him down. He felt under his armpits, his vest pockets, down his legs to his shoes and even groped his crotch. "I'm not wired," Koch said. "Should I give you the same inspection?"

"If you like." He didn't.

As a result, they got off to a slow start with the usual well wishes, the inquiry as to the success of the holidays, and the demands of work. Scott could tell that Koch seemed pressed to get to the matter at hand. As he poured Scott a little of a Bordeaux from Mouton Rothschild, he spoke of the bouquet, its superior terroir. Then he said, "It seems that the public can be easily intrigued with crossword puzzles."

"I presume it depends on how cross they are with the answers."

"We had thought you might use the information in a more direct way."

"More direct, but less titillating. I think it worked out alright."

"It has. It's created a storm in certain circles in Germany."

"By the way," Scott said, "I do want to thank you for the Honig family reunion in West Berlin."

"I hope they realize what you did for them."

"That's unimportant."

"And what is the reason you wanted to see me? These meetings need to be limited to the fewest possible."

"I can only write persuasive articles with good information. This low-level material that you gave me last time will not move mountains or shake foundations. I presume that you gave me a few eggs to see if I could cook an omelet. I accepted what you offered and essentially did what I could. Don't ask me to waste my time or my platform with unimportant tidbits. I want prima facie, original source material that I can verify. I'm not going to accept some roll of film that could be manipulated. And I don't want to be sued."

"I'm not sure I know what you're asking for."

"I believe you do. I don't think you trust me, so why should I trust you?"

"This is not a business based on trust. It's based on need."

"So it seems. Well I don't need to be rationed and managed."

"I can't make any promises," Koch said. "I'll see what I can do."

"And how do I know that what you're giving me is true? I have a lot at stake, so I don't want to be taken advantage of. If I detect any hint that you're planting false information, our deal will be over. It's up to you."

"I said that I would work on it. And by the way, I see from the guest list that you and your wife are attending a reception at the Soviet Embassy on Friday evening benefiting the historical restoration of a castle in the Loire. Do not be surprised if you see me there. My real name is Dimitri Rostov. I'm Russian. I think it would be better if we pretended not to know one another."

"Thanks for the tip, but I had already figured that out. And by the way, please stop your people from following me. My wife is suspicious, and she is perfectly capable of employing an investigator to get to the bottom of her curiosity."

THE NEXT MORNING, SCOTT WALKED FROM THE APARTMENT up l'avenue Foch to the Etoile, where twelve streets merge at the Arc de Triomphe, an intersection like no other. MacAllister was back in town and demanded a meeting. Scott was headed to the pickup point. He took a set of steps to an underground walkway provided for tourists to cross under the streets to arrive at the monument at the center of the intersection. Rather than taking the steps up to the monument, he took one of the other passageways to arrive on the other side, where a stairwell led up to l'avenue Wagram. Before going up the steps to street level, he waited to see if he had been followed. He didn't see anyone. A black Citroën limousine with tinted windows waited. He quickly got in, and it sped off. MacAllister was in the back seat. Wainwright was driving.

"Thanks for coming," MacAllister said.

"Did I have a choice?" Scott said. "Hi, Wainwright."

"I'm catching hell about your latest article, the crossword."

"It'll all be over soon, Mac. Show a little patience."

"I'm not clear on what you are doing. I'm beginning to think that you're planning something you're not telling us about."

"It'll be apparent soon. When we get closer to the strike price, you'll have only a few hours to make up your mind."

"Make up my mind about what?"

"Can't tell you yet."

"Remember, we're on the same team," Wainwright said.

"Tell me what's going on with Koch," MacAllister said.

"We have a system by which I receive information. He's in the process of evaluating my latest request."

"You met with him again? What new request? By God, Scott, if you weren't so involved with this Russian, I'd think about taking you off this assignment."

"But I am, and yes, we met on Tuesday. I saw your woman. Nice briefcase."

"You lost her at the Galeries Lafayette, and I think the Koch people too."

"I wasn't sure. I had to pick up something for Desirée. An amazing place, so many items of fashion."

"Cut the bullshit, Scott. What's the new request?"

"I'm asking for prima facie information, authentic documents with proof of legitimacy."

"He'll think twice about that. If he supplies that kind of crap, in some cases it could be traced back to the original source and more importantly to him. Jesus. But that's exactly what you're offering, isn't it? That's your plan."

"If you say so."

"Okay, I know you're not going to tell me until you're ready. Mark my words, he won't do it."

"What about von Ott?"

"Yes, what about him?"

"Did you find him?"

"We found him alright. Buried in the Stasi Memorial Cemetery in East Germany, 1947."

"Well, there goes that idea," Scott said.

"What idea?" MacAllister asked.

"It doesn't matter."

But, of course, it did matter—a lot.

And maybe MacAllister was right. Everything hinged on what information came back with the blazer. But the blazer was delayed at the cleaners, some excuse about the tailor and the button. They had to send it to Charvet to acquire a new button for the sleeve, saying the button he provided was broken. Of course, Scott wasn't fooled. He knew that it was a ploy to gain time for Koch to either decide on his own or go higher up to get approval to send the kind of intelligence Scott was asking for. Three days later, the blazer along with the other cleaning came back. When he reviewed the first few frames of the enclosed film, he could see right away that these were names with big titles but little importance. Apparently, Koch was playing hardball, or he couldn't get permission from his superiors to divulge more sensitive information, information that might pacify Scott but imperil others.

Thirty-three

On Thursday afternoon, he forwarded the new article to La Haye in Bern for publication the following Tuesday. It appeared on time, and, more importantly, as written. *Le Point Opposé* was dismissed by the Left as too moderate and accused by the Right as too liberal. This was the bane of being in the middle, and the primary reason it had been selected in the first place. Steinhausen was the first to call, followed by LeFebre, both asking why it was that when he was on to something with the previous crossword ploy, he suddenly veered off into this sensitive morass. Then Brigitte called. She wasn't good at keeping her emotions in check and informed Scott that he was doing damage to the cause, that the people he was singling out were for the most part helping her and others to battle the authorities.

Admittedly the thrust of this article was different—Soviet Co-op Leftist Institutions—and without going into too much background or detail, Scott had summarized the criticism of the more conservative journalists and political thinkers on the danger of the infiltration of Western leftist organizations by forces of Soviet Communist influence. He was sure that while his leftist supporters did not approve of this inexplicable change of direction, he acknowledged their concern. He rebutted their critique by reminding them that only by appearing to be a fair-minded journalist could he have credibility in either camp. They accepted his explanation, but they were not pleased.

What Koch had given him he hadn't used. This article was written as a protest aimed at Koch. The colonel had refused to give him the information he knew he was looking for, so Scott decided to show his displeasure by publishing an article about Communist infiltration into the West German government and student organizations. Koch would get the message. To underline his impatience, he sent a blue blazer rather than the black one to the cleaners. Two could play the game of obstinacy.

As luck sometimes dictates, that same evening Scott and Desirée were to attend the reception at the embassy of the USSR, the one where Koch had cautioned him to pretend that they did not know each other. Desirée was unhappy too. From her perspective, Scott's articles were creating notoriety and uncertainty—even unease—at the precise moment when she would be seeking Soviet support for one of her charities. He apologized and said he hadn't thought about it. He could sense that she knew that there was some other purpose.

When she met him in the salon of their apartment for a champagne toast to the success of the evening, he was reassured that her beauty and grace would overcome politics. She wore a silver lamé long dress with a plunging neckline trimmed in white ermine. A necklace of diamonds and more diamonds of an almost Czarist extravagance cozied up to the white fur. Her blond hair was in a coif resembling those in ball scenes from *War and Peace.* Long white gloves accented her slender arms and silhouette. He was in his uniform for such occasions, his tuxedo from Lanvin. Desirée was in a gay mood, revving herself up for her performance to come. Raising money is not easy. Neither Scott nor Desirée brought up the article that night. There was no reason to begin the evening on a sour note.

The Soviet embassy was in the 16th arrondissement, the same neighborhood where their apartment was located and only ten minutes away. The Russians must have seen the evening as an opportunity for propaganda. Their vaunted austerity didn't extend to evenings such as this one. They went all out, the theme being that of the grandeur of France with which this crowd was familiar and would heartily agree. Elaborate flower arrangements were strategically placed, gold brocade and bunting encircled the columns and mantles, and large banquet tables with bite-size canapés, as well as the pride of Russia, caviar—mounds of it—beckoned the guests. To reinforce the perceived Russian tradition of hospitality, circulating waiters, dressed in expertly tailored uniforms of gold and red, served ice-cold, 100-proof vodka along with champagne from Baccarat flutes.

Scott and Desirée always arrived a tad late by design. They emerged from the car, and a consular official greeted them and led them up to the entrance, which was flanked by a platoon of photojournalists and security personnel. Once inside, away from the blinding flashbulbs, they checked their coats and were led to the reception line, which consisted of the ambassadors of the USSR and France and their wives and a series of other cultural attachés of both countries, as well as the president of the French Historical Preservation Society.

Once through the gauntlet, Desirée led the charge, wandering from room to room, reconnecting with many of her Parisian friends and those of the Preservation Society. Then Le Marquis de Chambord-Benoit, the president of the society, cornered them, and in French said, "My dear Countess, can I count on you?" He also made a quick nod of recognition to Scott.

"Count on me, Andre, for what?"

"I want you to use your considerable charm to convince the embassy's cultural attaché to make a sizable donation to our preservation society and announce it this evening."

"Why Andre, I'm sure he would be more impressed by you."

"My dear Desirée, don't make me beg. Do this little favor for your favorite Andre?"

"Alright. But I will put a little mark down in my book of accounts."

"Oh, my dear, put two marks down, even three. I love owing you."

"Then which one is he? Point him out."

"There he is now," Andre said. "Let me call him over to introduce you."

The ambassador reached out and grabbed the consul's arm "Consul Rostov, please let me introduce you to Monsieur and Madame Stoddard. Madame Stoddard is very active in the Preservation Society as well as the arts and political life of Paris, indeed in France. Monsieur and Madame Stoddard, Consul Rostov is the chief cultural attaché of the Embassy of the USSR." After a brief exchange of *enchantés*, the Marquis added, "And I must warn you, Consul Rostov, that Madame Stoddard, the former Countess de Rovere, is not only one of the beauties of France, but an expert on medieval and baroque architecture and its restoration. I hope that she will be able to persuade you that the USSR should assist us in restoring treasures that are the world's, not just those of France."

Without even a stammer, Comrade Rostov said, "I would be pleased to consult with Madame Stoddard regarding the restoration project, and I will see what I can do. I say that in advance so that she will pity me and not turn her full powers of persuasion on me. And Monsieur Stoddard, I have read some of your articles. Very interesting, provoking even."

"I'm surprised and honored that you would remember something of so little consequence," Scott said.

"On the contrary, I have found them innovative, and it appears that you are as comfortable on *La Rive Droite ou La Rive Gauche,* the Left Bank or the Right Bank," he said.

"Please, my friends, no politics tonight," the marquis interrupted. "We are here to celebrate what we are certain to have in common."

Scott wasn't aware until it had already happened, but Desirée had deftly guided Consul Rostov to a small cached sitting area with only two chairs where they were engaged in what appeared to be a pleasant discussion punctuated by smiles and approving nods of the consul's head. Scott could tell that Desirée's hypnosis had begun, and when they stood and parted, Rostov not only clicked his heels in the practiced manner reminiscent of the Russian aristocracy's imitation of the traditions of French couturiers, but also raised her hand and kissed it. As Scott looked across the room, he saw the marquis witnessing the same event with a satisfied but subtle smile of contentment.

Thirty minutes later, Consul Rostov stood at a podium and in the most poised of ways let it be known that he had an important announcement to make. Gradually the crowd migrated from the adjoining rooms and encircled the podium, and the noise level subsided to where he might be heard. In French, *sans accent*, he said, "To the honorable ambassadors of France and the USSR, honored consuls and attachés, the Marquis de Chambord, ladies and gentlemen, I have been authorized by the USSR ambassador to France, the Honorable Sergei Litnov, to say that after detailed discussions with Madame Stoddard, the Countess de Rovere, the Preservation Society, and the Marquis de Chambord, the USSR will donate a sum of 300,000 French francs, to the Society's restoration fund."

The applause was broad, loud, and long. All the main participants in this little love fest had the good feelings that well up when a charitable impulse is satisfied.

Koch—Rostov—came toward them, smiling the smile of a self-satisfied man, expecting plaudits for his actions. The countess didn't disappoint.

"Consul Rostov, let me thank you on behalf of the Preservation Society for your generous gift," she said. "It will be spent wisely and judiciously toward projects that would make you proud."

"Madame Stoddard, I have no doubt, and I look forward to seeing your achievements," Koch responded.

"And since it is important that our donors see results," Desirée said, "I invite you to come to our ball next month to celebrate some of the progress that we are making at the Eglise a Val du Mont."

"You are too kind, but unfortunately, my wife and children will be joining me for an unexpected vacation in Austria, Lech to be precise. It is our anniversary."

"How lovely. I am very familiar with Lech, and I have shared with my husband my affection for a small chapel there, Sankt Nikolaus."

"Lovely indeed. It is where we were married some fifteen years ago."

"Well, you must come next year."

"I will look forward to it, Madame."

Scott gave Desirée an adoring hug that indicated both approval and amazement. Of course, he knew that there were other forces moving these tectonic plates. At the same time Comrade Koch—God, he had to be careful not to call him that—caught his eye. He knew that meant Scott should follow him, but not too closely. Scott excused himself. He left Desirée with a group of congratulatory members of the Society.

Rostov was headed toward the hall where the WCs were located. Turning left at the end of the hall would lead you to the loo. Scott looked to the right, down the other hall, and noticed that the second door down was slightly ajar. Guessing that this was a cue, he opened the door, and there, in a small library, was Rostov sitting in a chair, facing a sofa. Scott entered, closed the door, and locked it.

"The blue blazer wasn't subtle, even less so was the co-op article," Rostov said. "I thought we had an understanding."

Scott picked up a pen and a tablet from the desk. He sat on the couch and wrote, "Thank the ambassador for making it possible for the generous gift to the society. No names, please. I thought we did too. If you want to renew our agreement, then let's meet at the appointed place tomorrow at the agreed-upon time."

"By the way, the ambassador doesn't have that kind of money," Rostov said. "Until tomorrow then. Let's get back before we're missed."

Desirée was ecstatic that she had been able to persuade the consul, though she said that she suspected they had probably already decided in advance, but Rostov had been chivalrous enough to accord her some of the credit for the decision. Scott disagreed and told her that she was undervaluing her charm. And he of all people knew of its power. Now if he too could persuade the cultural attaché.

WHEN HE EXITED THE APARTMENT THE NEXT DAY, HE WAS TO meet Koch. He left before lunch, telling Desirée that he was going to the library for the afternoon and would pick up something to eat on the way over. He asked her if she wanted to come, and she smiled and said when they had lunch together, she wanted it to be a proper lunch with good food and good wine not something in haste on the way to the library. Of course, Scott knew this, which was why it was safe to invite her.

To arrive at Fauchon, he had quite uncharacteristically taken a series of trains in the Métro after a bistro meal at Chez Lipp in Saint-Germain. This tactic allowed him to take the Saint-Germain train to one of the largest transfer points, Le Chatelet, where even if he were followed, it would be easy to lose the tail in the milling Métro at lunchtime. He could mix in, change directions, buy a newspaper, purchase a ticket, change his mind once or twice, and at the precise moment race to the correct platform and take the purple line to la Place de la Madelaine, exit the underground, and cross through the sublevel parking to Fauchon on the other side. Anyone following him might think it unusual for him to take public transportation. After all, they had a chauffeur, and Scott had a Porsche, but he normally left Gustav for Desirée and Celine, and they also used any number of private car services. He knew it was wise to be unpredictable, never get into habits, and never take the same route, except he could abandon that approach when he went to the fencing club or his editor. They were known associations that did not need to be hidden. Even the paparazzi were familiar with these two destinations, and they weren't very interested in him when he wasn't with the countess.

Koch was already there with the usual setup of wine glasses and a number of vintage Bordeaux. He seemed surprised when Scott requested that they change rooms to one on the other end of the wine gallery, but he acquiesced and asked the sommelier to accord them the change. Scott made the necessary apologies for asking for something a little more private. Competitors, you know. His cover as a wine consultant was working. The wines he was choosing would support the image of a connoisseur of wines. Koch was probably making purchases in another name for the embassy. Fauchon didn't let you open a bunch of these bottles without expecting you to walk out with a few cases.

"Is that better?" Koch asked.

"Much," Scott answered as he patted Koch down.

"You're such a trusting soul," Koch said.

"I'm sorry really, I can't help it."

"So blue blazers and co-op articles aside, I can provide you with information you can't get, but maybe I can't get you all you want. But I thought you were interested in protesting the Vietnam situation. I can get you plenty of information on that."

"I'm still interested in the Vietnam angle, but protest of the war seems to be aggregating a lot of dissatisfaction from many different sources."

"But why can't you stick with that subject? It's what made you successful."

"Not if you read the response I'm receiving on the crossword and the co-op pieces."

"I don't know how many pieces such as co-op my superiors will tolerate."

"If you want to turn the hose in another direction, then let's have the information that I want, the names you're not giving me."

"Like what?"

"From what I see, there are two groups in the West German government with different aims. One is busy helping the government undermine student initiatives by alerting the Bundestag to pass laws that thwart the students. This has the effect of inciting them more. Now who would benefit from the resulting civil disobedience? And the other group in the government supports American policies in general and the war in Vietnam in particular, although the German public at large is against the war. I ask myself, why would elected officials support policies that the general public doesn't?"

"Do you have the answers?"

"I'm getting close."

"Dangerously close, perhaps."

"Perhaps you don't want to help me, or is it that you want to selectively help me? I would have thought you would be more than willing to give me information on officials in the West German government with dubious pasts who oppose your interests and are blackmailed by the United States to support theirs."

"Why not ask for the nuclear codes?"

"I'm not writing about those."

"Yet."

"By the way, how much do you know about a secretary in the ministry of defense, Kleinst is his name, I believe."

"Kleinst? Kleinst?" Koch asked while shifting in his chair and having more than a taster's sip of wine.

"Yes, Walther Kleinst."

"Oh yes, now I remember, a very low-level person. He has a big title with little responsibility and no access."

"I want to meet him."

"Why would he give you an interview?"

"I was hoping you would help me."

"No, I don't know him, but why him?"

"I can't remember exactly. Something I overheard at one of the conferences. He's not well liked."

"I can give you names that are important. So why waste your time with a little fish?"

"It was just an idea. What can you give me by the end of next week?"

"It will have to be this week. Let's meet in three days."

Koch hadn't passed the test. At first, he feigned ignorance of Kleinst, then he remembered but passed him off as small potatoes. Next he tried to throw Scott off the scent. Scott had a feeling that Kleinst was his man, but he was also Koch's man. He might warn him. That would be good. Then he would think he knew what Scott was after. Obviously, Koch, Kleinst et al., had penetrated both the student groups and the West German government. They had the inside track on both. Paradoxically, these students had the predilection of being leftist, but Koch and his associates didn't want incremental change, they wanted unrest and riots. The students were playing right into their hands. Poor Brigitte, she had no idea.

Thirty-four

DESIRÉE CAME BACK FROM SOME SHOPPING AND A little outing for Celine to La Chatelaine, a luxury store for children on l'avenue Victor Hugo. It was close to the aperitif hour and Scott suggested some champagne. Celine would celebrate her first birthday in Gstaad, where they would be in ten days. It had been almost two years since they had been there during the social season, and Desirée was determined that there would not be a third. They had already missed the Bal de Neige, where two years previously Scott had had his first unpleasant encounter with Desirée's ex, the notorious playboy Stefano de Rovere, whose philandering had cost him his countess.

"Is it a special occasion?"

"Well, I have some good news. My research has turned up the name of someone in the German government, a lower official, but he's connected to an important minister, and I want to try and get an interview with him."

"I'm happy for you, I think, but something tells me that if you want to interview him, he probably doesn't want to talk to you."

"He doesn't even know me. That's the problem. I was wondering if you knew anyone who might know him."

"Are you thinking of Uncle Pierre?" Desirée asked.

"No, I don't want to drag him into this. I was wondering if any of your lawyers or accountants have any contacts with German defense contractors?"

"I don't know, but I do know the French ambassador to Germany who was the former minister of the French Air Force, *La Force Aérienne*."

"He would do admirably."

"You must tell me exactly what you want and for what. I don't want to deceive my friends."

From this, he understood that his motives for the meeting must be pure, no obfuscation, no subterfuge, plain and direct. He told her that he wanted to have a meeting with Walther Kleinst, the private secretary of the minister of defense in West Germany. Scott was writing a story about student opposition to Vietnam, and West Germany was supportive while France was against the war. Perhaps an article needed to be written explaining the position of the West German government. If the article was presented properly and naturally and logically, then perhaps the government's hand would be strengthened. Scott thought that this kind of positioning might tempt Herr Kleinst. He'd be interested in anything to frustrate the students.

"An attempt at even-handedness then," Desirée said.

"I want to be completely candid. The answer is yes, it's an opportunity, but I don't have any high hopes for a direct answer."

"Well, he can refuse, correct?"

"No, you can't let him say no."

"I think then we need someone at Dresdner Bank," Desirée said. "They do most of the finance placements for the defense contractors in West Germany."

"My darling, you are such a good strategist, and you know everyone," he said, taking her hand in his and patting it.

"I guess I'm good for something."

"Yes, at least two things."

"You are miserable."

"I'm only miserable when away from you."

The next morning, Desirée was at her desk thumbing through her *petit annuaire,* her private telephone and address book. He told her he was going out for a walk and a coffee and when he came back, they would go to lunch. He thought she might like to be alone to make the calls.

As he wandered over to the l'avenue Victor Hugo, two photographers he knew by sight fell in behind him and then a third person he didn't recognize, lagging some distance behind the paparazzi. Scott didn't try to lose them, and he didn't look back. He got a kick out of wasting their time. He bought the morning's *Le Monde* and settled into it with a café au lait. Next, he went into a men's haberdashery store and took his time selecting two new pairs of gloves, one black fur-lined pair and the other a light camel color. Then he walked back home by going up to the Etoile and then taking l'avenue Foch back to the apartment. It was cold out, and he thought his shadow would be glad to see him heading back. Perhaps someone else would follow them to lunch.

Desirée and Francine, the nanny, were discussing what Celine was to have for lunch, where they should walk in the afternoon for some fresh air, and how she should be dressed for the cold. Desirée kept Celine at her side, always close, even with Francine around. She was determined that she was going to have more contact with her child than her mother had had with her. Scott tried to remind her that times were different then, and she shouldn't take her mother's absences personally. But the psychology of parenting was individual to each child and parent, and it wasn't up to him to make it right for her. She would need to come to her own conclusions on that score.

She wanted to know where they were lunching. And quite naturally, he was eager to know about the call, but he knew better than to ask. Desirée liked the dramatic. Everything had its own time. And it would drive her crazy that he wouldn't be so curious as to ask, so that she could delay his knowing immediately. They had understood each other perfectly from the beginning. And they enjoyed their little mind games of *coqueterie*. It was never boring. Theirs was a relationship of continuous flirtation.

"I thought we might go to Café Drouant. Isn't it one of your favorites?"

"I can tell you're trying to get on my good side."

"Always."

Café Drouant was a small restaurant in the 2nd arrondissement, that featured classic French cooking the freshest fish, prepared to perfection. It was favored at lunch by bankers and in the evening by artists and those of the literary world. Scott and Desirée often dined there when in Paris, but more in the evening than at lunch. When he had telephoned to make the reservation, the maître d', Jacques, let Scott know that he remembered Desirée's preferred table: "Ah, oui! Table 21."

When they entered a restaurant, it was not that uncommon that the room would look up from their plates and conversation to see who was entering, and it wasn't Scott that distracted them. He knew that, and Desirée didn't deign to notice. For the occasion, she was wearing a full, long, black leather skirt with camel-colored boots, a white cashmere turtleneck sweater, and a white fox full-length coat. Her jewelry consisted of pearls accentuated by diamonds. Scott wore a Christian Dior charcoal chalk-stripe suit with a vest, a soft blue Charvet shirt, and an Hermès tie with a design of cascading red and orange leaves.

As they sat down, Scott ordered a bottle of Krug from the sommelier. It arrived almost as if it had been anticipated, and he proposed the toast: "To my wonderful wife, to our improbable pairing, to our adorable Celine. I love you, my darling."

"You must think I've already got your appointment."

"Now don't ruin my toast. But now that you brought it up."

"I'll know by tomorrow afternoon. It appears to be no better than fifty-fifty."

"Those are much better odds than I had."

"If you don't mind, I think it's better that you don't know the details of the roundabout way this is taking place. If you're asked, all you will need to say is that it was a favor."

"Good idea. And I'm not curious anyway."

"Don't walk around with that delusion."

"Shall we have lunch and not think about it anymore until tomorrow afternoon?"

"Let's."

They had a lovely lunch of the sole munière with steamed potatoes, a green salad, and a dessert of pears, vanilla ice cream, and chocolate, Poire belle Hélène. They both had espresso and a Williamine, an *eau de vie* from Switzerland. They poured it from a Lailique crystal decanter that contained a whole pear still attached to a piece of the tree branch complete with two small leaves.

Scott was feeling exuberant. He asked Gustav to stop at la Place Vendome across from the Ritz at the jewelry store Mauboussin. Desirée balked, but Scott insisted. She reminded him that he didn't have the appointment yet. Jewelry was for effort, not success, he countered. They were shown to a private room, and Scott indicated he wanted to see a unique bracelet. The clerk brought out a number of bracelets, but the one Desirée liked was a 1950s gold knitted bracelet with a leaf motif. Ten carats of small white diamonds were embedded within the leaf. Desirée loved it at first sight. When the clerk was told to wrap it up, Desirée said she wanted to wear it out, and for once she didn't protest about the expense. But she did say it was too much, and he said that he had to spend his money from his articles somewhere. She laughed.

The next morning, Scott looked for something to keep him busy, something to keep him from pacing and fretting about when the telephone would ring. He had promised to keep MacAllister apprised of what Koch was doing, and the only way to do this was to meet with his publisher. Vincent was agreeable, he always was, and they would meet around 11:00. He left the apartment earlier than usual to avoid any of the reporters, but he wasn't out so early that he wasn't shadowed, by two people this time. He couldn't tell if they were together or even aware of each other. It didn't matter, given his destination. He wasn't trying to lose them on this occasion. He arrived at the editorial house right on time.

Vincent never seemed to pry. He waited, and only after a while would he ask a question or give advice. Their meeting lasted a little over half an hour. There were more pauses and silence than talking. Scott repeated what he had told Desirée about trying to identify a German official who would give him information, on the record preferably. He wanted to know why the German government supported the war in Vietnam and how they seemed to be able to anticipate the actions of the students. Vincent asked if he knew who the official might be. He fudged, saying he had an idea, but he didn't have an appointment and it was premature to single out anyone at this time. It sounded reasonable even if untrue, which was important, because he knew Vincent's report would be in Geneva by nightfall.

Thirty-five

DESIRÉE HAD GRACIOUSLY CANCELED AN APPOINTment for the afternoon in order to be in the apartment when the call came in. Thinking that she might want to be alone, particularly if it were bad news, Scott took a taxi to the Rond Point and the Champs-Elysées, a major intersection. From there he could browse the shop windows and pass some time distracting himself from the anticipation of the outcome. He decided to walk home, although it was very cold. He stopped at Le Drugstore, where he indulged in an American hamburger and picked up some political reviews in the store's bookshop. By the time he made it the rest of the way home, several hours had passed.

She didn't make him wait. "I have good news."

"Krug kind of news?"

"You'll have to be the judge. First, it's March eighth, not the fifth. And there are questions that you can't ask, and there may be questions he won't answer. He would prefer not to give you an interview, but he's doing it at the request and as a favor to one of the minister of defense's friends."

"It's definitely Krug time. Let's go out. Let's celebrate, dance. Let's go to Maxim's."

"Okay, darling, but I don't understand why you are so happy. There are so many conditions."

"Desirée, they all make conditions. It's their way of maintaining control. You've done more than your part, now it's up to me."

They went to Maxim's and danced until the early hours of the morning. They had the prerequisite caviar, the filet de boeuf garni, and for dessert, *oeufs à la neige* and Krug. They had seemed to reconnect since they were able to spend time together. And Gstaad was straight ahead, where they always were in sync.

As he left the house with Gustav at the wheel for his meeting with Koch the following morning, Scott saw out the window that he had two followers, one with a briefcase in his left hand and another a short distance down the street from his apartment building. That meant MacAllister was on the case again. But who was the short, swarthy man bundled up in an overcoat, scarf, hat, and unfashionable Eastern Bloc shoes that were heavy and unpolished? This was a new development. Did Kleinst and Koch work together? Maybe they worked together on some things, and then worked behind each other's backs as well. Koch didn't need to have him followed, because he knew where he was headed. He hoped they were ready for the chase. He had planned something special for them.

He asked Gustav to drive him to the underground parking of the Champs-Elysées. Gustav entered at the top end of the Champs-Elysées and maneuvered through the garage, traveling through the passages and tunnels from one level to another, and finally arriving at an exit some five blocks east of where he had entered. This trip through underground parking ran beneath seven blocks of the Champs-Elysées. But anyone seeing the car as it left the garage would have noticed that the passenger who had been in the car earlier was no longer there. Gustav had let him out in the garage by a staircase that Scott took to the third level, where he had parked a rental car the day before. Once inside the garage, it was easy to detect if you were being followed, and if the follower were in a taxi, there would be the hesitation to negotiate the parking fee. The difficulties posed by attempting to follow someone in this environment were multiple. There were just too many levels to the garage, too many exits, and too much competing traffic. He took the rental, put on a hat, glasses, and a scarf and slowly took the far exit only a few blocks from Fauchon. His pursuers might still be looking for him.

Koch was waiting for him at the entrance to the wine cellar. "I thought I'd let you choose the room where we will do the tasting."

Scott smiled, told the sommelier they would take number four, and soon the wines and glasses were set up. Koch asked the sommelier to open the wines and let them breathe for a while. They would call him back when they were ready. After the customary pat down, Scott said "What information do you have for me?"

"I have some of what you want, but I can't let you have the originals. What I can let you have is in the blazer being delivered this afternoon."

"Why no originals?"

"Because you can't take them to Berlin, anyway."

"Well, nobody's going to take my word for anything. I've got to have proof."

"I'm developing a plan for a contact in Berlin. It will be a woman. She will come up to you and say, 'I prefer the Pauillac wines of Château Latour,' and your answer will be, 'I prefer the Haut Brion.' She will be the one to get the documents to you, if I can manage it. Don't walk around with any documents on your person. She'll need to find a way to get them to your room at the hotel. Understood?"

"Yes. Did you have me followed today?"

"No. You are being followed by two sets of different people. We haven't been able to identify the new one. The one with the briefcase is CIA. You're not very popular with them. After all, Vietnam is largely their war. You are developing a lot of interested parties."

"Are the names you will be giving me West German government officials who were Nazis during the war?"

"You'll have to do some work yourself. I can't give you everything."

"Are you being coy?"

"You'll have to make your own deductions from the documents. I think it will be clear, and I don't want you quoting me," Koch said with some finality. He was becoming impatient.

If Scott was right in what he guessed Koch had been persuaded to provide, MacAllister would flip. Scott had purposely led MacAllister along, letting him think that all this had to do with the war in Vietnam. He was in for a surprise, and an unsettling one at that. It all hinged on whether Scott was right about what Koch would give him.

"Anybody on the list that might be undermining the students' efforts?" Scott asked.

"You need to leave that alone."

As they finished, they decided Scott was to leave first. He said, "Oh, by the way, I'm seeing Kleinst on March eighth."

He watched for a reaction on Koch's face, and he thought he saw the beginnings of a look of discomfort, but Koch was too professional to allow his expression to reveal his true thoughts. He, however, felt that he understood for the first time what was going on in the West German government, and it was much more complicated and treacherous than was commonly thought.

As he retraced his steps across la Place de la Madelaine into the galleries and stores along l'avenue Saint-Honoré, he began to organize the facts and make deductions. First, the stated agenda and the real agenda of the interested parties were quite different. Second, the interested parties at times were allies and at other times enemies. Third, the West German government was laced with former Nazis who had been recruited by the Americans to operate the government after the war. At that time, who else was available? These officials owed their jobs and their reputations to the Americans, which required the Americans to keep quiet about their unfortunate pasts. But there was a price for the silence: complicity and agreement with the aims and actions of the United States even in the face of popular opposition. And the principal aims of the United States were denying Soviet Russia of any gains in Europe and having West Germany's approval of the war in Vietnam. Fourth, the student groups, always more liberal than their elders, were being managed by the Soviets to oppose the West German government's approval of the war in Vietnam. What the students didn't understand was that members of the student groups sympathetic to communist objectives were feeding the Soviets inside information regarding the students' plans and strategies. At first Scott didn't understand this treachery, but then suddenly it was clear. The Soviets revealed the students' objectives so that the government would enact laws and initiate actions that were increasingly repressive. These actions would incite the students to a pitch, and with the addition of the Communist and anarchist elements within the student movement, would create the type of unrest necessary for political upheaval. The students were unwitting pawns to the Soviet's plans. Incremental change was not the goal. They weren't willing to wait on the ballot box. And, of course, Kleinst had insinuated himself into just the right position to keep Koch informed.

Thirty-six

One advantage of being in Gstaad was the privacy it offered Scott. Gstaad is a chic, small village in the Swiss Bernese Oberland that attracts a regular clientele of the international set, mainly Swiss, French, and Italian. Of course, there were the occasional Germans, the Iranians, and a few Moroccans, but if you didn't belong or didn't look like you belonged, you would be spotted immediately. Privacy, privilege, and protection were the cornerstones of Swiss hospitality and its banking system, and they had an abiding stake in its maintenance.

Gustav picked up the four of them—Desirée, Scott, Celine, and Francine—on Sunday at the Geneva airport, and they arrived in Gstaad a little before dark. Scott was glad to be away from the preoccupation and all the demands of spy craft: being followed, the messaging, the meetings, and the lying. Still, he had to continue submitting articles through the channels established to keep his supporters satisfied and, more importantly, propel his plan toward a resolution.

He had barely escaped Paris without having to meet with LeFebre, whose constant refrain was that there was too much accent on West Germany and not enough on the war in Vietnam or with the French Left's concerns, particularly those of the students. LeFebre saw the students as the arm of protest that might later agitate issues related to the trade unions. They all had an agenda to maneuver the students. He did, however, remark with unusual glee on the crossword puzzle article and reveled that there would be those in the West German government squirming uncomfortably; it was a perfect example of French schadenfreude.

Scott's German editors at *Westdeutsche Zeitung* were also clamoring for more of the kind of provocations that the crossword had generated. And with the new roll of film provided by Koch that had arrived in the black blazer just before Scott left Paris, there was plenty of material with which to charge the cannon. The tricky part was the timing and how much to reveal. How to strike fear yet protect himself against reprisal? Besides, he had to ration his ammunition for use with MacAllister.

Herr Kleinst would no doubt take a greater interest in the musings of journalist Stoddard than he had before. His reluctance to grant the interview would make him warily guarded, and articles that would appear prior to the interview could have the effect of either antagonizing or ingratiating his target. He wouldn't pander, but he could suggest without accusing. This would make him appear amateurish. Kleinst would like having the upper hand. He might even be tempted to instruct Scott. Still Scott couldn't alienate his following. These articles would walk a fine line and trigger his master plan to extricate himself from the service of MacAllister.

It took him about a week to draft and revise the first article. Mindful of its purpose, Scott wrote the article to deal with the recent decline of the West German economy, which had been booming for a period of nearly twenty years, beginning shortly after WWII. The resulting economic squeeze that radiated from this fall of the formidable German industrial and commercial sector was being felt disproportionately by the middle and lower classes, as so often happens. The government's response was to begin restricting and cutting expenses. And where did they think to begin their cuts? The services and benefits extended to students and other groups without political or economic power were the first to be trimmed. These cuts had the intention of reducing the time spent in gaining a degree and the abolition of certain courses that Germans felt central to a good classical education. The real intent was to quell protests and bring more discipline to the student population. But of course, it didn't work. It made the situation worse and played right into the hands of Herr Kleinst and his bosses.

It was clear that government officials were contemplating a strategy to draft a law that would make it illegal for students to participate in protests against the policies that were so unpopular with the students and the public at large. Additionally, there were direct communications in the form of transcribed telephone conversations in which government officials planned to try to turn the general population against the students. The aim of their propaganda was to accuse the students of being spoiled and unappreciative and fomenting unrest. And the government knew that for Germans, order is essential. All of these behind-the-scenes and largely secret projects were either being denied or impugned. Scott was certain that people like Steinhausen and Brigitte Fischer wouldn't be surprised that this was happening, but they would be surprised as to the degree of its perfidy. But who could tell which side anyone was on? For all Scott knew, any one of the people he had met could be an informer to either side. None of them had any idea that their friends, the leftists and Soviets, didn't mind if they sacrificed themselves on the barricades.

He wasn't ready—did it even fit into his plan—to accuse or even attempt to blame or indict anyone in the government. Instead, he would subscribe to the theory of circumstantial coincidence. This would eventually allow the interviewee, Kleinst, to deny and disclaim and make fun of Scott's hypotheses as connecting dots where there weren't any. Kleinst would mildly chastise Scott for stirring up emotions and remind him of his duty as a journalist that demanded he be more circumspect and responsible in his reporting. Scott would entitle his article "Anti-Democratic Teamwork in Bonn and Berlin?" The title or headline was a lot more jarring than the article itself, but that too was intended. A reader would be drawn in and then given a lot of innuendo without a lot of proof. Scott thought it would be the perfect come-on. Kleinst would reason that if he had proof, then why hadn't he used it? Therein was the trap. Scott would force him to deny that for which he had proof. Now for MacAllister.

It wasn't the best moment to do so, but Scott told Desirée that he wanted to drive down to Geneva for the day. He intimated a little research at the university library, but really it was Thursday, and he hoped MacAllister would be at the fencing club and lunch. To make sure, he called Kruger and asked him to inform MacAllister that he'd be at the club.

As was their practice, Scott met MacAllister in the dining room at their usual two-top, a little out of the way, but not so much that they appeared to be purposefully hiding.

"This is a surprise," MacAllister said. "I thought you had forgotten me."

"You won't let me." Scott handed him a copy of his latest article. MacAllister took it, and while reading it, he looked up from time to time. It was only eleven hundred words, not long, but to the point.

"At least you're off the war, but I'm not sure you're making any progress except that you're becoming friends with a lot of people opposed to United States policies and interests. We need you to learn more about their financing, and who's leaking information to newspapers and activists."

"I'm working on it. I'm going to interview Walther Kleinst. He seems to know quite a lot about what goes on in West Germany and elsewhere."

"I hope you don't think this article is going to get him to warm up to you. He'll see right through this."

"I hope so."

"What are you planning, or can I know? And how did you get the interview?"

"It was a favor. And I'm not sure of my plan, but you've never answered me about getting out."

"I have it under consideration."

"I'm not sure I believe you."

"We're not interested in Kleinst."

"I wouldn't think so."

"He'll just tell you that you've got it all wrong. Then what can you say?"

"I'm working on it. But there will probably be a time right after my meeting with Kleinst in Berlin that I may need your help."

"That would be a new development. You've never asked for any help. You're rogue."

"On another question, do you have more than one person following me around Paris?"

"No, just the person with the briefcase. We thought the other one was Koch's man."

"I did too, but I asked him the last time we met, and he told me that he thought it was CIA."

"Maybe you have more friends than you think."

"I've been wondering. Why does Germany support American action in Vietnam when the German electorate is against it?"

"Because sometimes the government is smarter than the people."

"I thought it might be something much more ordinary, like blackmail."

"Don't speculate. You're suggesting widespread corruption."

"Effective, isn't it?" Scott said.

Thirty-seven

THE END OF THE MONTH CAME AS SCOTT PUBLISHED another article, this one critical of the police reaction in Paris to the French students protesting the Vietnam War. This article was designed to prepare the way for a more congenial meeting with Herr Kleinst. He would approve of any article that would direct the light somewhere other than the German situation. Scott was to arrive in Berlin a few days before the meeting to give an opportunity to Koch's contact to deliver the other documents he had requested. And although Desirée wanted him to see Rheiner while he was there, he told her his schedule was too packed. But the real reason was that he didn't want to draw attention to Rheiner or the professor. He would be followed closely in Berlin, and there was no point in giving his pursuers any more fodder to fret about. And of course, Brigitte would need nurturing while he was in town. Fortunately, Steinhausen was away at a family funeral. He wasn't obliged to keep them informed about the visit, but if they discovered later that he had been in Berlin for the purpose of interviewing Kleinst and hadn't called them, they would be cross. That he didn't need either.

After he checked into his hotel, the Savoy, a message from a government courier was brought to his room. The communication was from Herr Kleinst. He was changing the meeting site to a conference room at the Dresdner Bank very near the Brandenburg Gate. Scott presumed it would be less official and less visible. He was certain that Kleinst wouldn't want to be seen with a journalist contributing to the

Westdeutsche Zeitung. Meanwhile, Brigitte insisted on lunch at a small café, Kürzen Stubel, on Kufürstendamm Strasse, the main shopping street of Berlin. She reassured him that it was a quiet place where they could talk. She also indicated that Helga, the woman he had met before, would join them.

Brigitte was correct about the restaurant being small, but at lunchtime it was filled with what appeared to be a hungry gang of German men determined to put away a few steins of beer to brace for the afternoon. With the din, it would have been impossible for anyone to overhear their conversation as they had a difficult time hearing each other. Helga did not vary from her role as surveyor in chief. She listened very attentively, following the conversation between Scott and Brigitte much like a spectator at a tennis match. She showed no emotion and didn't demonstrate approval or dissent. Her reticence prompted Scott to be more guarded than he would have been had he been alone with Brigitte.

When Helga excused herself, Brigitte, sensing Scott's displeasure, apologized for having brought her to the meeting. Helga had insisted on coming, saying that she wanted to hear more from the man who was writing these articles critical of the administration. Scott reassured her that it was fine, but Brigitte wondered out loud why he was in Berlin. Was he there to see Steinhausen, Rheiner Honig, who? He saw Helga returning to the table and said that he was interviewing Walther Kleinst, but he couldn't discuss it. Brigitte looked shocked. As Helga sat down, Scott shot Brigitte a look to convey that the Kleinst discussion was over before it began. Lunch ended, and Scott knew that Brigitte would like to talk more about the Kleinst matter, but he indicated that he was in a hurry, leaving no opportunity for her to pull him aside. When the first taxi rolled up in front of the restaurant, Helga got in and said to Scott, "I could drop you off at your hotel. I'm going right by it."

He accepted; there was no reason not to. He almost welcomed the offer just to get away from Brigitte's questions. They didn't speak for a few minutes. Then Helga broke the silence: "Thank you for allowing me to have lunch with you and Brigitte. I prefer the Pauillac wines of Château Latour."

"I prefer the Haut Brion."

"What is your room number? I will be up and slip the documents under your door two minutes after you arrive. I will knock once. You will knock three times in response."

"I may need to get a message to our friend."

"When?"

"I'm not sure yet."

"If you leave the hotel any morning during your stay here in Berlin without your glove on the hand that grips your briefcase, then I will have him find a way to contact you. You are being followed. But I guess you know that. By the way, I was told to tell you that your other shadow is the Stasi."

"Tell Comrade Koch thanks."

"Can I trust you to keep my secret?"

"I mind my own business."

Scott wondered why Koch had let Helga tell him about the Stasi tail. Koch probably was honest about this to build his own credibility with Scott. A refusal to lie about the things that don't matter is a path to overall trust. The Stasi were involved because of Scott's interview with Kleinst. And Brigitte didn't realize that the KGB was privy to everything she was doing. No wonder the students were stymied. They didn't have a leak; they had a flood.

A few minutes after Scott returned to his room, first the knock and then the envelope came sliding under the door. He slit the seal and carefully spread the papers on the desk against the wall. Naturally Koch hadn't provided any information about Kleinst. One of two pages consisted of a list of five neatly typed names, three of which were easily recognizable and two others that were unfamiliar. On page two appeared a list of annotations, footnotes almost, five in all that apparently alluded to the list on the first page. But a caveat, typed in italics, indicated that the annotations were not necessarily in the order that would correspond to the order of the names on the first page. A quick perusal of the annotations indicated birth dates and highest rank attained in either the Nazi Wehrmacht or the Luftwaffe.

Koch was clever. He had furnished incriminating evidence, but as he had advised, Scott would have to do a little work as well. He would need to synchronize pages one and two. These pages, if left together, would be explosive in the wrong hands. He needed to find a safer place than his room to store them.

He wondered why Koch was not using this information for his own purposes. Maybe he was. But it was more plausible that both sides were respecting the dead bodies of the other in a kind of spy standoff, an odd *code de guerre* between enemies. Who could predict what unraveling would take place if even a single thread were tugged too hard in this elaborate fabric of subterfuge? Koch wouldn't mind if it appeared that Scott stumbled onto it, but he wouldn't want his fingerprints on it. This was Scott's leverage with Koch as long as he used it in a counterintuitive fashion.

Thirty-eight

THEIR MEETING WAS FIXED AT 10:30 IN THE MORNING. This hour of day for an interview indicated that it would be strictly business. There would be no food or drink to promote cordiality. Scott could expect nothing more than strong black coffee and that would only increase the palpitations of his pulse. From other photographs that he'd seen, Walther Kleinst, in his early fifties, was in good shape, slightly balding, and had a fair complexion and penetrating eyes. He was a graduate of the University of Leipzig, mathematics Scott seemed to remember, and a man who was always the assistant, never the chief. Obviously, this was by design. In his metamorphosis from Günther von Ott to Walther Kleinst, there were no apparent blemishes on his record, no missteps. The development of his biography had been carefully engineered to promote his bureaucratic career. The path by which he had navigated the shoals of the unpleasantness of Germany's National Socialist past was at lower levels, as a functionary. His term while residing in the Stasi ended when a more important assignment had been found. In that new mission, he had made a steady but sure ascent in the democratic West German government to his current position. And being an underling, a second fiddle in effect, meant that he could enjoy all the perks of inside information without undergoing the scrutiny had he been at the top. Now he was the private secretary of the minister of defense of West Germany. And the defense ministry was not only the seat of the limited military of West Germany but also the department in charge of the intelligence service having knowledge of the United States defense strategies of Western Europe in the event of a Soviet attack. Kleinst was in a position to know about everything there was to know about all things going on in West Germany. No wonder Koch had tried to deflect Scott from homing in on Kleinst.

THE DRESDNER BANK, ONE OF THE OLDEST BANKS IN GERmany, occupied a building in the center of Berlin very close to the Brandenburg Gate. It was an imposing baroque structure projecting the security and solidity of a bank. When Scott entered the building, a uniformed attendant approached him, addressed him by name, and asked him to follow. Scott was ushered into a conference room of human proportions, large enough to be impressive, but not so grand as to overwhelm. He'd only been seated for a moment when Herr Walther Kleinst joined him, entering from a door opposite where Scott had entered. He wore a medium-gray suit, a white shirt, and a dark green tie. He didn't smile.

Scott had left the chair at the head of the table vacant, taking one off to the side. Herr Kleinst, as if by right, sat at the commanding spot. They shook hands and went through the necessary but obligatory sequence of greetings, expressions of gratitude by Scott, and declarations of mutual respect, and the wishes that good things would evolve from their meeting. Herr Kleinst also mentioned Scott's articles, apologized in advance that he disagreed with them, and doubted that he could add or subtract. He reiterated that as a government servant his duty was to all the people, and it was a responsibility that he had sworn to uphold and one that he took very seriously. He summed up by asking if Scott had any questions.

"Yes, I was wondering if you find it odd that whatever the students decide to protest, the government seems to be counter to their objectives by arresting their leaders or confiscating their communication materials. How does the government so correctly anticipate the students' plans?"

"Two things, Herr Stoddard. First, the students are rebellious and led to protest by foreign entities. The government has a duty to keep the peace. Second, the students telegraph what they intend to do. It is not difficult to see where they are going. What are you suggesting?"

"I'm suggesting that one might suspect that somehow the government is obtaining advance notice of the students' intentions and that their efforts are being preempted."

"The students make no secret of their intent. And there isn't money for all their demands. Students are a notoriously dissatisfied group."

"Very true, but many of them get arrested and held overnight or expelled."

"As you wish, Mr. Stoddard."

Scott knew that he wasn't going to get anywhere in this interview, but he still had to go through the motions. "On another subject, the Vietnam War, I wanted to ask you why the government supports the United States while the students do not, and there's every indication that the population at large may substantially oppose it as well."

"I don't believe those who protest have a very good grasp of what's at stake."

"Maybe it should be explained."

"It's very complicated."

"It isn't complicated to see who might benefit from the unrest and the undermining of West Germany."

"I don't understand where you are going with this."

"I'm proposing that the current situation, if continued, could bring down the government. And I believe entities beyond the Wall within the Soviet orbit of influence could well be hoping for such an outcome."

"Well, of course, they aren't interested in helping us."

"But that's not the point. Is there someone on the inside of the government assisting them and promoting the government to subvert itself?"

"Herr Stoddard, are you a troublemaker?"

"I could be."

"Then when you have facts instead of hypotheses, we can meet again."

"I have facts, one in particular. I'm just not ready."

"That sounds like a threat."

"Does it?"

"I believe that our meeting is over."

After leaving the Dresdner Bank, Scott settled into a taxi for the ride back to the hotel. He was certain that MacAllister would not have approved of his taking Kleinst to the edge. Admittedly, there was no way that Kleinst could know that Scott wasn't just speculating. And, certainly, he might not think that Scott was accusing him of being an informer or worse, but it wouldn't matter. Scott's digging around was the real threat, so what could he anticipate from Kleinst? In Berlin there were kidnappings all the time. People disappeared. Granted it was rare for anyone with diplomatic immunity to be harmed, but Scott wasn't in that category. The number of spies and illegal agents in Berlin from Western intelligence services, the KGB, and all the other services of the Soviet Bloc was legion. It was clear that after this Scott would be under constant surveillance. His room might be bugged; the telephone was for sure. He was a threat, and they would want to know where he was and what he was doing at all times. He had to be very careful. He couldn't let them know what he knew until the last moment. Otherwise the danger to his life was considerable. Journalists did not have the public's highest esteem. One more or less wouldn't make a difference.

As he walked back to the hotel along Kurfürstendamm Strasse in the middle of Berlin, thinking of perhaps buying a little something for Desirée and Celine, a large black sedan cut in front of him at a side street, and a tall man wearing a heavy coat and a brimmed black homburg exited the car. Scott was slightly irritated, as the car had stopped in the pedestrian walkway. The man turned directly toward him and said, "May I walk with you a block?"

"Do I have a choice?"

"No."

He took Scott by the arm and began guiding him down the street. "Once upon a time you were a good American, Scott. Stop poking around in things that are none of your business."

"Are you threatening me?"

"I'm advising you."

Suddenly three large men with their hands in their overcoat pockets appeared out of nowhere, and one asked in French, "Is this man bothering you, Mr. Stoddard?"

They grabbed his walking companion and escorted him away, but they couldn't stop him from one last blast, "You found a way to stay with your wife and child. Don't fuck it up."

"Let him go," Scott said.

As quickly as they had appeared, they were gone, all of them.

The first guy was American, probably CIA, another part of the CIA unfamiliar with Scott's role or MacAllister's people since he had alluded to Scott's avoidance of the draft. They had to be worried that he was getting too close. They were only interested in scaring him, this time. Had MacAllister put them up to this? But who were the other three, his protectors? They must have been following him all along. He hadn't seen them, and he had been looking. And weren't they French? LeFevre perhaps? No, it couldn't be him.

That evening he made a careful survey of his room, his clothes, his briefcase, and his luggage to see if anything was askew. All appeared as it should be. Good, they hadn't searched his room yet. He had to hide the two pages that Koch had given him along with the photograph of Kleinst. He couldn't afford to be stopped or arrested. Without that photograph it would be impossible to accomplish what he had in mind. He couldn't walk around with a briefcase full of incriminating evidence, nor could he leave it in the room.

Thirty-nine

THE NEXT MORNING, AFTER A GERMAN BREAKFAST OF sausages and eggs, he took his shower, carefully placed the two pages and the photograph into a folder and left the rest of the more mundane material in his briefcase. Then he opened the second smaller case he had brought and began putting on clothes that he hoped would allow him to leave the hotel without notice. It took a few minutes to get everything right, but finally he slipped into a black overcoat, put on a pair of large black horn-rimmed glasses, and pulled a black Fedora over his forehead. He didn't button up the overcoat completely. It was important that the black suit and vest with the white clerical collar be visible. He looked in the mirror, stuffed the folder into his pants at the back, picked up his cane, checked to see if anyone was in the corridor, and descended the stairs at the end of the hall down to the lobby.

Looking around as he walked toward the front door, he spotted two heavyset men, apparently of Slavic descent. They manned both sides of the lobby, intently monitoring the elevator and the entrance. They were probably looking for that journalist, Scott Stoddard. As he moved toward the entrance, he was greeted by a number of hotel guests in a kindly manner. He asked the doorman for a taxi and gave the address of Saint Hedwig's Cathedral. When he arrived at the cathedral, which was modeled after the Pantheon in Rome, he moved up the steps and waited for a while, but apparently he had not been followed. After remaining in the sanctuary for an hour, he caught a taxi to Tempelhof airport, where he found a series of storage lockers designated for travelers and selected one that was available at the corner where two rows of lockers came together. He placed the folder with the evidence inside, closed the door, and extracted the key. He placed the key inside the lining of his hat. It wasn't a perfect location, but at least it wasn't in his pocket.

Next he called his editor from a public telephone cabin. After a few rings, his secretary answered. Fortunately, Vincent was in the office, and finally Scott heard on the phone, "*Allô, Vincent ici.*"

"Vincent, no names, tell my friend Copenhagen, Thursday, urgent," Scott said and hung up. "Copenhagen" was the agreed-upon replacement code word for Berlin that Scott and MacAllister had developed. Scott knew that MacAllister would understand, but he wasn't sure if he would come. Though probably monitored, the call had lasted only twenty seconds, and even if it could be attributed to Scott, it would be difficult to determine what it all meant. Because of what he had planned for tomorrow, he would let all his admirers follow him today as much as they wanted.

His diversionary tactics had taken more time than Scott had imagined. It was getting late, and he wanted to return to the hotel to let his admirers, the CIA, Stasi, or otherwise know where he was. The hotel personnel were busy with check-ins and the concierges with dinner reservations and the like; he was not recognized by anyone at the front desk or the concierge station. International, crowded, and vibrant, the Savoy was a good place to stay. He took the elevator to the fifth floor and then took the stairs down to the third floor and his room. It didn't appear that anything had been touched, although it didn't matter if it had. In some ways there would be a benefit to their rifling through and discovering nothing.

He took a shower, redressed in his normal attire, and called Desirée. At first, she said that she was worried when he hadn't called the evening before, and she had tried calling twice during the day. He apologized, saying that he should have called, and he agreed that he needed to think more about her and Celine. She asked how the interview had gone, and when he hesitated, she reminded him that after all it was she who had negotiated the interview in the first place.

"It was difficult," he said. "Herr Kleinst didn't like some of the questions. I need to stay a couple days to clear up a few things."

"I'm worried you're stirring up trouble with these articles."

"Oh, I don't think so. Maybe there's a little discomfort, but nothing really serious."

"Then why was that man threatening you on the Kurfürstendamm Strasse yesterday?"

Now Scott understood. Desirée had hired French security personnel to watch over him while he was in Berlin. An absolute crowd was following him. But the French guys were good. He hadn't seen them. Maybe she had them tailing him around in Paris as well. He should have known.

"He was giving me advice."

"Please come home."

"Desirée, you must give me two days, darling. Two days."

"All right. But promise me you won't try to lose your security."

"I promise. I'm not going to ask why you set all this up."

"You don't have to."

WHEN HE WENT DOWN TO DINNER, HE SAW THEM IMMEDIATELY. One was pretending to read the newspaper while the other was standing by some luggage in the grand hall of the Savoy. Scott didn't tarry. He went directly into the dining room and asked for a table in the middle of the room. He ordered a split of champagne and surveyed the menu for quite some time, asking various questions about the preparation of certain dishes and discussing the merits of each. He finally decided on smoked salmon, followed by a pork roast with red cabbage and potatoes. The sommelier came and Scott went through the whole pretense with him as well, purposely conferring back and forth, regarding the best vintages and attributes of the wines in question. He chose a heavy burgundy. He took his time over his meal, wanting to give the appearance of nonchalance. He extended the evening with some Viennese pastries, coffee, and cognac. He slept like a baby.

THE NEXT MORNING, HE DRESSED AS SCOTT STODDARD AND decided to have breakfast in the dining room of the hotel. With the morning came two new babysitters who had probably received a report on the activities of the evening before as well as MacAllister's sleuth clutching a briefcase handle with a bare hand. He didn't see Desirée's contingent. He hoped they weren't hungry, because they were being forced to watch him eat some very delicious food. After breakfast, Scott caught a cab to the library at the Free University of Berlin. Once inside, he went to the information desk, presented his press credentials, and with the young woman's assistance, soon amassed a stack of books relating to the Second World War and the division of Berlin to the present. Most of the books were in German, but there were also a few in French and English. His pursuers had followed him into the library. It appeared their fare was more of the periodical variety.

Scott would select a book from the pile, turn the requisite number of pages, make a few notes, leave the book open to a certain page, and then move to the next book. He repeated the procedure for a couple of hours. He hoped that the report would read that he was heavily into researching subjects connected with post-WWII Berlin. When he was finished, he made a neat stack of the books, passed by the information desk, thanked the librarian, and asked if he could assist her in returning the books to their place. She thanked him, but said that it was part of her job, and that she hoped he had found what he was looking for. He responded that he hadn't.

He hailed a taxi, noticing when he exited the library that he was followed by only two of his earlier trackers. Careful circumspection also revealed the three musketeers at a discreet distance. He reasoned that one had remained behind to list the names of the books he had been reading. He decided to go back to the restaurant Kürzen Stubel. His shadow waited across the street in a doorway. It was a busy place, and it would be easy to get a taxi back to his hotel.

Back at the Savoy, he went to the front desk and asked if there were any messages. There weren't. He didn't expect any, but it would be something that a guest might routinely do, particularly one who could communicate in an open manner. Scott was not that guest.

He turned the key in the door and put his briefcase in the closet in the foyer. As he entered the room, he saw MacAllister sitting on the sofa with his finger set across his lips indicating silence. He handed Scott a key and a note that read, "Come up at 1:00 AM." Scott wrote on a piece of paper, "No. Meet me tomorrow at 10:00 AM at Tempelhof Airport, the chapel, lower level." MacAllister nodded, checked the hallway, and left.

The next morning, after his rather ostentatious breakfast, Scott returned to his room, donned his priestly attire again, and escaped the hotel without scrutiny. The terminal at Tempelhof was crowded with civilians and military personnel. He went to the locker and took the folder with him to the lower level, where there was a small chapel served for travelers. For those flying in and out of Berlin, there might well be a reason to pray.

He sat in plain sight in one of a row of chairs against the wall outside the chapel pretending to read a magazine. He wanted to monitor the chapel and also to see if MacAllister, who by nature was an observant person, would spot him.

Scott was early by twenty minutes, yet no one went in or came out of the chapel. With luck, they would have the space alone. Inside there was a modest altar, a few rows of pews on either side of a central aisle, and two confessional booths, one on each side of the chapel.

Just before 10:00, a woman and two small children appeared and sat in chairs down the row from Scott. A few minutes later, Scott saw MacAllister. He sure looked like a spy in his gray overcoat with his hat pulled down over his eyes. He was walking toward the entrance to the chapel, looking behind him and to each side from time to time. He casually glanced toward Scott and the children before entering the chapel.

One of the children began to cry, and the other was jumping up and down. The mother had her hands full. She wasn't paying any attention to Scott. After a few minutes, he walked into the chapel. Placing his hand on MacAllister's shoulder, he said, "Would you like to confess my son?"

"I wouldn't wear that getup too often," MacAllister said.

"I don't plan on it," Scott said.

They moved to some chairs against the wall of the sanctuary. Scott thanked him for coming, and MacAllister said, "You said urgent. How did the meeting go?"

"As expected."

"What happened?"

"I think he thought I was there to discuss the students' plight, but he was surprised when I proposed that someone probably from the Soviet side is working inside the West German government."

"You really know how to get along with people."

"He didn't seem angry."

"He couldn't afford to."

"He asked if I had any proof."

"And you said?"

"I said no, but that I thought I was close."

"So that's the reason half of Germany is following you."

"Speaking of that, one of your associates threatened me in the middle of Berlin yesterday."

"I know. I heard about it. But who were those other three that barged in? Koch's men?"

"Don't ask. My wife employed them to protect me. I didn't know about it."

"I think my wife would let them have me."

"I don't blame her."

"Very funny. Where did you go the day before yesterday?"

"I went to church, and then I came out here to the airport."

"And what did you find at the library yesterday?"

"Nothing. Of course, I wasn't looking for anything."

"Kleinst won't be impressed with anything less than absolute proof."

"Will he be impressed with this?" Scott slid over the photograph.

MacAllister looked at the photo, then he looked at Scott and said, "Where in God's name did you get this?"

"Someone gave it to me. Von Ott looks good in uniform, don't you think?"

"Scott, a photo like this can get you killed."

"No one but you and I and, of course, the source knows that I have it."

"What do you plan to do with it?"

"At first I thought I might show it to Kleinst. But once it's published, he's a goner anyway. Why give him advance notice?"

"What's your idea? I know you have one."

"Are you ready to bargain?"

"It's not enough."

"Oh, I didn't think it would be."

"You have something else?"

"I want to show it to Koch."

"Don't do that, my God. He'll warn him."

"No, he won't."

"And why not?"

"Because he's going to defect."

"He'll never defect. His family. Besides we'd rather have him as a double."

"Not possible. He'll be blamed for the Kleinst outing."

"I don't see how."

"Because I know something you don't."

Scott explained that he would be sending a message to Koch to come to Berlin. That it was urgent. In the meantime, MacAllister needed to put Koch's family, currently vacationing in Lech, Austria, under surveillance with the intent that they could be scooped up in a minute's notice once Koch agreed to asylum. Without the assurance of his family's safety, Koch wouldn't defect. It was a unique opportunity. MacAllister thought that it might be possible, but Koch was very high up in the KGB. His experience told him that it was rare that one of these lifers would betray all they had been about for the last thirty years.

"I guess when the options are between something and nothing, the unthinkable becomes possible."

"I'm bringing in Wainwright and a team here to Berlin to protect you. No disrespect to the countess. I better look after the Koch family myself. We'll take them to a safe spot where we can protect them."

Forty

SCOTT GUESSED THAT HE ONLY HAD A DAY OR TWO TO make his plan work. He called Brigitte and asked her to lunch and suggested that she bring Helga. She was surprised, but she agreed to his request. He told her that they'd had a nice chat in the taxi, and he wanted to understand better the new law restricting the students and what it might contain. Brigitte was pleased that he was so interested. He could imagine that she was thinking that from this luncheon an article would surely flow.

He figured Helga was smart. And he was right. She showed up thirty minutes before the time of their luncheon. They sat at a table waiting for Brigitte.

"Thank you for coming," Scott said, "and thank you for coming early. I didn't have time to use the glove signal."

"It's fine. Quickly, what do you want?

"I need Koch in Berlin tomorrow or at the latest the next morning. It's urgent."

"He's on vacation with his wife and children."

"I know, but it's urgent."

"Where do you want to meet?"

"In the chapel of Saint Helvig."

"I'll do my best. He'll want to know why."

"Call him now."

She left and came back after Brigitte had arrived. They had a very pleasurable lunch. It was particularly satisfying because when Helga came back, she gave him the nod that it was arranged. He hoped she would tell him which day before they went their separate ways.

Helga played her role well. Scott and Brigitte listened attentively as she explained how the government planned to reduce the time required to earn a degree from the university. On the surface it sounded good, but when examined, it only contracted the time frame by reducing some of the core courses that Germans considered to be central to an education. The effect would be to depreciate the value of a university degree. The government was more interested in reducing the cost per student than in the quality of the education. Scott asked a few questions, and then Helga went into great detail regarding the proposed law. Brigitte was excited to hear the back and forth as well as adding her own particular viewpoints.

When lunch was over and they were waiting for taxis, Helga inquired how much longer Scott would be in Berlin. He responded probably only two days. She said that if he had the chance, he should look on page two tomorrow of the *Berliner.* There might be a piece she had written. He said he would be sure to look for it.

Scott understood from this that Koch would be at Saint Helvig the next day at two. He didn't dwell on how she had arranged it so quickly. It seemed that the word "urgent" was a good word to use when you wanted some action.

The next morning as he sat down in the dining room for breakfast, a man walked up to his table and said, "Scott? Scott Stoddard? I didn't know you were in Berlin. Do you mind if I join you?" Scott played along although he didn't know the man. He must be representing one of the players, but which one? He spoke English with a heavy German accent. The maître d' came over and the man ordered a coffee with milk and the bread basket.

"Do I know you?" Scott asked.

"It's not important, but we have a friend in common. A friend who is worried about you."

"Tell him I feel fine."

"Our friend thinks it is time for you to leave Berlin and get back to what you know best."

"I would like to, but I still have some digging around to do."

"But digging is backbreaking work. We don't want you to hurt yourself."

Before Scott answered, the man got up and left. He had hardly drunk any of his coffee, and the bread basket remained untouched.

Forty-one

SCOTT WENT UP TO HIS ROOM, THEN CAME BACK DOWN into the lobby, bought a number of newspapers and magazines, and returned to his room. Around noon, he left the room carrying a small suitcase and took the elevator to the second floor and then accessed the back stairs reserved for the maids and room service and jogged down to the basement of the hotel. An employee stopped him, but he made him understand that he was expecting a delivery of several cases of champagne at the loading dock. The employee showed him to the ramps leading to the back dock. Scott thanked him, and in two minutes he was out in the street without being noticed. He took a taxi to Tempelhof to retrieve the photo.

The taxi dropped him at Saint Helvig. He used the side entrance and chose one of the front pews down by the altar. Under normal circumstances he would have enjoyed gazing at the cavernous ceiling and the beauty of the architecture. The cathedral had recently been reconstructed faithful to the original, which had burned to the ground during the war.

Koch entered the chapel right on time. Scott could tell that it took his eyes a few moments to adjust to the darkness in the church. He saw Scott and soon sat beside him.

"So, I'm here. What's so urgent?"

"I'm afraid there are some new developments. Developments that worry me. I think someone threatened me at breakfast this morning."

"I told you to tread softly."

"Yes, I think I made a mistake to tell him I thought there was a Soviet mole high up in the West German government."

"Why would you tell him that?"

"Because I think it's true. And now I think he may blame you."

"Me? Why me?"

"Because I found this," he said, sliding the photograph across the pew. Koch took one look at it, and his face turned ashen.

"Where did you get this?"

"Someone gave it to me."

"Have you shown this to anyone?"

"Yes."

"Who? Not your newspapers, I hope?"

"No, not yet, but that will happen in the next day or two, after Kleinst is arrested."

"Who have you shown this to?"

"My CIA contact. He was as surprised as you."

"CIA? What do you mean?"

"Isn't it clear, Colonel Rostov? I work for the CIA. People might think you're helping me."

"Helping you? How?"

"Somebody might think you gave me this photograph. After all, now your fingerprints are all over it. You can deny it, but someone will wonder where it came from. And you've given me all those other names. I wouldn't think it would take too long for you to become a suspect. And no matter how many times you protest, someone must take the blame. It could well be you. You've been giving a CIA operative certain documents."

"You tricked me. You've put me and my family in a terrible position."

"Colonel Rostov, you were using me as well. We're even. But once the scandal begins, I'm sure you'll be recalled to Moscow. You'll have some explaining to do."

Koch stared at Scott with penetrating eyes. Scott could see him wondering if this was the only copy of the photograph or if there were others. He appeared to be sizing up the situation, trying to anticipate what he could do to escape what could very well be an almost certain death sentence and the punishment of his family. Scott looked over his shoulder, and he and Koch saw them at the same time. Wainwright and his team had moved into the back pews.

"Of course, there is a way out," Scott said.

"Which is?"

"To defect, to seek political asylum, perhaps to move to the United States and establish a whole new life and a new identity."

"I couldn't do that. What about my wife and children? Do you know what would happen to them?"

"I do. And that's why we have your family under close surveillance and protection in Lech. If you agree, then we're prepared to move them immediately to a safe house."

"How much time do I have to think about it?"

"You're out of time."

"If I agree . . . but how can I disagree? The disappearance of my family from Lech and Kleinst's arrest will condemn me in absentia." His mind was racing now. "Berlin is closed off. How do I get out?"

LESS THAN AN HOUR LATER, THEY WERE AT TEMPELHOF. FROM a secure line, Scott called MacAllister, who was heading up the Lech operation. Their conversation was short. "Conditions perfect," Scott said. "All runs are open."

Scott and Koch, who now was dressed as a colonel in the United States Army, boarded a military cargo plane. Koch was silent for a time, probably contemplating his future, which he well knew meant hours of interrogation. The reality of what Koch was to endure was difficult for Scott because he hadn't been doing this long enough to become a total cynic.

"I totally misread you. I never thought someone your age in your situation could be an agent," Koch said. "It was a big mistake."

"I think that's why they recruited me. I had no choice either, if it makes you feel any better. It was either do what I was told or be sent to Vietnam."

"A nasty war."

"Aren't they all?"

"When did you first think of it?"

"Of what?"

"Of compromising me?"

"When you wanted to keep me away from Kleinst." Scott didn't have the heart to tell him that he had thought of it from the first moment he met him in East Berlin.

"I knew I hadn't fooled you, but I didn't think it mattered."

"It didn't."

"They won't let it rest until I tell them everything."

"If I were you, I'd do it right away. Save a lot of time and protect your family. That's why I did what I did."

"Do you think my family will be all right?"

"Yes, we've had them under close watch since yesterday before Helga called you."

"Can I speak with my wife?"

"As soon as we land."

They arrived in Stuttgart shortly after six in the evening and were driven from the military airfield to the same base—CIA headquarters in Europe—where Scott had originally been tested for what he thought was the Army. That was well over a year ago, but it seemed much longer.

Scott understood that with the beginning of the next day and many days thereafter, Rostov would be questioned at length about every aspect of his knowledge of the KGB, which he had served for over twenty years. He had been posted to many of the most critical and dangerous stations in the world: Vienna, Bern, Berlin, and Paris. He would have detailed knowledge of past as well as current operations. He could deliver the names of agents and counterespionage agents. If Koch really wanted a new life for himself and his children, there would be no secret that he could withhold. They would question him again and again looking for any incongruities or inconsistencies in his answers. If he supplied a date, they would trace back through the CIA files and find if he was where he said he was on that date. And if they found out that he was lying or even not being as forthcoming as they would like, he would be threatened with return to the Soviet Bloc, which was, in effect, a death sentence.

But Koch hardly needed anyone to explain the situation to him. He had played the other hand many times. He was a formidable opponent, one who had turned many agents and had experience with interrogation and the uncovering of secrets.

Scott asked one of the agents if they could call MacAllister. Soon he was on the line from a dedicated phone. MacAllister recounted the events of the day in some detail to Scott, who was anxious to know the specifics. At first Madame Koch did not understand. She and her children had been waiting for a bus to take them up to the lifts for an early morning slalom run. The bus that stopped for them was not the one they expected, but rather a coach of the CIA. The wife and two children, the driver, and two others plus MacAllister had been the only passengers. Madame Koch was more scared than combative, but it had taken some time to convince her that she and her children would not be hurt and that her husband was safe. It took them just under three hours to drive to the safe house, where they could be protected.

Scott asked if Koch could speak with his wife. He handed Koch the phone and a tearful reunion began. Scott had some pity. This is exactly why he wanted out of this situation. He didn't ever want Desirée or Celine to be subject to this kind of anxiety.

Forty-two

THE NEXT MORNING SCOTT CALLED LA HAYE OF *LE Point Opposé* and told him that he wanted to apologize to him in advance because he was submitting a story to Steinhausen and LeFebre that would appear in their next editions. La Haye needed to understand that it is was urgent and couldn't wait until *Le Point*'s publication date the following Tuesday, although they were welcome to run the article then if they saw fit. In compensation to *Le Point*, Scott would write a follow-up story that would help offset being scooped by the German and French papers. La Haye didn't want to understand the urgency, and Scott couldn't possibly explain it to him.

MacAllister had arranged for a courier to take a copy of the photograph and Scott's story of the fall of Kleinst to both Ian Broder in Munich and LeFebre in Paris. The couriers had explicit instructions as to the time they would make the delivery, and each courier was only to deliver the package into the hands of the intended recipient. To make it easier, Scott had called the evening before informing them both of an important story that would be hand-delivered the next morning. LeFebre had pleaded that he had an appointment, but Scott refused to allow the courier to leave it with anyone else. Scott gave him the choice. He relented. Scott told him that he wouldn't regret it. Broder asked about La Haye and *Le Point.* Scott said he would handle the matter with La Haye. It was a story that couldn't wait.

MacAllister also told Scott of Kleinst's arrest that very morning. Since Kleinst had such a listening post within the intelligence branch of the West German government, it was decided that a special unit of federal police flown in from Bonn would make the arrest for treason. They surprised him in the garage of the office building where he worked. He was always early to work, so the arrest took place without any resistance other than the protests from Kleinst that someone was making a huge mistake. Of course, he hadn't seen the photograph of himself and his two East German friends of the Stasi. They could hold him incommunicado for up to twenty-four hours without charging him, which would give Scott the time he needed. MacAllister said that he would be in Stuttgart with the Koch family around two in the afternoon.

Scott then called Ian Broder at the *Westdeutsche Zeitung.* The receptionist asked him who was calling. Scott gave his name. Broder was instantly on the phone, "*Mein Gott,* Scott, what is this?"

"Listen carefully, Ian. Kleinst has been arrested this morning for crimes against the state. He's in custody. Have you read the story?"

"I was reading the story when you called. But the photograph, is it real?"

"Very real. It all checks out. He's been telling the East Germans what the West Germans have been planning for years. His real name is Günther von Ott."

"How did you get this photograph and the other parts of the story?"

"It was tied to a brick that came through the window."

"It would help if we knew the source."

"But you're not going to. Be happy with what you have. Will you print it?"

"Of course. Page one, top of the masthead. I'm surprised we haven't already heard of his arrest."

"You will shortly, but you have the why of his arrest. No one else has that except LeFebre."

"Let me go, Scott. I have work to do. Where can I reach you if I have a question?

"You can't. I'll call you again at two this afternoon."

His next call was to LeFebre, who immediately complained that he had been trying to reach him for the last few minutes. LeFebre wanted to know where he was. He hoped it was not Berlin, which could be dangerous. And he, like Broder, wanted to know where the photograph had come from. He was disappointed that Scott wouldn't answer any of his questions.

"Don't be petulant. I'm not the story," Scott reminded him.

"Not for now, but you could be." It was a worrisome thought.

THAT AFTERNOON, MACALLISTER AND COMPANY ARRIVED IN a three-car caravan with the wife and children of Dimitri Rostov. There were tears—lots of them—and Scott understood. Rostov was not embarrassed. He and his wife were relieved. The children appeared a little bewildered, but they had the rest of their lives to recover from this uprooting. On one hand, they had survived a dangerous game. On the other, they faced an uncertain new life without the benefits that they had enjoyed previously. MacAllister had thought ahead to have some refreshments and food available, and soon the parents and their children seemed to be discussing more practical issues. MacAllister, who surprisingly spoke Russian, gave Scott the gist of the discussion. As the party wound down, MacAllister said, "You may want to say goodbye. We have a plane to catch."

Scott caught the eye of Koch, who came over and said, "Is it goodbye?"

"I'm afraid so, but you're in good hands."

"Time will tell. I'm still angry with you. But I must also thank you."

"I understand. It's a dirty business."

He clicked his heels, saluted, and said, "My regards to your wife."

SCOTT AND MACALLISTER ARRIVED IN GENEVA LATE IN THE evening. Scott had wanted to discuss the next steps, but he knew that these issues could not be discussed in public. He didn't have luggage; his suitcase and other effects were still at the Savoy in Berlin. He would spend the night in Geneva and go up to Gstaad early the next morning. At least he had been able to telephone Desirée and tell her he was on his way back. But he didn't tell her anything about leaving Berlin or being in Stuttgart. She was unhappy. Her people had informed her that he was an uncooperative subject, that he had continually lost them.

In parting, he asked, "How about our deal, Mac?"

"We'll talk next week."

THE NEXT MORNING, HE ENGAGED A CAR AND DRIVER TO DRIVE him to Gstaad. Desirée was on the phone when he entered the chalet. She quickly ended the conversation and ran to him and threw her arms around him. He kissed her long and hard on the lips and then her neck and face.

"Are you still mad at me?" he asked.

"I should be."

She was always beautiful, but particularly after he had been away. It was the sensation of missing someone you loved. Helga brought in Celine, who was all smiles and little noises. How nice to be so innocent and unaware. When she saw her papa, she became excited and struggled to get away from Helga and take those unsteady last steps to him. He gathered her up and held her above his head, then let her descend into his cradling arms. She giggled and cooed. This was what he had been missing. They sat on the sofa and enjoyed the warmth and flicker from the fireplace. Desirée asked if he were tired, but although he was, he knew the question presaged a request for him to do something. He said that he wasn't particularly tired, what did she have in mind. She hadn't known he was coming home until late, she explained, and she and the Goosens and Father Kohler had planned to have lunch. Would he like to come along or would he rather stay at home and get some rest? He knew she wanted him to come, so he told her that he looked forward to seeing them all.

It was mid-March, and the crowds around town were thinning day by day as the ski and social season came to an end in Gstaad. Even they would be moving back to Geneva in a week, so in a way it was the final get-together of the season. It was a beautiful day. It hadn't snowed in a week, and the rush of water in the streams coming down the mountains announced that the spring thaw was in motion.

There weren't many people having lunch in the Palace dining room. They took a lovely table with a floor-to-ceiling window that displayed a panoramic view of the valley and the peaks beyond. Scott was in a mood to celebrate and ordered Krug to get things started. Then he ordered caviar and smoked salmon and fresh-shucked oysters. "Scott's having a good time," Louise said. "Are we celebrating something?"

"Just being back home with my two girls," Scott said.

"I thought you might be celebrating your article in yesterday's evening edition of the *Westdeutsche Zeitung*," Louise said.

Scott froze. He hadn't told Desirée yet. Well, he had told her there was an article coming, but he had left out its explosive contents. After all, he had just arrived. He had been trying to find the right moment, well, more than the right moment, the right way to tell her. He was basking in the homecoming, not wanting to spoil it, not wanting it to end. Leave it to Louise.

"What article?" Desirée asked.

"Your husband is very modest," Louise's husband, Jon, said. "The article is on the front page of the paper. Actually, it's all over the papers. It reads, 'Kleinst arrested for Treason,' and it has an old photograph of Secretary Kleinst with two Stasi officials."

"Wasn't Kleinst the man you went to Berlin to interview, Scott?" Louise asked.

"Yes, Kleinst. I had some dealings with him when I was at the Vatican," Father Kohler said. "Something about refugees, I remember."

"I didn't realize the story was out yet," Scott said. "It was all quite a coincidence, the interview, that old photograph someone found somewhere, and his arrest."

"And to top it off, French television is reporting this morning that the Russian cultural attaché in Paris, I think his name is Rostig or Rostov or Koch, something like that, has disappeared," Jon said. "And even his family is nowhere to be found. Poof, gone, just like that."

"Rostov, Koch?" Desirée asked.

"Yes, Rostov. That's it," Louise said. "He was in Lech. He went to Berlin. From there he vanished apparently."

All eyes turned to Scott, and these were not the eyes of those waiting for an answer. These were the eyes that knew the answer and were waiting for an explanation. They asked too much. He couldn't deflect their suspicions or their curiosity with some reasonable concoction, because there was none, but he didn't have to answer either. It was an unsatisfactory solution, but it was necessary to preserve his secret. Even they couldn't fantasize the truth.

"Can I order for everyone?" Scott said. "I was thinking the mixed grill. And a nice Bordeaux, one from the Pauillac estates, a Château Latour." This was in honor of Helga. In one way, Scott hoped that Helga used the good sense she was known for and got out of Berlin into the East sector before she was compromised by either Kleinst or Koch.

Scott knew that Desirée was bursting with anticipation, holding it in until they were back at the chalet. He was certain that CIA operatives would be slightly less intense than she would be. Her version of mixed grill would begin the moment they were back home.

She started with those ominous words, "I think we need to talk." He didn't resist, because she was correct. He had to make this right with her. She led him to the library at the far end of the chalet away from the servants and Celine and the nanny. She closed the door, and she started to say something, but Scott preempted her.

"I have a confession to make," he said.

"Good, it's about time."

"This journalism thing has really mushroomed into something that I hadn't expected, and obviously it put me in some situations that are suspicious. Suddenly, because of the subjects I write about, people want to attribute to me everything that might happen that surrounds the people I know, talk to, or interview. Well, I'm tired of being accused of every little thing that happens. I'm quitting the journalism field. I'm going to find something less political," Scott said.

Desirée looked a little puzzled. "And that's your confession? That's it? I think there's more going on here than you're telling me. I have my own idea."

"I know it's been hard on you and Celine. I'm telling you that I'm quitting, it's over, *fini, basta, kaputt.* I'm calling them all and telling them that I quit. I'm tired of having to defend myself every time someone gets arrested."

"Stop it. You're working for the CIA. Now how are you going to quit that?"

"I was thinking of a nice letter of resignation."

"That's not funny. They don't let people quit."

"Countess, I have a plan. But how did you know?"

"Because I've been around it all my life. Why do you think my father moved to the United States? Once his identity became known, he couldn't stay in Europe."

"And Uncle Pierre."

"Of course."

"I'm surprised they haven't enlisted you."

"How do you know they haven't?"

"Now you're not funny. How long have you known?"

"I was suspicious from Bern on, but when I saw someone following you in Paris, it was confirmed. That's when I put the security on."

"Are you angry?"

"No, I spoke to Uncle Pierre. I understand the why and the how of it. They're like that."

"They are."

"What's the plan?"

"Will you trust me just a little while longer?"

"Yes, but how long?"

"Until next week."

It was a long week, but she was a woman of her word. They didn't discuss it anymore. When they were back in Geneva, he went to his fencing club. It was a Thursday. MacAllister was there, and Scott found him at their usual table.

"We've moved the Kochs to Washington. He's better than expected," MacAllister said.

"Better than who expected?" Scott said. "I knew that he would be great."

"And Kleinst is giving up everything, hoping not to be shot."

"I didn't think they did that anymore in the new Germany."

"They don't, but he doesn't want to tempt them."

"So, Mac, you got two for one. Now you have to give one up."

"But you're a great agent."

"Correction, I was a great agent."

"I heard that you resigned from *Le Point.* You broke La Haye's heart."

"This too shall pass, but I've written one last article as an insurance policy. It's a really juicy one. I'm sure they'll run it."

"And why do you need insurance?"

"To make sure you follow through with our deal."

"Must be a policy with a double indemnity clause. What's it about?"

"The title is 'Five Card Stud.' Want to read it?" He slid a sheet of paper across the table.

MacAllister didn't get very far into the article—maybe two sentences—when he said, "You can't publish this! You'll bring the West German government down. Where did you get these names?" Scott had included the five names Koch had given him via Helga. He hadn't written in the last name, but with the first name and government titles,

MacAllister filled in the blanks easily. He looked up at Scott for some explanation. Scott gave him one.

"In five card stud, is the ace a good hole card?"

"How can we be sure you won't publish it anyway?"

"Because I want to stay alive. As long as I'm healthy and happy, you can relax."

"Okay, a clean slate, your U.S. passport returned, but on one condition."

"A condition?"

"Yes. In the future, if the need arises, you'll hear me out before you say no."

"Okay. I'll listen, but it won't mean much."

"By the way, where did you get the photograph?"

"A little birdie gave it to me. Actually, it was more like a bee."

"I don't get it," MacAllister said.

"Look at the photograph sometime. You'll notice that it was taken from inside a car, in essence through the window. There's a ghost reflection of a hand, and on that hand is a signet ring. On its surface is the engraving of an insect, a bee."

"So what?" MacAllister said.

"Bees make *Honig.*"

"Ah!"

Forty-three

DESIRÉE MUST HAVE HEARD EITHER THE SQUEAL OF the tires or the downshift to a lower gear of Scott's Porsche as he came up the driveway, because she was standing at the door of their house in Geneva, waiting for him. It was only the end of March, and it was still cold, but the sun was strong and provided comforting warmth. The lake alternated between dark greens and blues. He parked the car in the turnaround rather than in the garage. She was on top of him as soon as he opened the car door.

"You went to see them, didn't you?"

"Yes."

"I knew it was today."

He knew that this was not the time to tease. "It's over."

"But how? They never let anyone go. There must be some strings attached."

"Yes, and I'm holding them. But I have agreed to listen in the future."

"But that doesn't mean you must do more than listen, right?"

"Correct."

"But darling, I want to know how."

"I told them you had found out and wouldn't permit me to do it anymore."

"Very funny. What are you going to do now?"

"I'm going to give up fencing."

"I don't blame you. It never seemed like your thing."

"School's out, too tame. Banking's out, too boring."

"So, what's it to be?"

"I'm thinking arms dealer. I can use some of my contacts."

"Yes, I can see your fitting in."

"By the way, if you were so suspicious, why didn't you say something?"

"But I did. I told you someone was following you. I questioned the coincidence of the Honig release. I hired security for you. How much more could I do?"

"You could have said, 'Honey I liked you better when you weren't a spy.'"

"And I do. Now where were we before the CIA interrupted us?"

"I remember."

"Really, where?"

"Let's go inside. I'll show you."

Epilogue

THE LAST LITTLE GUESTS, CELINE'S CLASSMATES AT her nursery school, were leaving, their parents or chauffeurs or both picking them up after Celine's fourth birthday party.

Scott and Desirée had been working with Helga, Francine, and the caterers to make sure everyone had a piece of cake and a present. Celine's playmates had arrived in their winter finery, darling wool coats with fur trim for the girls and macho leather jackets and coats for the boys. The prerequisite games were played, and remarkably little crying or arguments had broken out given this privileged group. None of the little ones would leave unhappy. Desirée had made sure of that.

Celine's proud parents stood on the steps in front of the house, saying goodbye to the last one and relishing the success of the party. The sun was rapidly descending in the south over the vast Lake of Geneva. They both were surprised when a car drove up the driveway and parked in the turnaround in front of the house. The driver remained in the car, the brake lights indicating his foot was still on the brake pedal.

Scott walked toward the passenger side of the car, looked through the window, turned, and waved to Desirée, saying it was a friend. He got into the car. He stayed there for a half hour or so. Finally, he got out of the car, said something to the driver before shutting the door, and waved goodbye.

He watched as the car backed up, turned around, and headed down the driveway.

"Was that MacAllister?" Desirée asked.

"Yes."

"Don't!"

About the Author

GARY DICKSON IS AN INVETERATE traveler and a Francophile sans merci. Educated in the United States and Switzerland in history, literature, and the classics, Gary lives in Los Angeles with his wife, Susie.